Stay

Mildred Gail Digby

*Quest Books
by Regal Crest*

ISBN 978-1-61929-422-6

First Edition 2019

9 8 7 6 5 4 3 2 1

Cover design by AcornGraphics

Published by:

Regal Crest Enterprises

Find us on the World Wide Web at
http://www.regalcrest.biz

Published in the United States of America

Acknowledgments

I would humbly like to acknowledge the help and patience of the Regal Crest team. Without their help and untiring dedication I would not be able to present such a polished and readable finished product.

Dedication

This book is dedicated firstly to my wife, who continues to support and cheer me on even when I get a bit strange and start having arguments with myself while frantically scribbling down random snatches of dialogue in my notebook.

Secondly, I want to dedicate the tough parts of this book to the ones who, at some time in their lives, faced a road they thought was too hard to travel but found the strength to keep going forward instead of taking the off-ramp. You are not alone.

Chapter One

THE STILLNESS OF the night broke with a series of taps on the door. While the individual impacts were quite light, the attack went on long enough for Jade Mayflower to raise her head from the scattered papers on her desk. Outside of the circle cast by her desk lamp, she could just make out the outlines of the two chairs stiffly waiting in front of her.

Jade blinked into the streetlight-tinged darkness as her eyes adjusted. The collection of mugs and a small Thermos were a black mass on top of the small folding table in the corner. The glowing strip underneath the door indicated whoever was outside had turned on the light in the hallway outside Jade's office. She scowled. She did not like interruptions. Jade raked back a handful of long hair, shit brown and straight as a stick, and wished for one of those damn clips she was always losing. With an annoyed snarl, she dragged the trailing bangs out of her face as the determined knocking continued.

"Is that you, Ben?" Jade asked in a tone just shy of a growl. "I'm busy!"

The pattering sounds paused. The door swung open to admit a young man with a bright smile on his face. Haloed by the fluorescent lighting behind him, his streaked blonde hair was fashionably tousled and his slender body was swathed in a long, form-fitting denim coverall liberally decorated with rainbow patches. He held a tinfoil-wrapped plate in one hand.

"Not too busy for some yummy leftovers from my café," Benny sang. He pranced into the room, seemingly unaffected by the fierce scowl Jade aimed at him. He set the plate down in front of Jade and rested his backside against the desk, facing her. "I have two cinnamon scones for you plus a scrumptious onion bagel. I know you'll be up half the night anyway, so here's a bit of fuel."

Still scowling, Jade picked at the foil. She was about to dismiss the young man when she felt it, the subtle drop in the room's temperature, the whisper of chill electricity across the back of her neck. Jade rose to her full height of nearly six feet, towering over her desk. In one quick motion she threw her arm out and corralled Benny behind her. He let out a squeak.

"Stay quiet and still," Jade snapped. She held her breath and waited.

The air thickened. A thin mist gathered in front of Jade's desk and slowly took the shape of a young woman. She gave off waves of cold and she was almost transparent. Jade could make out the shape of the chair behind her. The young woman's form was almost devoid of color, like an antique photograph. She had pale, shoulder-length hair that waved around her face like she was underwater, grayish eyes, and too pale skin. Her nose was small and slightly upturned, her mouth sweetly full and delicate.

As she hovered in front of the desk, the young woman's gaze was unfocused, her posture small and shy, as if she wasn't entirely sure if she was going to remain there or blink out. Jade needed to change that.

"Thanks for coming tonight," Jade said in a conversational way. She kept Benny behind her. The visitor didn't look dangerous, but Jade wasn't taking any chances. Sometimes they changed without warning.

"What's going on?" Benny whispered. "Oh my god, it isn't one of...those things you see? That's so cool!"

Jade shushed him with an upraised hand. The woman's mouth worked as if she was trying to say something. Like a candle fighting against a cold breeze, she guttered and faded before she re-solidified.

Help me.

The words stained the air. Jade felt them in her mind more than she heard them.

"Try again," Jade said. She pitched her voice low and softer than usual. "It's okay, you're safe here."

"I need you to help me." The words seemed to cost the woman a great deal of effort. She stopped, clenched her hands into fists, and tried again. "I need you to find out who did this to me."

"You've come to the right place, I can help you," Jade said. She grabbed up her datebook and flipped through it. "I'm free from—"

"What are you talking about?" Benny scooted around the

desk and looked like he was one second from heading out the door. "Are you seriously going to take this...ghost as a client? Jade, honey, this is what you get from hanging out at the morgue all the time. I told you, you need to get a hobby, or at least find clients who aren't dead."

As she let out a slow breath, Jade coaxed herself down from giving Benny a little smack across his cute but noisy face. "This is a legitimate case. One only I can take, all right?" She knit her fingers together, crushing the datebook in an iron grip. "It's her last chance for justice. I can't ignore that."

"Hooray for you, that's very noble." Benny still didn't look convinced. "But noble doesn't pay the bills."

"It's not like I need the money."

"That's good to know," Benny said with a toss of his head. "Because what, is ghostie going to pay us in *boo* dollars?"

"She can pay us in whatever she can. I'm used to taking payment in lots of different forms."

"I'm sure you are," Benny huffed. "But cigarettes and bodily favors don't pay the rent here."

"In case you forgot, you're the only one paying rent here." Jade let loose with one of her well-practiced glares of painful death and he raised both hands and took a step back. Rid of the young man's effervescent interference, Jade returned her attention to the visitor. She shoved the foil-covered plate out of the way and perched on the desk. With a wave in front of herself, Jade said, "Please have a seat."

The young woman sank down and started wringing her hands. Jade was ready for her to begin wailing or gushing blood from inappropriate orifices; however, none of that happened.

"What can you tell me?" Jade fixed the flickering apparition with a calm expression, prepared to wait. She swapped her rather crumpled datebook for a black professional-looking notebook and absently fiddled with her pencil.

"I don't really know much, I'm afraid," she said.

"That's okay," Jade told her. "Just give me what you can. Don't worry about anything you don't know right now. Let's start with a few basics. Can you tell me anything about yourself? Like your name maybe?"

"Connie," the woman said. She started flickering again as Benny bitchily turned on the overhead light.

"Shut it!" Jade yelled, scaring everyone.

"Sorry," Benny said in a languid drawl. He tossed his head and flicked the light off with a sigh.

"Connie. Good start." Jade wrote the name down. "How about what year is it? It might help if we can establish a date."

The apparition faded, the woman's face blurred and nearly disappeared.

"Incense!" Jade hollered over her shoulder.

Benny plopped down a small dish with a smoking incense cone on it.

"Thanks Ben, I need to get her a bit more stable," Jade said. She bent over the dish and blew on the umber-colored cone. Obligingly, it glowed a bit brighter and a near-solid plume of smoke rose from it.

"Is that gonna do something?"

"I don't know. It's not like I know what the hell's going on either." Jade muttered a string of curses as she waited for the incense to get going.

"You using 'beep' words every few seconds isn't helping," Benny said.

Jade ignored him and fanned her hands over the dish in an effort to direct the fumes across to their visitor. A musky, medicinal scent filled the room along with the skeins of smoke. Like searchlights streaming through fog, Connie became stronger in the thickened air. She stopped flickering and color seeped into her form. Golden blonde stained through her softly waving hair and tiny freckles came to life on her cheeks. Her once-grey eyes deepened to green. Connie's true beauty shone through like a slowly blooming flower and hit Jade like a wallop to the chest. Jade's breath caught in her throat.

"I gotta tell Amber her incense stuff actually works," Jade said. She focused on Connie once more and smiled in what she hoped was a calming and knowing way even as her heart thudded in her ears. "How about that date?"

"Oh gosh, are you serious? You want to go on a date with *me*?" Connie squeaked. Her face went pink. "But I just met you!"

"I mean today's date."

"Yeah, I knew that." The disembodied spirit looked sheepish. She sank into the chair behind herself. "This is all very new and strange to me."

"That's all right, just tell me something that can help us find out *when* you're from. Like some recent local news for example."

"I seem to remember something about the mayor going to the pier. Umm, for some kind of dedication maybe?"

"Google!"

Benny jumped and his phone fell from his hands. "Jade, you made me drop my phone!"

"Help me out for a minute here. You've got that damned thing out already, make it useful." Jade relayed the information Connie told her.

"You could look this up yourself you know," Benny said.

"You're faster. Plus. I hate that fucking touch-screen," Jade gritted. Benny plopped into Jade's vacated chair with a dramatic sigh, but Jade focused on the apparition of the young woman in front of her. "What year were you born?"

Connie froze. She hugged her arms to her chest. "I don't know," she cried out. "I don't remember!"

"It's okay, calm down, Connie. Let's take a look at you," Jade said.

She put her notebook down and studied Connie. Her clothes were modern but not flashy. The ghostly visitor was wearing a simple, long-sleeved green top with a small ribbon-held gather at the base of her throat and slim-fitting jeans. Her moonlight-pale skin wasn't adorned with any type of jewelry. The absence of a wedding band wasn't very telling due to Connie's age. She looked young, probably early-twenties. She had delicate, almost elfin features. Connie was, in fact, quite attractive in a subtle way that often got overlooked. Jade gave herself a mental shake. She had to keep things professional. A client was a client. Even if she did pay in boo dollars.

It struck Jade how they were almost polar opposites. Jade, in contrast, was tall and lanky, her long limbs cinched tight with muscle, her own features broad and somewhat plain. While she could never claim to be cute, a few people called her handsome, which Jade didn't mind at all.

Her initial survey finished, Jade said, "How about telling me anything you remember."

"Darkness." Connie's blonde head dropped into her hands. "I'm cold and it's dark. Empty. I can't get out." Her head came up, eyes blazing. "I want to find out who did this to me. It's not my time yet, I want to live. I wanted to so badly. That's all I have. Just this....feeling."

"And the fact that you're here when, no offence, you kind of shouldn't be."

Connie looked at Jade defiantly but didn't respond.

"Okay peeps," Benny's voice sang out from behind the desk. "I got something about the mayor, it would help if I knew *which* one though, but there are three occasions where a mayor visited a pier. One of them is in India and two are in the eighteen hundreds. Jade, is your little ghostie friend wearing a corset or a sari?"

"Nope," Jade said.

"In that case, I'd say my searching abilities have failed us."

"Cuntwad fucknuggets," Jade spat. Both Connie and Benny looked at her.

"Sorry," Jade muttered, compelled by their shocked faces to offer an apology. She kept forgetting to at least wear the veneer of manners in civilized company. She glowered and gripped her pencil as if she was going to throw it at someone. She shook her long hair back one more time and thought the curse words instead of saying them.

"Keep an elastic around your wrist so you always have something on you to make a ponytail," Connie said. She leaned forward in her chair, a genuine smile on her face. Her attention roved over Jade's form in a slow tour from Jade's face, down her long body and back up again.

"Good idea." Jade got a flash of heat from the thoughtful words and smile. Most people didn't talk to her like that. Most people didn't look at her like that either. Discomfited, Jade scooted behind her desk. She shooed Benny out of her chair before she sat down and rummaged around in the drawers. After a moment, Jade came up with a plastic hair clip and a few mints. She held the clip up with a triumphant look before she dragged her hair back into a messy twist. Free from distraction, Jade faced her guest again.

"Do you think you could give me any more info? Are you from around here? Got any friends or family? Pets?"

A long moment passed without movement. Connie looked like she'd been put on pause.

With a bored yawn, Benny left his post next to Jade's desk

and wandered around the office with his phone in his hands. He waved it around in the air.

"What are you doing with that?" Jade asked.

"Taking a video," Benny replied. He pouted at the screen. "But I'm only getting static."

"Quit that." Jade stopped herself from adding an explicit statement and scowled at him instead.

"Somebody's bitchy!"

"Go." Jade waved her hand, "Just go away somewhere for a while, would you Benny?"

"Whatever you say." The young man was absorbed in his phone screen as he wandered over to the coffee corner and leaned back against the wall. "I can't believe this, the one chance I get to have a genuine ghost video and it doesn't turn out. *Hmf!*"

"Don't care," Jade sang under her breath. She looked up as Connie began to speak. Jade guiltily abandoned the mint she'd been teasing from its wrapper and returned her attention to the apparition.

"The only thing I know is I needed to come here," she said. "I felt drawn to this place. The clearest thing I remember is passing by here so many times, wishing and aching to come in but not being able to make myself cross the threshold." Her voice got stronger the longer she stayed around. Jade wanted to credit her own magnetic presence but figured it was probably the incense. "I wanted to go in but I never did. There was something leading me here. It seemed like a place I should be. A place I wanted to be. And now finally I am here and there's something significant in that. There has to be!"

"So you never came here before?" Jade tensed. "Are you sure of that?"

"I'm sure. I've only been outside," Connie said. She shrank back at the harsh tone and Jade felt like kicking herself. Head down, Connie twisted her hands together. "I'm not good with new places and new people. Everyone seems so free and happy here. I didn't think I'd fit in."

Benny's phone chirped. At the sound, Connie recoiled violently with a look of fear on her face. Jade reacted instinctively. She jumped up from her chair and rounded the desk in an instant to put herself between Connie and the source of her alarm.

"Manner fucking mode, Ben," Jade snapped.

"Whatever you say." Benny stashed his phone and announced, "Not to belittle our magnificent guest from the other side here, but it *is* past closing and I need to do the books for the night. Such are the trials of a young boy-wonder. A cute and helpful double-agent if you will."

"All right, do what you gotta do." Jade dismissed Benny and he trotted off. With the other warm-bodied individual gone, the air chilled and Jade realized anew who she was dealing with.

Jade leaned back against the desk and let her gaze rest on the young woman in front of her. Connie looked up and their eyes met. A shiver that wasn't unpleasant rolled down Jade's back and a tight, choked feeling rose in her throat at the loneliness she saw staring back at her. That had never happened to her before. Jade usually didn't give a shit about what anyone else was feeling. She must be getting soft in her old age. She had to focus on business. Jade hid her unease by crossing her arms over her chest in a nonchalant way.

"Tell me about yourself, Connie. Anything at all. I'm listening."

Her hair waved about her face as she shook her head. Connie bit her lip in a way that had Jade getting a jolt all over again. She looked so lost but so damned cute at the same time. Like a stray kitten left out in the rain.

"I'd rather hear about you," Connie said. She leaned forward as well, echoing Jade's posture. A tiny smile quirked up her lips that emphasized the sweet, kissable curves.

"Shit, there's not much to tell," Jade said. She sat back in her chair, desperate to put a bit of distance between them. Why a ghost and why *now*? Jesus Christ. Her knee jiggled under the desk.

"Please," Connie whispered and Jade's resistance vanished.

"Don't blame me if you get bored," Jade said. She cracked a grin as her usual bravado flooded back. It *had* been a damned long time since anyone looked at her like that, like she was a person and not a project or a subhuman pain in the ass. Jade leaned her chair back as far as she could, propped one foot up on the desk, and said, "I was gonna be an accountant but that didn't work out." She shrugged and let herself relax, buoyed by the way Connie gazed across at her. "Maybe it was a good thing because I hate all that office bullshit. Managers, *pfft*, more like—" Jade let loose with a filthy Yiddish epithet from the restricted section of her library of profanity. She followed it up with a rather long and colorful description of office hierarchy and several suggestions to what those hypothetical managers could do with themselves.

Connie clapped her hand over her mouth and Jade stopped mid-rant, worried the young woman was offended beyond belief until Jade heard a stifled laugh. That small sound alone soothed something inside of Jade she hadn't known was aching.

"But seriously," Jade said. "Connie, is there anyone out there who would want to hurt you?"

"I don't know," Connie said. She pulled her arms to herself and lowered her head, which broke the connection that flowed between them. She put a hand over her face. "I don't even know where to start. I just know I want to stay here. I have nothing left out there."

"Hey, don't think about that," Jade said, alarmed as Connie started to flicker. "Think about something nice. How about lunch? Everybody likes lunch."

"Yeah, lunch is pretty good," Connie said with a shy smile.

"Are you the lunchbox type or do you like to go out?"

"Out," Connie said. Her eyes were unfocused and Jade took that as a good sign. She seemed to be remembering something.

"Where do you like to go?" Jade fished around for ideas. She hoped Connie had classic tastes as Jade's knowledge of the landmarks around Traynor's Port was twenty years out of date. Connie didn't answer and seemed to be struggling, so Jade changed tacks. "What do you see?" she breathed. "Work with me, come on Connie. It's noon, people are bustling around, the place smells great. Maybe it's quiet and you're—"

"Red and white awning. Formica tables, like a real nineteen fifties diner." Connie's voice was small. She didn't appear to be all the way there. "The jukebox hasn't got anything past the eighties and pretty much everyone is a regular."

"How's the food?" Jade asked.

"Not great, but they have the best apple pie."

"Pie?" Jade sat up ramrod straight. "Did you say pie?" As the starved, overeager tone of her own voice reached her ears, Jade attempted to put her cool face on again. She waved a hand and said, "Tell me more."

"I want to stay there, slip into the past and never leave."

"Okay, what's outside?" Jade's mind raced.

"Buildings, trees," Connie said, still in that odd fugue-like state.

"No help there," Jade muttered under her breath and used the young woman's distraction to shove a mint into her mouth. She tucked the mint into her cheek and asked, "Are you with anyone?"

Suddenly Connie snapped back to the present. It was odd seeing a ghost do that. A smile that tore at Jade's heart slipped over her face. "I'm alone. I'm always alone. Even when people are with me I always feel like I'm alone."

"Nothing wrong with that. At least you don't have anyone stealing bites of your pie," Jade said in the jolliest voice she could muster. "Hang on, I wanna take some notes."

She looked away for a moment.

In the space of a heartbeat, something changed. Jade raised her head to find the chair across from her empty. Pale moonlight competed with the orange streetlight coming in from the window, bent on throwing everything in the utilitarian room into a harsh artificial illumination. Even as she fought the emptiness Connie left in her wake, Jade finished her notes as best she could. First of all, she needed to find out who her client was. Usually when potential clients withheld information from their investigators, it was because they were afraid of their husbands or bosses or whoever finding out, but not because their only perception of reality was through a fractured and unreliable barrier.

Jade was not in the business of taking usual clients. Connie wasn't the first of her kind Jade had dealt with and she wouldn't be the last. She was, however, significantly cuter than the regular ones and something about her interested Jade. More than interested. She felt drawn to the young woman. She wanted to banish the sad look that plagued her, make her feel cherished and not alone. All the better if pie was involved. Jade could really sink her teeth into this case. She caught herself and stopped that line of thought cold.

Jade got to her feet and snuffed the incense. She hesitated in the doorway of her office. She debated going down the hallway to where her private rooms took up the rest of the second floor but decided against it. The conversation with Connie left her restless and her mind full of conflicting thoughts. Jade left her office and went down to the first floor where Benny's bookstore and café lived. She discovered Benny in the tiny, cluttered office cubby behind the café counter with his head bent over the glowing screen of the tablet he used for bookkeeping. He wasn't exactly businesslike, but quite capable nonetheless. He ran the store well — even in the age of eBooks and online shopping he managed to turn a profit. A lot of that was due to his bubbly personality and the hopping business his café did during the day. Benny's phone lay next to him and occasionally he snuck glances at it.

"So did you perform an exorcism?" Benny wanted to know. "Or did your guest drift away on the breeze?"

"She just kind of vanished," Jade said. She hitched herself up on a stool at the counter and plopped her notebook down in front of herself. With a frown, she flipped through her scant notes. "If she comes back I'll try to get more information. I can at least cross-check some things in the meantime."

"So, you're really going to do this?" Benny asked.

"Of course. You know that's what I do. I told you that from the start. I'd see them anyway, so it's to everyone's benefit if I help them out." Jade paused and her mind went back to the young woman who had appeared so suddenly in her office. She couldn't stop the half-grin that tugged at her lips. "I have a feeling this one is different, Ben. Connie's not like the others. She's special."

"Oh?" Benny raised his eyebrows. "So what's she like? Young? Old? Cute?"

"She's about your age," Jade said. "And yeah, she is pretty cute."

Benny tilted his head. "Any pings on the Gaydar? Do you think she bats for our team?"

"I don't know," Jade snapped. She hated the heat that rose to her cheeks as she remembered how Connie's eyes stroked over her.

"For the record, even if you're not getting paid, I'm all for it if it gets you out and about," Benny said. "It's been a year, honey. You know you're free to go anywhere you want. You don't have to stay cooped up in here all the time."

"I know," Jade said in a tight voice. With a flash of annoyance, she stood up and pocketed her notebook. "And I'm going out now, actually."

"All right, take care. Don't do anything I wouldn't do."

Jade blew out a raspberry. "That doesn't narrow it down at all, Ben."

As Benny graced her with his tinkling laugh, Jade wandered out of the store into the night. She heard Benny lock the door behind her. Her car, a boring and nondescript middle-of-the-line four-door sedan, was waiting for her in the scrubby parking lot behind the building.

While she could afford a new car, Jade decided to go with a used model so she wouldn't feel bad when she dinged it up backing into stuff and doing her lousy attempts at parking. She'd kept it in pretty much the same condition as when she'd bought it a month ago without bothering to make it fancy. The car was good enough for her limited drives around town. One day Jade planned to take a trip out to the ocean when she felt like spending a bit of time with the Atlantic.

Next to her car, Benny's little red Honda was plastered with all sorts of stickers and decorations. Jade noticed a new one—a plain white sticker with sparkly purple letters that read: "If I had a dollar for every gender, then I'd have infinity dollars".

Jade dug out her keys and fell into the saggy driver's seat of her car.

While the clunky engine warmed up, she prodded at the GPS screen in an attempt to communicate her ideas to it before she gave up and went with her instinct. For once, it felt good to be outside. She didn't want to admit it, but Benny was right about her not getting out enough. She couldn't seem to shake the unease that chased her outside of confining walls.

Even though Traynor's Port was the second-largest city in Nova Scotia, it was still pretty small. On a good day, Jade could hike from one end of the downtown area to the other in half an hour, including a stop for coffee and muffins. The city crouched on one side of the St. Lawrence River and was connected to the sprawling, refinery-laden city of Portsmouth on the other side by a gigantic lumbering bridge.

Jade drove around without any real destination but kept her eyes on the dark shops on either side of her. The road was empty and wet with the night's damp exhalations. The darkness outside was quiet—too quiet.

Jade could almost hear a soft breath coming from behind her.

Silence fell once again. She hated when they lurked. Just fucking come out and get it over with. Jade suppressed a shiver and dialed up a cheerful FM radio station. The action took her attention from the road for a second.

"Shit!"

A frantic twist of the steering wheel threw the car to one side with a squeal of tires. The car jolted to a stop and Jade clutched at the wheel. Her shaking breaths filled the car. A grey column stood on the road in front of her, staring mournfully.

After her heartbeat went back to non-lethal levels, Jade rolled down the window and hollered, "Christ, Connie! You nearly gave me a heart attack. Get in the damn car."

The young apparition drifted over and stood outside the passenger side door. Her hands went to grab the door handle but passed through it. Halfway through the cracked brown paneling, Connie stopped with a look of disbelief and embarrassment on her face.

"Fuckity McFuckfurters," she muttered.

Something ignited within Jade at the singular ray of humanity. An emotion Jade had never felt before burst into life within her chest and filled her with warmth.

Lightheaded and a bit shocked, Jade made a few unnecessary adjustments to the GPS as Connie's form drifted through the window and folded itself into the passenger's seat. She struggled with her hands going over her chest and shoulder for a while.

"Connie?" Jade glanced over. "Are you all right?"

"Yeah." She looked adorably sheepish. "It's just, I can't really grab anything. I guess I don't need the seatbelt."

"No, I guess not."

"I'm sorry, were you going somewhere? I can leave if you're busy."

"No way. I'm glad you showed up." Jade drove the car over crunching gravel and got back onto the road. "I was thinking about tracking down that diner you mentioned and I could really use your help."

"But it's in the middle of the night," Connie pointed out. "I don't think it's even open."

"That's fine, I just want to get a feel for the area. Maybe you could give me a hand. Do you remember anything else about it? Can you try and get a picture of it in your mind? Think about what it looks like from the outside. Are there any other shops nearby?"

Connie nodded and lowered her head. Her hair fell forward over her face.

The radio had a female DJ crooning through it in a sexy voice that gave Jade inappropriate thoughts, so she fiddled with it for a while and then left it on some country station. A song about "My Daddy's Car" started playing and Jade kept time on the steering wheel with her thumb.

She glanced at Connie, who had gone completely silent. The passing lights streaked over her in otherworldly waves. In the darkness between them Connie was reduced to nothing more than a smoldering shadow.

"We're going around in circles," Connie said. "Is that okay?"

"Yep. That's the plan. If you go there for lunch, it's gotta be close to where you work, which is always a good place to find clues and stuff. I figured we'd come across it on one of these streets. This is where most of the little shops with awnings are, kind of the old part of town. How about you tell me a bit more about what you did...um, what you do." Jade hoped she hadn't broken a rule by using the past tense. She made a mental note to go see Amber in that new age hippy shop of hers.

The car rolled through an intersection and as Jade was checking for oncoming traffic, Connie started flickering. She looked concerned and made little motions like a moth batting around a light bulb.

"What? Do you recognize something?"

"This isn't the way —" and she flickered out.

Cursing, Jade hauled the car around. The next stroke of a streetlight revealed the young woman was back in the car.

"Sorry about that, Connie," Jade said. She spared a quick, worried glance at her passenger to check if she was worse for wear from her abrupt trip to somewhere and back.

"That's all right," Connie said. She gave Jade a smile that reassured her to no end before she vanished again.

"Oops, not this way either," Jade mumbled and threw her arm over the back of the seat as she slammed the car into reverse and frantically backtracked.

Over the next half hour or so, Jade was able to narrow down the focus until Connie was beside her, still and sure in the moonlight with no flickers or fading. Jade breathed a bit easier. They were definitely getting close.

"What did you say you do for work?"

Connie looked startled as she said, "I—I don't know. I mean I do know but I can't remember." Her head fell into her hands as she mashed at her hair. "I mean, I spend a whole lot of time at work. I go there every day! I know I do have a job. I do. I'm not a bum!"

"Neither am I," Jade told her agreeably.

"But why don't I remember?"

"It'll come back, don't worry."

"I must do something? I must maybe...make something?" Connie slouched in the seat and stared into space. "Type...something. The phone rings. Yes, the phone is always ringing." Her body went rigid and her eyes snapped open. Ghostly hands grabbed at Jade but passed through her with a whisper of ice. "There's a fire, always a fire! Someone needs to put it out. Please, someone's going to be hurt. They're trapped. God, I'm sorry, it's all my fault!"

The next instant, Jade was lost in the memory of gritty concrete under her body. She struggled to move but couldn't. Orange flames spilled from a wastepaper basket, swiftly crawling up the walls. They reached for her like ravenous tongues. The sleeve of her jacket burst into flames and pain swallowed her. It was too much. Against her will, Jade screamed and stomped the brake pedal into existence. The vision faded into a white blanket and Jade swore a streak to herself. She concentrated on breathing as she shivered and hugged herself. God damn! Why did it have to be fire?

"Are you okay?"

Dragged back to the present, Jade looked up. Connie hovered over her.

"I'm sorry," Connie said. Her brow furrowed and she shook her head. "I did that, didn't I? I'm not good at talking to people. I said something wrong."

"No, we're cool. This is my problem, Connie, not yours." Jade got both hands back on the wheel and her foot on the gas. As streetlights swung by, she tried not to notice the way the light glistened unnaturally off the skin of her left hand. "Just try and think about daily stuff. Things you do or see."

"Okay," Connie said. She went silent again and Jade left her in her own world. Jade had to admit it wasn't unpleasant at all being with Connie. She didn't feel like she needed to be on guard around her. Jade didn't trust many people, but she trusted Connie. She hoped she wasn't making a huge fucking mistake.

"Here! It's here!" Connie's voice pierced Jade's own soft musings like a knife.

Startled, Jade swerved and the car jumped up onto the sidewalk. She sucked back the string of curses that wanted to explode out of her mouth as she twisted the wheel. The bumper scraped over the curb before the tires plopped back onto the road.

"I'm sorry. Your car," Connie said

"No problem, this thing is a piece of shit anyway." Jade let the engine idle and slung an arm over the back of the seat so she could face Connie. "So where are we?"

Connie pointed and Jade let out a breath of triumph. They had stopped in front of a rundown diner that had obviously seen better days but the awning was red and white, and square Formica-topped tables could be seen lurking within, illuminated by the streetlights. Even at that late hour, Jade thought she could smell the lingering ghosts of homemade gravy and apple pie. Her mouth watered at the thought of pie. She swallowed. That was the place all right.

"Woo! We did it!" Jade howled in triumph and held up one hand for a high five before she could stop herself. She tried to make it look natural as she changed directions and ran the hand through her bangs. Her eyes locked with Connie's and Jade couldn't help laughing as Connie sputtered out a few giggles. "Shit, sorry. Now that wasn't very suave, was it?"

"That's okay, not everybody can pull off suave," Connie said.

"I can," Jade groused. "I just need a bit of a running start is all."

"You're fine even when you don't try," Connie said. Her voice was soft but it still echoed through Jade's entire body. "I like you the way you are."

"You do now?" Jade straightened up and pulled a face in the rearview mirror, just in case anyone back there was listening in. "I'm glad someone thinks that way."

"You mean you don't, um have anyone?" The question was so hopeful and yet so shy that Jade felt something within herself melt. Something she should probably not let defrost.

"Nope. Most people don't really want to have anything to do with someone like me."

"And what is a person like you?"

Jade wondered how to answer Connie without scaring her off. While the thoughts fought a battle inside her head, Jade stretched her arm over the back of the seat again and leaned a bit closer. She got the urge to wrench herself back as she realized what she'd done. If Connie had been solid, she would nearly be in Jade's arms. The moment drew out. Connie looked up at Jade with utter trust and Jade held her breath as a jolt of something hot and electric woke up in her chest. For an instant, Jade wanted to trust Connie, to let down her barriers and willingly accept whatever the young woman wanted to give her.

Her survival sense took over and Jade steeled herself for betrayal, the sudden attack. She had left herself open and physically vulnerable once. That was mistake one. With a quick jerk, Jade retrieved her arm and braced both hands on the steering wheel. She hated herself for the look of confusion on Connie's face, but twenty years of hard-won instinct took precedence.

Connie blinked. She twisted to look out of the window. "Things are kind of coming back now. I remember where I work. In that building over there."

Jade didn't want to think about what had just passed between them. Instead, she concentrated on driving and soon the car rolled to a stop in the parking lot of a four-story concrete building. It had a number of non-descriptive company names displayed discreetly on etched metallic plates mounted on a large black granite plaque stuck to the front of the building. The first floor appeared to be some kind of artsy studio from the shadowy forms of lumpy pots in the window. A sturdy fenced-in corrugated-iron shed crouched on one side of the parking lot. It was decorated with keep out signs and looked singularly unwelcoming. The rest of the floors seemed to be office-standard from the glimpses showing through the windows.

Jade pocketed her keys before she creaked the car door open and stepped out. Her white leather cowboy boots parted the lingering fog gathering on the damp asphalt as she walked up to a side entrance.

Connie was beside Jade. She held herself with nervous tension and her movements, although rather wispy, held purpose. It looked like they had a winner. They stopped in front of a side entrance and Jade watched as Connie's hands made a swiping motion by the door's card reader. For one second, Jade actually expected the door to open.

"Duh, of course not," Jade breathed the words.

She got down on her haunches and yanked out her handy "key maintenance" kit. She flicked on her penlight and stuck it in her mouth. While Connie went through several confused motions, Jade's fingers were busy at the lock. The side of her closest to Connie was cold and goosebumpy, not a pleasant sensation. Jade squirmed and nearly dropped her penlight. She felt the old tumblers slip into place and with a click that seemed very loud, the lock opened.

"There must be something wrong with the card reader, but it seems to have fixed itself," Connie said as she wandered into the still and dark hallway with Jade close behind. They came to a lobby of sorts. It was illuminated only by the green emergency exit sign and boasted a water fountain and two dilapidated potted plants. Jade was relieved to note a security station wasn't one of the amenities provided.

"After you," Jade said and gestured to the stairwell. She didn't want to take a chance with any cameras in the elevator and she figured Connie was the stairs type of girl from the toned look of her tight little butt. Jade's theory was proven as Connie turned around and ducked into the stairwell, displaying a decidedly nice view.

Following Connie's pert ass, Jade scrambled up the stairs. While she knew it wasn't the most prudent move to ogle a ghost's rear end, Jade hadn't had the pleasure of seeing such a nice one in a while and allowed herself the small luxury. It didn't help her peace of mind at all that the cute tush was attached to a person with an equally cute personality.

Suddenly Connie turned around and Jade raised her eyes with a guilty jolt.

"You were checking me out?" Instead of sounding angry, Connie seemed confused. Her cheeks were flushed.

"Yeah, you caught me," Jade said. She wasn't going to lie.
"Why?"
Jade raked a hand through her hair and shrugged. She was

more than curious and decided to test the theory that Connie was indeed batting for her team, as Benny had put it. She let her lips quirk into a crooked grin as she held Connie's gaze.

"Because you're the sweetest thing I've had in front of me since I don't know when."

Connie gave a squeak and clapped her hands to her face, blushing wildly.

Jade cocked an eyebrow before she held up both hands in a peace-making gesture and said, "But I don't want to make you feel uncomfortable. Say the word and it won't happen again."

Connie flushed more before she said, "It's okay. You can check me out anytime, as long as you don't mind payback when I check *you* out. You're pretty sweet yourself." She gave Jade a shyly mischievous smile before she resumed her journey upstairs at a good clip, leaving Jade standing there with her mouth open.

After she recovered, Jade took the stairs at a dead run to keep up with the rapidly vanishing figure who made inhumanly good time. She caught up just as Connie drifted out of the stairwell at the fourth floor. Jade followed her, only to end up alone. She looked up and down the hallway for some clue as to where Connie had led her. Jade didn't blame her for disappearing. If she'd been in Connie's place of revisiting her old workplace, Jade didn't think she would be too happy hanging around for long either.

Two different establishments were housed on that floor. One was a language school while the other some kind of small-time manufacturing company. A dusty, glassed-in display window near the entrance housed a row of metal canisters.

On a whim, Jade chose the manufacturing company and slipped through the unlocked office door. Jade repressed a shudder. Offices sucked. They were thankless and soul-stealing. Connie was probably better off dead if she worked in one.

Inside the office, Jade pressed her back to the wall and shone her penlight around, careful to avoid the windows. She'd never been a burglar, but she did have a lot of experience slinking around and avoiding attention. Taking care not to make too much noise or knock anything over, she walked around and studied the scattered detritus of a normal work day. Most of the computers were clunky and out of date. Only two of them looked new. Jade guessed those were for the big-wigs who probably didn't even know how to use them.

She tried not to think back to her own working days. The all-too-short time she'd sat at a desk like those and written up meaningless reports and tried not to sleep during meetings. That was in another lifetime, one she'd left behind.

Jade was sufficiently distracted by finding out which desks were whose to drown out the lingering unease of her past life. Obviously the private office was the boss's. It was locked and Jade didn't feel like trying her luck with her picks again. Connie didn't seem like a boss-type anyway. She shuffled through a couple more desks and looked around for any reminders of the pale young woman.

A sudden shadow by the window startled Jade and she dropped her flashlight. She swallowed the curse words and let out a breath of relief as she realized who it was, not missing the irony of being relieved to see a ghost.

"Hey Connie, fancy meeting you here," Jade said in a weak attempt at humor. She paused and asked, "Are you all right?"

"No. Something's changed." Connie paced the floor. She wrung her hands and looked very much like the tortured wraith she should. Even though she felt sorry for Connie, Jade took a moment to clinically admire the scene. It was something straight out of a made-for-TV horror movie. She actually hated those for their inaccuracy, but she had become quite familiar with them, as well as the never-ending series of airplane panic films they'd shown on Friday nights.

"What's changed?" Jade asked as she continued her methodical catalogue of the desks. Two more seemed to belong to accounting types with the flotsam and paper mountains of trivia the job attracted. Photos on the desks showed respectively a smiling dark-skinned woman ringed by three young boys and a middle-aged and somewhat overweight couple. They were wearing matching polo shirts and had some kind of badges pinned to their shirts, which they were pointing at.

Jade rounded the recycling station and found a giant stash of fire extinguishers in a closet before she continued her tour. From time to time, Jade looked over to see what Connie was doing. Of course Connie's footsteps made no sound, but she did manage to cover a lot of ground as she paced back and forth. Jade left her to carry out her anxious ritual without interference. It couldn't be easy to be a ghost. Probably a very new one from the looks of things. The older ones tended to mellow out in time. Get their routines down. Stake out their turf.

"You okay?" Jade called out.

"Not really." The words were hollow and baleful. Jade felt the temperature of the room drop. "I wish I knew what was going on."

"Don't sweat it, Connie. It takes anyone a while to get used to being in a new situation." Jade said as she swept over to the last desk in the long row by the windows. The wall bedside it was cluttered with photos of a pretty, smiling young woman with short, permed blonde hair and amazingly blue eyes. Dark brows hinted at her original hair color. She posed for the camera, making a duckface and casually draping her arm around the shoulders of other people in the photos. A few were pretty young things in lipstick and eyes ringed with mascara smudged from club-sweat but most of them were striking, androgynous-to-butch women, some of them in suits with the ties pulled casually open at the throat. Jade found herself looking far too long at a few.

There was no reply, and Jade continued, "If there's anything I've learned, it's that people can get used to anything. And sometimes you think you've got the short end of the shit-stick, but it's really just one end of a two-ended shit-stick. If you know what I mean. Sometimes the alternative is just as bad."

"That makes a lot of sense, actually." Connie stopped her pacing and looked at Jade with a quirk to her lips. "Not that I'm a connoisseur of shit, on a stick or not."

"Leave the shit to me," Jade drawled. "I'm an expert on all of it, particularly the kind that hits the fan."

"Ooh, I hope we avoid that!"

"Me too, but sometimes there's nothing to do but take a face-full," Jade said. "If that ever happens, you stand behind me, Connie and I'll take the brunt." As Connie nodded thoughtfully, Jade wondered where the bullshit spilling out of her mouth was coming from. She wasn't usually so smarmy. But she had to admit it felt good, almost flirting with the disembodied spirit. The little smiles her words sometimes elicited kicked Jade hard in a place she wasn't used to getting kicked. If she wasn't careful, she was going to get used to it.

Connie drifted over and stationed herself at the coffee

machine. "It seems to be empty." She gestured at it. "Otherwise, I'd get you a cup. But then again it's kind of late, you might not be able to sleep."

"Don't worry about it," Jade said. "Coffee tends to make me sleepy anyway. Just one thing, though. Don't take this the wrong way, but I don't think you actually work here."

"No! I do!" Connie swept up and down the aisle. "I remember clearly. Let's see, I always punch in here and say hi to everyone." She went through the motions before she came back through the little office. "I snag a coffee and come over and put my bag down...here." She came right toward Jade and stopped, confused as she looked down at the desk. "This is my desk. I was safe here, safe from...him." Connie's voice trailed off and she hugged her arms to her chest.

Jade picked up the note of panic in Connie's voice. "Who?"

Instead of replying, Connie drifted over her desk. "Where is my stuff? Why is Vickie's stuff all over? I told her not to put her pictures on my desk."

"Maybe you moved?" Jade shrugged, feeling unhelpful. "Um, where was this Vickie person before?"

"Over there, at that little table behind the bookshelf."

"I can see why she took over this desk," Jade muttered as she gave the cubby a quick look over. The bookshelf was stuffed with bulging files and printed manuals plus a bunch of small-publisher books on fire prevention and burn analysis. Fire. Burn. Damage. The words swam in front of her face like a swarm of angry flies.

Jade took a step back. Her breath caught in her throat as she tried to coach herself back to normalcy. And to think, she'd gone through all that therapy. Jade's chest got tight. She couldn't breathe. Fuck.

She had to get out of there. Clues or no clues. Thundering footsteps heralded Jade's hurried descent down the stairs. Before she knew what was happening, she was back in the safety of her car, gunning down the street as country songs poured from the radio.

As Jade's heart got back to normal, she turned over the night's events in her mind. She left so abruptly, she hadn't even thought to say anything to Connie. Still, Jade figured Connie would either drift off somewhere or stay in the office, possibly giving her coworkers quite a turn in the morning. The mental image summoned a sickly grin. But Jade had more to do than simply hang out in a strange office. She decided she needed to go home and sleep first so she could be ready to start fresh and give the investigation the attention it deserved.

Chapter Two

JADE SLEPT LATER than usual and after she shrugged into her clothes, she was lured downstairs by the smell of coffee and cinnamon coming from the café corner of the bookstore. A large plastic crate sat on the counter, full of the daily delivery of baked goods. In the sports aisle, Benny was busy with a feather duster in his hand, looking like an industrious male Tinkerbelle. He paused in his work to strike a pose, hand on hip and head cocked to one side.

"Good morning, sunshine," Benny chirped. "How did things go with the ghost?"

It was too early for her to appreciate cuteness. Jade scooped up a newspaper before she kicked a chair away from one of the three tables and threw herself into it. "Look Ben, I don't know if we should use the G-word around her. You never know, it may make her act strange."

"As opposed to what? I seem to remember not too much happening in the realm of 'not strange' last night," he said. "Have a coffee. You look like you need one. Couldn't sleep?"

"I was up late with Connie," Jade said. She picked up the mug Benny set in front of her and started ruffling through the paper.

"Oh, I bet you were. Having fun with your new friend?"

"Don't fucking get on my case, Ben," she gritted. Her fist clenched around the newspaper. Benny was saved from finding out how Jade dealt with annoying bugs by a rotund and curly-haired older lady who popped out of the stairway with a clatter.

She passed the café counter and leaned intrusively over Jade's table. "That smells great, where's mine?"

"Get your own damn coffee."

"Jade! You need to be kind to your aunt. She's the only one you have."

"That's right, Benny. You hear him Janie?"

"How many times do I need to tell you it's Jade," the owner of the name spat. She wrapped her fingers around her mug and squeezed tightly to stop herself from hurling it. Suddenly wary, Jade forced herself to relax her posture to a harmless and submissive one. Showing aggression could get you a Time-Out in the box. Then she stopped. Of course not.

"One of my special brews, coming right up." Benny swept over to the café counter and to Jade's relief, Addie followed him. While Benny was busy behind the counter piling muffins into a basket as the coffee machine whirred, Addie heaved herself onto one of the stools and flipped through their local community newsletter. She put it aside as a mug appeared in front of her.

"Oh my, just what I wanted." Addie blew across the surface of her coffee before she slurped up a mouthful. "Benny, you are such a good boy."

"I try, Aunt Addie." He preened. Jade ground her teeth together. "So, did Jade tell you about who visited us last night?" Benny asked. He scooted out from behind the counter and pulled over a chair from an unoccupied table. He sat down and crossed his legs with a showgirl flourish.

"Janie never tells me anything." Addie helped herself to a muffin from the basket beside her. "I don't know if she's coming or going. Back in my day a gal her age woulda had at least three kids in school. Look at her, she ain't so hard on the eyes. Even with what's happened, I bet she could get herself a good man who'd take care of her no problem."

"The problem my dear Aunt Addie," Benny said and tilted his head with a grin, "Is that Jade likes women."

"Even so," Addie huffed. "There's no reason why she can't find someone nice and settle down and start a family, responsible-like. They're letting anybody get married nowadays. And don't get me started about the fact that she's not getting any younger."

"Yes, how about we don't start that," Jade said in a conversational voice. She side-eyed the bread knife that was lying on the counter. She wagered that if she got a jump start, she could totally grab it in one smooth motion. Perhaps sensing this, Benny put it out of sight with a forced titter and offhand remark about keeping things tidy.

"Anyways, what's this about a mysterious caller last night?" Addie asked.

"A client," Jade heard Benny say. Jade, meanwhile, stalked

up and down the science fiction aisle. She noticed someone had moved all the bibles there. Again. With an aggrieved sigh, she shut out the prattling voices of Benny and her aunt and slinked into the women-for-women romance section. With a slim, independently-published novel in her hands, Jade leaned against the solid oak shelf and sullenly thumbed through it.

After a while, she heard Addie saying, not yelling, but saying in a very loud voice, "If the client don't pay then there ain't no reason for you to help them. Benny-boy here doesn't give his books away for free and I'da thunk you'd have just as good sense as him. I guess not."

"Nobody has as good fashion sense as me," Benny told the room in general. He wiggled his derrière over to the front door and unlocked it. He flipped the sign and threw the door wide open. He called out a cheerful, "Good morning! It's a lovely day!" to the few people shuffling around on the sidewalk outside.

Jade stayed in her bookish refuge until she heard the door to the stairway shut with a bang, followed closely by her aunt's heavy footsteps as she plodded up to her third-floor living area. Addie wasn't having a temper tantrum but simply seemed to be incapable of moving around or doing anything without making a noisy fuss about it. Jade wandered back to her table and downed more coffee. After a while, she found a muffin on a napkin beside her, which she shoved into her mouth whole, ignoring Benny's agonized cry of "Chew, sweetheart!"

Her notebook was open on the table in a warm square of sunlight, and Jade looked at the few facts she'd managed to get. This case was unusual, even for her. More than anything, she needed an ID. If she was investigating a recent murder, the morgue would be a good place to get answers. If not then she'd have to go digging around, hopefully not literally, for older information.

Cheerful voices swirled around her. The café corner teemed with regulars, and Benny chatted with them while handing out rounds of coffee and fancy drinks. Something warming up in the toaster oven filled the room with a cheesy aroma. Jade tuned everything out and concentrated on the case.

At least Connie was a local. With most of her money tied up in mutual funds and boring stuff like that, Jade didn't have the cash to self-finance a fact-finding mission to anywhere far on short notice. She wrote down the date and time of Connie's first appearance. It could prove useful to keep a timeline.

In the time she'd been hiding in the bookshelves, Benny had put away the newspaper Jade was reading so she stifled her muttered swear words and went over to the newspaper rack. She yanked out the morning edition of their local paper. Most people called it the "Chronic Horrible" and it was full of stuff the volunteer fire department did and school projects by random elementary school students. It might have been either too early or too late, but there was nothing about a young woman being murdered in that day's issue. Even the police blotter was as bland as usual. The Mancuso family's pita shop had burned down again and the river-cleaning project using inmates from a nearby low-security men's prison was reporting great success. No surprise there. Even if you were hauling slimy tires out of a river, getting the hell out of those four walls was a blessing. Something you did not want to fuck up.

She moved on to the regional paper and shuffled though some of the thicker national papers, but Jade couldn't find anything other than a whole bunch of accidents, incidents, and murders that didn't match her client's. She did her best to return the papers to their original order before she plopped back down at her table to stare out of the window. She rested her chin on one fist, eyes focused inward as Benny rushed over and started rustling around in the newspaper section, refolding everything.

He looked over as Jade got to her feet.

"Going upstairs?" he asked.

"Yeah, I want to work on some stuff in my office."

"Gotcha. Jim's working today, so I'll send him up with your lunch at noon. The usual ham and cheese on whole wheat okay?"

"Don't bother, I'm going to be out and about all day," she said as she sidestepped past the customers at the counter. "In fact, I'll probably be doing stuff all this week, so cancel lunch until I say otherwise."

"Sure thing, honey," Benny said and saluted with a flourish.

Jade stopped in front of the door to the stairway. She studied the lettering on the glass pane with her hands at her sides. Mayflower Investigations. Pretty swanky, if she did say so herself.

She didn't make a move to grip the brass doorknob.

"Um, you know that's not an automatic door," Benny pointed out helpfully. "And we don't have a butler. Well, besides me, I guess. I'm more of a concierge, though."

"Fuckity McFuckfurters." Jade exhaled Connie's phrase in a throaty growl.

Her shoulders came up and her head went down. She had to get over that goddamned habit of waiting for the guard to open the door. It came back when she least expected it and every time Jade wanted to smash something. It had only taken her a week to get over the fact she could switch lights on or off any time she wanted.

Jade was already through the door and halfway up the stairs before she remembered she'd forgotten to put her coffee mug away. She sighed. Ben would give her shit about having to clean up after her as usual. Jade knew she was supposed to be looking after Benny, but she wondered if it wasn't the other way around most of the time.

Back in her office, Jade hauled out what she liked to call her mission pack, a bunch of different colored Post-It notes and a big piece of brown paper. The paper got tacked up in her walk-in closet/auxiliary bedroom and the various items of information she'd collected got written down and stuck up on the paper. She'd originally wanted a clear writing board like they had in those detective TV shows, but the price was prohibitive and even trying it out in the hardware store had given Jade a headache. Not helping at all, the ass-for-brains hardware store guy's condescending remarks made Jade want to throttle him. Something she was sure her counselor would not be pleased to hear about, so she settled for telling him off and stomping out empty-handed.

By the time she'd gotten the scant facts down, Jade realized she really didn't have a whole lot of leads to go on. She needed to pay another visit to Connie's office, this time in the daylight. She sat on the low cot she kept in the closet for power naps and looked at the poster, wondering if Connie would show up. It was useful having the crime victim around. That was the reason Jade gave herself for wanting to see the young woman again.

There was the note about fires, but that seemed to be more about the office than anything else. Jade glared at the poster. She didn't want to remember the cute way Connie smiled, how the smallest innuendo from Jade could send her into a blush. She didn't want to think of how her body reacted when their eyes met.

At any rate, Jade had a bunch of things on her to do list that day and mooning over a ghost, no matter how cute, was not at the top. She slung her canvas messenger bag over her shoulder and headed down the stairs, ignoring Addie who wanted to know where she was going and tried to make her take a sweater.

"I folded your shirts from the laundry and you never even put them away." Her aunt's voice rang out querulously from the third floor.

"Yeah, whatever," Jade gritted.

"Janie? You listening to me, Janebeth?"

"Addie, for the last time, that's not my name!" Jade shouted over her shoulder as she stomped down the stairs and escaped into the street. Rage pounded through her veins. As far as Jade was concerned, Janebeth was long dead.

Her anger faded as Jade drove through the narrow streets of the town. She considered swinging by Amber's shop and then thought better of it. Facts first.

In the daylight, the squat grey office building was even more boring and utilitarian than at night. At least in the darkness the mist lent it a nice, spooky air. The fact that a ghost hung around at the time definitely added to the special feeling. The parking lot was half full and Jade took note of the cars, particularly the ones in the VIP spots.

Jade got into the elevator and studied her reflection in the mirror. In the too-short time between the first and fourth floors, she tucked in her shirt and tried to give a kindly smile to two young Asian guys who got in ahead of her. They clutched at their book-bags and backed away with looks of terror on their faces, which Jade took in stride. She was used to people being afraid of her. It came in handy sometimes.

Almost as an afterthought, Jade tugged down the rolled-up sleeves of her denim shirt, covering both the rich sprawl of tattoos on her right arm and extensive scarring on her left. One of the young men hammered at the "open" button. Both of them jumped off the elevator and scrambled away the moment the doors slid open.

Jade exited the elevator at a much more leisurely pace. She remembered her own days of dashing in and out of elevators. The firm where she'd worked was much larger than the one Connie worked at. It took up the entire six floors of the building that

housed it, and Jade ran ragged ferrying stuff from one department to another and scurrying to and from stupid board meetings. She used to call them "bored meetings" in ironic emails with
her coworkers. But that was another person and another reality.

In the daylight, Jade saw the company's name for the first
time, grubby letters against the frosted glass of the door. Goode
Fire Extinguishers Inc., which explained the fire thing at least.
Jade wandered in, hands in her pockets, then pulled them out in
an instant. Not allowed. Fuck it. She shoved them in again.

"Hi," Jade said to the unwelcoming face of the receptionist.
"I was wondering if you could help me."

"'Pends on what it is." The woman was wearing a vest with
the company's logo embroidered on the front over her blouse and
unflattering slacks combination. A clear plastic nameplate on the
counter in front of her read: Murel Finch.

"Well, Muriel," Jade began. She stooped just a bit to bring
herself closer to the receptionist's level. "I was—"

"It's not a typo," the woman said in a disagreeable voice. Her
face puffed up as her lips scrunched together. "It's Murel. MUR-
rel."

"Sorry about that." Jade resisted the urge to walk out. Instead
she continued, "I'm a private investigator and I'm interested in
one of your employees."

"Huh. All right, which one?" Murel's granite face didn't
change. She was getting paid to wait and had all day to do it.
Behind her, similarly vested people populated the cluttered and
bustling office. A lot of them shuffled papers and some of them
were on the phone. All of them carefully pretended not to be
interested in the visitor looming over the reception desk.

"I want to ask you a few questions about a young woman
named Connie—" Jade stopped and hoped that Murel would help
her out with the next bit.

"You mean Connie Mason? What's she done?"

Victory! However small.

"That's confidential for the moment. Would it be possible for
me to see her desk? I need to collect anything of hers that's here."

"Nope," Murel said. "She ain't got one no more. She quit."

"She did?" Jade gawked. That explained a few things anyway. "When did you last see her?"

"Last Thursday. That's the last anybody's seen of her, far as I know. We hadda goodbye party for her and everything," Murel told her. "What's your name again? And who hired you?"

"It's Jade Mayflower. And that's confidential between myself and my client."

"What's this about Connie?" An angular and almost painfully thin woman came over from the inner areas of the office. Her face was older than her years and she'd obviously made some kind of effort with her hair as it was teased into an artificial brownish orange halo around her head. She caught sight of Jade and flinched as if startled just by the existence of another person. "I'm Nathalie Gallant," she blurted out. "I took over for Connie after she left. Who are you again?"

"She's some kinda cop," Murel's loud voice boomed over the office before Jade could reply. "Something's happened with Connie. Mebbe she finally went off the deep end and killed someone. Allus the quiet ones, I say."

Movement in the office stopped. Everybody's face went blank. The disinterested pretense dropped.

"So you said she quit last week?" Jade prodded. She had to keep them talking. That was all she could think to do. She wasn't used to Q&A with the living.

"Yep. Can't say I blame her." Murel's attention went back to her computer screen. "Working here, that's gotta be a good reason to want to get away and go somewhere else."

A young woman with an armful of files pattered up to the little gathering. Jade recognized her from the photos on her desk — the one that used to be Connie's.

"What happened? Oh my God, was there an accident?" The bleached-blonde girl peered up at Jade who drew in an involuntary breath at the startling force of her blue eyes.

"Did you know Connie very well?" Jade asked.

"No, not really. She was kind of a loner. I really hope nothing's happened to her. She was always nice to me. I'm the new girl. I was always bugging her to help me with this and that. I kind of hoped we'd be friends."

"You're Vickie, right?" Jade wanted to take a step back as the girl came around the desk to stand next to her, but she didn't. You didn't back down when somebody tried to get into your space unless you wanted to make a habit of it. Jade's nose filled with the sweet, powdery scent of her makeup.

"Yes, that's me. Vickie Bourne."

"Didn't she say she was going on a trip or something?" Murel didn't bother to look up from shuffling through papers at her desk as she spoke. "That's why she quit? She said she was going on that Peace Boat thing. Bad idea, I told her but did she listen? Nope. You never know what's gonna getcha if you go on those things. I hear they make them volunteer in nasty, dirty places where they got no water. You know those places they allus show on TV with the kids eating that gross rice stuff with big-ass spoons? Ain't that right, Nathalie?"

"I heard the volunteers help a lot of people." Nathalie rocked slightly in her shoes. "So what brings you here? Connie doesn't work here anymore and she didn't leave a forwarding address or anything. We don't know where she is or even how to get in touch with her."

"That's the problem," Jade said. "Nobody else knows either."

"Oh my land," Nathalie breathed as she went back to her rocking.

There was a clatter as an inner door opened and released four coverall-wearing workers in various stages of scruffy, along with a suited man whose neck appeared to be nothing more than an arbitrary delineation by his necktie. The coveralled group immediately converged around the coffee corner where they poured packets of sugar into cups while making a string of loud comments and inside jokes that bordered on sexual harassment.

The suited man came over to the small gathering at reception with an annoyed look. His glasses reflected the harsh fluorescent lights and made his face look even less pleasant than it already was.

"So this is what you all do when I'm in a meeting. You girls having some kind of hen party out here instead of doing work?" He drew back and stared at Jade as if seeing her for the first time. "Look here ma'am, we have a no-solicitation policy. If I were you, I'd take my business elsewhere."

In a taut voice, Jade introduced herself and received the name Barton Butters in return.

"She's here 'bout Connie," Murel told him. "Apparently she's got herself kidnapped or missing or some other such fool thing. Came here for Connie's stuff she sez. Not that there's anything left."

Jade shifted from one foot to the other. All the talking was making her antsy. She wanted to move, do something physical and real instead of just gabbing.

"May I have a look around anyway?" Jade asked. She stepped forward and almost got past the reception desk before Murel was in her path.

"Why? You looking fer clues?" Murel only came up to Jade's mid-chest, but she was built like a dump truck and made an effective barrier.

"Sit down, Murel, it's okay," Nathalie wavered from where she was hovering over a desk. She looked like she'd fall over any second as she continued her nervous rocking. "What if there's something really wrong? I think we should do what we can."

"Suit yerself." Murel went back to her work. "There ain't nothing left to find anyway. Not like I care about trespassing laws. You okay with that, Mr. Butters?"

"Actually I have a letter for Ms. Mason here," Mr. Butters said. "She didn't fill out the final employee survey like she was supposed to so I have to mail it to her. Wherever she is, she's still gotta do it. HR needs this information."

"Not like they care either," Murel muttered just loudly enough for everyone to hear but quietly enough that they could pretend they hadn't.

"I can take that to her," Jade said. Her pulse quickened. That had to have an address on it. "Save you guys wasting money on a stamp." She appealed to the cheapskate living inside of every boss with what she hoped was a friendly smile on her face. Obligingly, Mr. Butters handed over the envelope. Another victory. Jade mentally high-fived herself as she stashed her prize in her bag.

"But you said she was missing." Vickie piped up from behind Jade. "Kind of like—well like something happened to her."

Oh shit.

"I'll hang onto it until we, uh, find someone with the responsibility to take it." Jade said a whole lot of bad words inside her head. She needed to brush up on her lying skills.

"Kin I see your business card?" Murel had a florid hand out.

"I prefer not to carry them."

"Likely story." Murel snorted to herself. "Funny the police haven't been around or anything. Just you. And this is the first

I've heard of the whole thing."

"When did," Nathalie started. She paused. Her mouth worked soundlessly before she asked, "When did it happen?"

"I'm afraid I can't give out any details," Jade said. She didn't care to elaborate that the reason was because she didn't know herself.

"Excuse me, but we have a business here to run." Mr. Butters shoved himself into the conversation.

"Yeah, I can see that," Jade said. "So you make fire extinguishers?"

"No, we make big red flowerpots," Mr. Butters said in a way that had Jade clenching her fists inside her pockets. "What the heck do you think all this is?"

Jade took a deep, slow breath and let it out. Taking a swing at the man was not an option, no matter how much she wanted to.

One of the engineers came over with an apologetic smile. "Mr. Butters means to say we make the pin that you pull to get the foam to come out. We assemble and distribute, and also do maintenance of our units. We gotta 'nother place out near Truro where they manufacture the canisters." He had both hands shoved into his coverall. Underneath his grayish stubble he looked friendly. His smile was genuine and unrehearsed. "But we do all of the product development here. Me and the gang were out back testing a bunch of new stuff the other day. We set a whole sofa on fire. I guess that's not really the important thing here, but it was a lot of fun."

Jade just replied with a sick grin. There was nothing remotely fun about setting shit on fire.

"Howsabout I show the lady around?" The last question was directed to Mr. Butters.

He grunted, "Do whatever you want." Without another word, Mr. Butters wandered off.

"Bill Glass, head of R&D." The big man came around the front of the reception desk and offered his hand to shake, which Jade did. "I'll introduce you around. Maybe someone can help you out."

"That's decent of you," Jade said. "I appreciate it."

"No prob. Connie's a trouper, a real fighter. I always thought she deserved better than what she got stuck with here. It kills me to think she might be in trouble and I'll do anything I can to help out."

The words of gratitude stuck in her throat as Jade followed Bill's creased coverall through the computer-heated maze between desks. She had to walk extra carefully to keep her butt from sweeping piles of papers off the desks as they passed. For his bulk, Bill managed the journey extremely well. "That's our engineering team over there. Those guys are Bob Hurley, Dan Brinkle, and Nora McAllen—"

"Not a guy, but thanks all the same," the person referred to as Nora shouted back from where she and the other engineers were tinkering with the coffee machine. She didn't look too offended.

After a slow tour of the office, they ended up at Vickie's desk. Jade looked down at the curly-haired girl who was working on some kind of chart on her computer.

"So this here's Connie's old desk. I dunno if there's anything she left in it, but Vickie'd know."

"It was cleaned out really well." Vickie's eyes were big. "She didn't leave a single thing."

Jade had expected that. "How did Connie get along with everyone here? Any trouble?"

She didn't miss the look that passed between Bill and Vickie. Vickie opened her mouth to speak, but Bill gave her a little shake of his head. Jade narrowed her eyes. He didn't look guilty or upset. If anything, he seemed sad.

"No one comes to mind." Bill shoved a hand under his cap and scratched at himself thoughtfully. "Connie was a pretty quiet gal, never had much to do with any of us at the office, but not in a bad way. Just kept to herself. She went out with you a bit, though, right Vickie?"

"A little. She showed me around to some of the, um, the bars in town."

Jade wondered why there was a pink flush on the girl's face.

"Uh, how about I give you two gals some alone time?" Bill gave Vickie a thumbs-up sign and a broad wink, and then wandered off.

"Thanks Bill," Vickie said before she turned the full force of her deep blue eyes back to Jade. She stood up and leaned one hip against her desk, never breaking eye contact.

Uncomfortable under Vickie's single-minded attention, Jade

glanced around. The rest of the office was oppressive in its heat and bustle, but that corner was almost pleasant. The desk had a wall behind it and a window to the right. The building faced east and the morning light filled the room with golden slashes through the blinds.

"Nice spot," Jade said.

"I'm lucky, I guess," Vickie said. She gifted Jade with a sparkling smile and leaned into Jade's space. "I really want to know what's going on with Connie. She was kind of like a mentor to me. She showed me the ropes and got me introduced and settled and all. It's just, God, it's so weird to think something might have happened to her." She paused and fluttered her lashes at Jade. "Um, can I give you my card?"

"Sure." Jade fought the swell of unease as Vickie also gave her a lingering once-over. There was something predatory in the way she looked Jade up and down. Jade at once felt that her denim shirt and baggy jeans combination was both too butch and not nearly butch enough.

"My mobile number's on the back," Vickie said in a soft, intimate voice that had Jade wondering if Vickie was making a play for her. She decided to take a gamble.

"I wish it was always this easy to get pretty girls to give me their phone number," Jade said in a low voice as she leaned in closer to the young woman.

As Vickie handed over a business card, Jade let her fingers brush over Vickie's. Her cheeks flared red. Bingo. Vickie looked down and flinched back from the contact. Her eyes were fixed on the puckered skin on the back of Jade's hand.

Reflexively yanking at the cuff of her shirt, Jade cursed in her head. She'd had over two decades to get used to her scars and she forgot the effect they had on other people. A second later, Vickie was smiling again.

"I don't usually give out my number so easily. But I'll make an exception for you," Vickie replied, just coquettishly enough to set off Jade's flight reflex.

The moment of disgust as they'd touched passed so quickly Jade was almost convinced she'd imagined it. Whatever else was going on, things were beginning to get interesting. Vickie continued, "Anyway, if you find out anything or need to ask for any information, just let me know. I've only been here for a few months, but I kind of get what's going on."

Jade wanted to say she did too, but didn't. Instead she asked, "What did Connie do, exactly?"

"She handles—I mean, handled, replacement parts and customer complaints," Vickie said. She oozed forward again until her shoulder was almost brushing Jade's arm. "Nathalie's taken over most of her duties."

"You get a lot of complaints?"

"Who doesn't?" Vickie grinned, showing small, white teeth. The front two gapped slightly. Even though she was at work, she was made-up like she was going out. Her lips were pink and sparkly, her long lashes black with mascara. "But, yeah, when you make safety equipment there's a lot you have to answer for. And it seems like there's been nothing but problems lately. Connie, well, she took a lot of it personally. Like she felt responsible if something went wrong. Recently she's been, I don't know exactly, but she'd go off and come back with red eyes. She acted all right, but there was something off. It might have had something to do with some problems with our new products. Or maybe she just couldn't stand to be here anymore after—um, what happened." She stuck her thumbnail in her mouth and gnawed at it. Her eyes were fixed on a desk across the room from them. It held the slouched figure of a young man Jade hadn't met yet. The fear in Vickie's expression gave Jade pause. She put a trip across the room on her list of things she wished to accomplish that day.

Just then, Mr. Butters poked his head out of his office and shouted some instructions at Vickie. She turned and scooped up a pile of papers. "Um, I gotta go. Anyway, let me know what you find out."

After Vickie disappeared into the meeting room, Jade took advantage of her un-chaperoned situation to make a slow tour of the room. She ended up in front of the young man's desk. His mousy hair was greasy and unkempt and his worn corduroys looked like they'd seen his ass through a few days already. While he was lank and gawky, his face was heavy-cheeked and set in a surly expression. He had a portable music player on his lap and he grunted along to it, drumming on one thigh instead of even pretending to do work.

"What do you want?" His watery eyes stopped before they

reached her face and he addressed the third button of her shirt. "Is Jade Mayflower your real name?"

"It is now," she said.

"Sounds like a stripper." His lips were slightly parted and a thread of saliva hung between them.

"What's your name then, son?" Jade wasn't taking any crap from that whippersnapper. He could stare all he wanted. Enjoy the view she wanted to say. He looked like he was fresh out of college, so Jade had about twenty years on him. She also had a lot of butt-kicking experience and was sure she could take him in a fair fight. Hell, she could take him in an unfair fight. She'd let her hair get long and dressed pretty low-key, but that didn't change the fact that she was still a stone-cold butch inside, ready to deal out a good pounding at any time it seemed necessary.

"Gord Holloway. How come you're here? Did Connie's family hire you? I don't know anything, so just leave me out of it."

His eyes never left the front of her shirt. Jade resisted the urge to return the favor and fake-leer at the most likely unimpressive junk stashed behind the fly of his grubby pants. He was just another young guy who thought his dick was the center of the world. She didn't want to talk to him and wouldn't have in any other situation. However, the unappealing specimen was high on the list of suspects that had Connie upset and feeling unsafe.

"How long have you been working here?"

"I don't think I have to answer that." He fiddled with his music player as he spoke. Tinny noise swelled from his earphones.

"No, you don't," Jade said amiably. "However, you're making yourself more interesting to me. I might just have to do some digging and find out for myself."

"You do that." Gord didn't look at her. He slouched lower in his chair.

"I will."

After the unsatisfying meeting with Gord, Jade wandered back into the thick of the office, determined to stay there as long as she could stand. She chatted with the other people there and was invited over for an impromptu coffee-drinking contest with the engineers. They apparently revamped the coffee machine to shoot out jets of espresso and took turns filling shot glasses and passing them around.

Mr. Butters retired into his office and could be heard having a loud conversation in Chinese behind it. Jade eavesdropped and wished she'd picked up some more of that. Portuguese and Quebecois, no problem, but the only Cantonese she knew was bad words. Maybe she'd get a Chinese girlfriend next.

At one point, Jade noticed Nathalie hunched over her phone, speaking intently and at length about some kind of problem, a misfire, if she made out the words correctly. It seemed like she was apologizing and almost in tears about it. Yeah, fire sucked. Jade reflexively crossed her arms and tucked her left hand into her armpit.

Jade hung out until the oppressive office atmosphere drove her to escape. She was waiting for the elevator when Vickie came out of the office. She stood just a little bit too close to Jade, who decided not to move away, this time not to protect her turf, but because she didn't feel like there needed to be a lot of distance between them and it seemed Vickie agreed.

"So I guess you met Gord?"

"Yeah." Jade suppressed a grimace. "Not exactly a catch, is he?"

"I don't like him." Vickie crossed her arms and shivered. The motion brought her arm flush with Jade's. She didn't seem to notice Jade froze in place as she said, "He's always had this weird thing for Connie. Like, he had a bunch of pictures of her in his desk that Bill found and made him throw out. Nothing illegal. He'd just picked them out from the ones we took at company events and stuff. Anyway, that's how Connie got to move her desk into that nice spot—she used to sit with her back to Gord and he was always trying to smell her hair. He cut off a bit of it one day and that was it. He said it was an accident but come on."

"Lovely fellow," Jade said. The elevator came and Vickie stepped back. Her eyes flicked to the opening doors. Jade didn't move and the doors slid silently closed. "Did he ever do anything to her? You know, anything that would make her feel threatened?"

Vickie chewed her bottom lip before she said, "I don't know if Connie would want this to get out, but about a month ago we all went out one night for drinks and Connie got really drunk. Like falling down, staggering drunk."

A jolt went through Jade. She had a sick feeling where the

story was heading and she didn't want to hear it.

"Anyway, we were just talking and suddenly she was gone and I went to find her but I couldn't. I got really worried so I went back in and got everyone to come out and help me." Vickie chewed at her thumbnail again. "Bill and Nora were the ones who found her. She was lying on the back seat of Gord's car with her skirt up and her panties down."

"Jesus Christ," Jade breathed. "That fucker."

"He said he didn't do it," Vickie said in a rush. "He said he didn't even know how she got in there and some random guy must have grabbed her or something. Mr. Butters believed him but it messed Connie up. She was so worried about, like diseases and whatever. I was with her when she went to the hospital but they didn't find anything. Whoever did it, he must have used a condom. She wasn't even, you know, torn." Vickie gave an awkward giggle and Jade fought a wave of nausea. "Guess that means he's pretty small or Connie was more into it than she let on."

Jade couldn't speak past the fist of sorrow and rage in her gut. It took all of Jade's willpower not to barge back into the office and pound Gord into mush.

"Anyway," Vickie said in a breathy voice that had Jade uneasily wondering if it was for her benefit, "would it be okay if I gave you a call to, I don't know, to let you know if anything comes up here?"

Jade didn't have a chance to reply before Vickie held out a pen and her exposed wrist. With her eyes trained on her task, Jade scribbled her number on Vickie's bare skin.

"Thank you," Vickie said with a smile. She lingered against Jade for just a second too long to be meaningless before she pulled away and trotted back to the office.

Once she was alone again, Jade lunged for the button and called the elevator back. She showed herself out of the front entrance and was heading back to her car when a voice stopped her in her tracks.

"Miz Mayflower, got a minute?"

Jade stopped and looked around as she tried to figure out where the voice had come from. Bill poked his head out from the fenced-in shed in the parking lot and gestured for her to come closer.

"Me and Nora were just gonna light up a bunch of stuff. Try

out some new products. How about joining us? I think there's
something you should see."

Jade took an involuntary step back and grabbed at her left
arm.

"Oh no, I don't think so."

Bill's eyes went to the ridged and puckered skin revealed by
her cuff.

"You've had some experience with fire, huh?"

"Yeah, just a bit." Jade bit off a curse and shoved her hands
into her pockets.

"Think of it as therapy. Come on, it'll be good for you."

Unable to think of a way to get out of it, Jade unwillingly followed Bill into the enclosure. After giving Jade a nod, Nora
squatted down in front of a bound stack of papers with a Zippo in
her hand. Jade tried to stop herself from flinching as the lot of it
went up in a merry orange blaze. The edges of the papers crinkled
and turned black as the fire devoured them. Her breath came
harder as the hazy memories of waking up on hard concrete in
the middle of hell came back in full force.

"Okay, here's our new extinguisher." Bill held up a shiny red
cylinder. "Same as the old one on the outside, but the inside is
different." With a practiced pull, he yanked out the pin and
aimed the nozzle at the fire. A sizzling sound came out followed
by uneven puffs of white smoke. The flames didn't die down, in
fact, they seemed to be getting stronger.

Jade took a step back and collided with Nora's comforting
bulk. "Isn't that supposed to be a bit more effective?"

"Yup." Bill tossed the extinguisher to the ground. "That's the
new filler Mr. Butter's got in all our new units. Some factory in
China makes it and I have no idea what the hell's in it. He won't
let us take any samples."

"Why would he do that?"

"It's cheap as shit and for a real small fire, it does the trick.
Anything more than say a candle and you're talking a crisis situation."

Jade breathed a series of words that sizzled just as much as
the plastic binding on the newspapers. She clawed at the fall of
bangs that hung into her eyes.

"Hey Bill, you know those papers are really going up over
there. How about you get something else and put that fire the hell

out? Like, now?"

"Go ahead." Bill grinned. He nodded and Nora handed Jade another fire extinguisher.

"Pull the pin and hold here." She gestured with cool efficiency as she said, "Squeeze down in short bursts while aiming low. Got it? Aim for the base of the fire, not directly at it or over it. Don't worry, this is one of our old ones. It won't let you down."

As if she was warming up for some softball pitching, Jade shuffled her feet and bounced her shoulders a few times. She gripped the fire extinguisher and did as she'd been instructed. Even in her shaking hands, the cloud that erupted from the nozzle was powerful and snuffed the flames with only three bursts. Jade looked at the gently smoking pile with satisfaction. She rubbed one hand across her forehead and came away with a wristful of cold sweat. An exhilarated feeling of victory sang through her and Jade didn't feel the helpless fear that usually froze the shit out of her around open flames.

"Take that, fire! Thought you could get me, did ya? Ha!" she shouted and pumped one fist into the air. The two engineers looked at her with big grins and she shot off a few more frothy blasts, just to make sure. "Now that's what it should be doing!"

"Yup," Bill said. "Look, I don't know how much they told you, but it used to be Connie's job to deal with the fallout when our products failed. We switched to the new stuff around the start of the year, and three months ago we had our first fatality."

Jade hissed a breath through her teeth and steeled herself for the rest.

"A family. Two kids. Could have been prevented. She held herself together until closing, but then she just had a meltdown. Vickie had to take her home. Maybe that might have been the last straw? Make her want to get out of here?"

"What about that other incident?" Jade blurted out. The words tasted foul. "You know which one."

"So you know about that." Bill's face fell. "I know it shook her up a bit, but Connie's tough. She came back, held her head up, and kept going like nothing happened. They never did find out who did it. Far as I know, the case is closed."

"Why did you try to hide it from me?" Jade asked in a sharp voice. Beside her, Nora looked at the ground.

"Look, maybe I should'a told you from the start," Bill said. He put a hand over his face. "But Connie was ashamed enough when it happened, and I didn't want to be the one to dredge it up. I feel awful that we all had to see her like that. It's not easy for me to talk about it. I got two daughters myself and every day I worry about them and what's waiting out there."

"Fair enough," Jade said. The man seemed to be genuinely upset. Jade knit her brows together. It seemed like life was out to get Connie. Even so, the light hadn't gone out in Connie's heart. She still laughed at Jade's jokes, got flustered when Jade flirted with her, and above all, reached out for life with a hunger that kept her from the other side.

"Okay people," Nora interrupted the somber mood. She held up red ball. "Who's up for a little smoke grenade demonstration?"

"I sure am," Bill crowed. He looked over to Jade who shrugged her consent in kinship with the two scruffy engineers.

Chapter Three

AFTER SHE LEFT Connie's workplace, Jade sat in the car and wondered what the hell was going on. The fact that someone appeared after their death and hired her to investigate it was quite beyond her scope for understanding. She was no stranger to seeing things, knowing things she shouldn't, but this situation was a first. None of the ghosts she'd seen ever approached her like this. It was almost as if Connie wasn't a ghost at all but something else. Jade took the steering wheel of the car in her hands and soon the road was purring under her tires.

"Sucks to be me."

Jade jumped at the voice. Connie's slender figure was beside her in the passenger seat.

"How do you mean?" Jade tried to keep her tone level. She needed to get used to these sudden appearances.

"I had to force myself to go there every morning. Sometimes I would get a stomachache and nearly faint in my car before getting there. So many times I thought about not turning into the parking lot. Just keep on driving until I ran out of road. It's actually kind of nice to not have to go there anymore. I totally understand why you ran out of there last night."

"Sorry about that. I just got triggered," Jade said. "It wasn't personal, you know that, right?"

"I hoped it wasn't because of me," Connie said. She gave Jade a sideways glance. "I would hate to think my presence makes women run screaming into the night."

"Not at all, sweets," Jade said.

On a whim, she rolled down Connie's window and let the car fill with the fragrant morning breeze. It was a splendid late summer day. The sunlight was warm and the air was full of the musk of burning leaves. Connie closed her eyes and leaned out of the open window.

"I heard about what you did for your job," Jade said. She didn't want to bring up the incident with Gord. Not yet. If Connie was repressing the memory, Jade didn't want to risk having her bolt. "Tough work."

"Yeah. It sucked the life right out of me. Day in and day out having to apologize over and over. And when something goes wrong—" She broke off and squeezed her eyes closed.

"Aw honey," Jade murmured. "Bill and the other engineers seem okay."

"Yeah, those guys are good people." Connie perked up. The grin she sent Jade brightened her entire face. "Vickie's all right too."

"Yeah, she is." Jade was strangely reluctant to bring up the young woman in front of Connie.

Jade stifled the nervous, uneasy feeling and concentrated on driving. It was unnerving how she could read passing road signs through Connie. She focused on getting the radio tuned to something other than the Christian Rock channel as she didn't want to accidentally exorcise her client, especially now she seemed to be remembering things and was more grounded than the previous night.

Connie's voice interrupted Jade's thoughts. "Did Bill let you go out back and help him set stuff on fire?"

"Yeah, he and Nora let me try out some things. The smoke grenade was pretty spectacular. Like poof and the place was completely white, that was cool."

"That's what I really love about my job. Trying new stuff out and seeing how it works. Especially the smoke grenades. I bet you had a good time."

"Actually, I'm not all that okay around fire," Jade said. She figured what the hell, ghosts can't blab. It wasn't like she was trying to hide it either. "I got burned pretty bad back when I was—" What? When she was an innocent kid? A clueless schlep more like it. She settled on the nebulous, "When I was younger."

"I know. I saw your scars. I'm sorry that happened."

"It was a long time ago," Jade said. "Being burned is like nothing else. You wanna die but can't quite make it. And I was lucky. I didn't lose my fingers. It was more my back and my arm. The jacket I had on spread the burns around but it sure hurt like a sonovabitch picking all that polyester off me." Jade resolutely yanked the steering wheel around. She wondered if she should just shut up right then, but her counselor always said it was good to talk these things out. Besides, Connie seemed like she'd understand.

Jade signaled to turn and said, "You people and your extinguishers are doing a good thing. I wouldn't wish the pain of being burned, the skin grafts and all that horrible stuff that goes with it, on anybody. I spent some of it in a coma, but after I woke up, sometimes it just got so bad I—went someplace else. It was like I would *slip* out of my body and kind of hover around in this in-between place. I would always end up getting yanked back, but it was like less of me came back every time. Even now there's something stretching me between here and there." Jade shook herself back into reality before she said, "But I got through it. Not everybody does."

"I'm glad you did." Connie looked at her. She flickered gently as they passed under an arch of trees. "You seem like a really nice person, helping me out and all. Even though I can probably only pay you in boo dollars." Her grin was quick, but it illuminated her face in an instant. Jade gulped. Her heart sent a bolt of liquid heat straight to her crotch. Fuck. She did not want to realize once more exactly how cute Connie was.

"Aw shit, you heard that?"

"I hear a lot of things." Connie stared down at her clasped hands. "I wish I knew more to help you out. I don't think anyone's ever been as nice to me as you are now. That's the truth. I feel it in my—I was going to say in my bones but I don't know where those are."

"Honey, I got a feeling we'll find those eventually. You have to stay with us for that long, okay?"

There was no answer and Jade looked over to see an empty seat. A visit to Amber's House of Woo-Woo was definitely in order. A few U-turns later, she pulled the car into the gravel parking lot. Amber's shop, named Womyn's World, was one in a line of redone cargo containers donated by the shipping companies that operated out of the port. The one to the left of Amber's was home to a makeshift deli-counter that served kosher hotdogs Jade had a fondness for. It was too early for lunch and Jade noted the Closed sign on the door with a twinge of disappointment. The shop on the right was also closed; however, that wasn't much of a surprise. Ross generally kept irregular hours and didn't show up unless he had an appointment. As she hopped up the three wooden steps to Amber's place, Jade wondered if Sky was around. While Jade wasn't a huge fan of anklebiters in general, she had to admit that kid was all right.

Jade wandered into the store and froze in the entrance as she always did. She needed a moment to get used to the heady scent of incense and the multiple depictions of fleshy orchids all over the walls and ceiling. One other customer was there, a woman encased in a black and crimson corset who was sitting moodily on one of the little mushroom chairs Amber had placed about her shop. It was probably a wig, but the woman had long, pure white braids that spilled over her crouched form and fell to the floor.

The jingle of the door was barely over when a smiling and plump redhead hustled out from the handmade jewelry-laden counter. A Batik sheath dress hugged her curvy figure and brushed the floor. Jade could see her mustard-yellow Birkenstocks flashing under the hem. She smelled like cinnamon and dried saliva, some kind of weird independent brand perfume that was all the rage with the Pagan crowd at the moment. Amber tried to sell her a vial of the stuff the first time Ross introduced them. Jade found it nothing short of nasty and pitched the glass thing out the front door where it smashed into a little spackle of stink on the sidewalk. Amber never tried again.

"Jade!" Amber came over and Jade found herself enveloped in a squishy hug. "I was just thinking about you and you appeared!"

"Hey Amber," Jade coughed as Amber released her. "I happened to be in the neighborhood and thought I'd stop by."

"It's always nice to see you. I hope you're well?"

"Yeah, I'm doing pretty good," Jade said. She stuffed her hands in her pockets and said, "Actually, I need to talk to you about something kind of weird."

"That's fine, you know I'm always around and ready to talk about anything."

As the sullen corseted woman wandered over toward a rack of books labeled Vegan Cooking, Amber appropriated the mushroom chair she'd vacated. She dragged it over to a small, round table with a collection of tea-related equipment on it. Amber hovered as she poured hot water from an electric kettle into a glass teapot. Loose tea leaves swirled around inside it. Jade relaxed in silence for a moment. She appreciated the leisurely ritual. Finally, Amber poured for them both and passed a cup over to Jade.

"So," Amber said. She fixed Jade with a patient look. "What's on your mind, then?"

Jade stared into her cup and studied the leaves floating around inside it before she swallowed her tea in a scalding gulp. After the entire thing went down her gullet, Jade wondered if it was good idea to have drunk the leaves too. With a mental shrug, Jade dismissed the thought. She'd ingested a whole lot worse in the past twenty years and nothing had killed her yet. It wasn't like they were going to grow into trees in her belly or anything like that.

The silence dragged before Jade blurted out, "There's this girl I need to talk to you about."

Amber's pearly face glowed with smiles. "Don't tell me you've found yourself a lady friend."

"Not exactly," Jade said. "I'm being haunted."

Suddenly Amber was all business. "What kind of entity? Is it self-aware? Is it causing any electrical disturbances in nearby appliances? Does it have an effect on physical items?"

"She's hired me to solve her murder."

Amber stopped, her expression frozen in a mixture of surprise and disbelief. "That seems quite self-aware enough. Is she like the others?"

"No." Jade shifted. "I don't just get visions, and instead of the usual few words, I get whole conversations. She actually communicates with me. Answers questions, remembers stuff I've said, and that sort of thing. She doesn't remember a whole lot of her life before, but I've been able to find out a number of things about her."

"So she's a real person?"

"Yeah, she is. Stuff she's said pans out in real life."

Amber held out the teapot once more and Jade allowed her cup to be refilled. Jade figured she'd be toilet-hopping on the way home, but drank the steaming tea anyway.

Jade continued, "She's been around since last night, actually. I went to her work today and they knew her. I got a name, an address, and everything. Also, I think I just saw her going behind that rack of magazines."

"There's a Presence in my shop!" Amber leapt to her feet and looked about herself ecstatically. "That's a first. Do you think I could get a picture of her?" She already had her phone in her hand.

"I don't know," Jade said. "Benny tried to take a video of her last night but didn't get anything."

"That's a pity," Amber said and stowed her phone in her bosom. "How stable is she?"

"More than the usual ones." Jade stretched her hands over her head but stopped as the taut scar tissue on her left arm gave a twinge. "When she first appeared, she was pretty faint and flickering, so I lit that incense shit you gave me and I guess that worked. But even without it she seems to be getting stronger as time passes. Don't know why, exactly."

"That's your influence," Amber said. She fluffed herself up like a proud mother hen. "You've got this pull to you. The lost ones recognize you and they come to you. They are drawn to you and are nourished by your aura."

"Sure wished that shtick worked on gals in the world of the living," Jade cracked.

"What would you like me to help you out with? I can't beat you in the channeling area, but I can give you some tips on how to help her over the threshold."

"No, I need her here. She's pretty much the only lead I have in this case." Jade didn't want to admit the flash of panic that welled up at the thought of Connie going away forever. The strange ache of loss.

"All right. But when the time comes, you have to let her go."

"Yeah, I know that. But in the meantime I was wondering if you had something, like more incense maybe, that would help Connie. She seems to struggle a lot just to be here. I guess that's normal, but if I could make it a bit easier on her that'd be great."

"Well, I do have a special candle," Amber began, and then raised her hands at Jade's glare. "Not that one—I know how you feel about Sapphic Magicks."

"No fucking way I'm burning something shaped like a hoo-ha in my house," Jade muttered. "No matter how much pussy I'm supposed to get from it. Smelled like someone took a dump on top of a bunch of rotten squirrels."

"So you did light it!" Amber clapped, delighted. "All right, no candles then. I do have something in mind that may help you."

She quickly sobered and went behind the counter where she reached into a box and pulled out a black velvet bag. She shook a few clear, polished stones into her pink and moist palm where she rolled them against each other as she studied them. Finally, she chose one and poured the rest back into the bag.

"This crystal is good for grounding energies and taming wild Magicks, especially when coupled with chanting and meditative dance."

"Enough with that magic crapola already." Jade was slowly but surely losing patience. She should have known Amber would just try to preach some kind of stupid woo-woo shit to her.

"Don't dismiss it out of hand, Jade. This is good for your Connie," Amber said as she held the crystal up to the light. "Consider this crystal a gift. I support your otherworldly interactions. You are the bridge between worlds and a sacred line in the Mother's all-seeing eye."

"What the fuck is that supposed to mean?" Jade bitched. "This isn't like that time you tried to get me to jump my naked ass over that bonfire at your Goddess camp, is it? Because I'm Protestant. I told you that."

"Of course your faith is valid. The Goddess smiles on all womyn."

"Yeah yeah," Jade said. "By the way, is Ross coming in today?" She flipped up her right cuff and absently stroked the small tattoo of a sparrow on the inside of her wrist. In contrast to the sharp details and vivid colors of the others around it, the bird was faded and the lines bled into her skin. "I was thinking of going ahead with that touch-up he offered to do."

"That's wonderful to hear," Amber said. "But I'm afraid today he's chaperoning Sky on her class trip to the science center. He'll be in all the rest of the week, though. I'll pass on your message."

"Thanks," Jade said.

Jade drank some more tea and used the "Womyn's Room" then looked at some naughty magazines that were pretending to be art while Amber wrapped up her crystal. She came back with a small paper bag which Jade obligingly shoved into the back pocket of her jeans and schlepped out.

BACK IN HER office, Jade added the new information to her case wall in the closet. When her store of facts was exhausted, she pulled out some weights and did reps while she studied the scant information. She focused on working her upper body, breathing slowly as the good kind of burn rippled through her. Even after all that time, her left side still struggled to keep up with her right.

Muscles taut and glowing, Jade chucked the weights back into their corner before she sprawled out on top of her little cot in the closet and closed her eyes. She had a perfectly good bed just down the hall in her bedroom, as her aunt constantly reminded her, but Jade preferred to camp out in her closet. She just couldn't get comfortable in that vast expanse of mattress. It was too big, too fluffy. Too empty.

Just as Jade was sleepily deciding between snacking on the peanut butter crackers she'd stashed in the basket under her cot or venturing into her kitchen for actual food, her cell phone rang. Startled, Jade yanked it out of her pocket and promptly dropped it.

"Piss-flaps gloryhole shit plunger," Jade snapped as she raced after it. She managed to scoop up the phone before the voicemail bullshit kicked in and answered in a breathless, "What?"

"Hi, it's Vickie. Are you okay to talk now?"

"Yeah, sure," Jade said. She furrowed her brow as she wondered why Vickie was calling her.

"I just wanted to see if you were busy tonight."

A jolt of nerves hit Jade in the gut, but she fought it down. "Nope, I'm free."

"Oh that's good. You see, a bunch of us gals were meeting up at Sunny's and I thought it would be nice if I could get you to come along too. Connie first took me out there and I, well I had the feeling it was the kind of place you'd like to go."

Jade had never been there but she'd heard of it. Sunny's was the local lesbian meat-market and popular with the younger crowd. Just the other day Amber urged her to go there and try her luck with the local "Gay until Graduation" set.

"Goddamn it, Vickie," Jade said as she flopped back onto her cot. "I'm an old lady to all you kids. I'd probably get laughed back out onto the street if I even set foot in there."

"No way," Vickie said. "Lots of us like older women." The phone went silent for a beat, then Vickie continued, "Sorry if that was too forward. I didn't mean anything by it."

"That's okay." Jade knew she'd end up going, even though

just the thought of going out was incredibly daunting. After all, her counselor and Amber both agreed that it would be good for her to be involved in a normal, i.e. mutually consensual, relationship. Maybe some of Vickie's friends were old enough for Jade to actually consider them a possibility. "I know where the place is. What time?"

A high-pitched titter bothered Jade's ear as Vickie gushed, "Oh, I just knew you'd come out with us. Actually, it'll be just me from the start, but a few girls are coming later." Her bright voice paused. Jade twitched in impatience. Her time was going to run out and Vickie still hadn't gotten to the point. With an angry shake of her head, Jade dismissed the thought. She could talk all day if she wanted to. "I hope that's all right," Vickie said.

"Sure, no problem," Jade said, more to reassure herself than the girl on the other end of the phone. "I'm cool with that."

"Great! You know what, I'm just about finished here, do you want to meet up for dinner? Do you know the Italian restaurant down the street from Sunny's? I think it's called La Tomatina or something like that."

"Sure, sounds good," Jade said with a calm possession she didn't feel. She forced herself to participate in the inane, normal telephone chatter. Jade was back in high school and had the nervous hormones to prove it. She was already on her feet by the time Vickie hung up. In three bounds, Jade went up to Addie's domain on the third floor. She was dozing on the sofa in front of the TV but managed to wake up and demand to know why Jade hadn't left enough bread for sandwiches.

"I don't fucking know," Jade said. "Look, I have to go out tonight and, um, could I ask you to keep an eye on things until I get back?"

"A date?" Addie sat up and adjusted her glasses.

"No, not really," Jade snapped. "Just make sure nobody gives Benny trouble when he's cashing out."

"Sure thing," Addie said.

Jade was already running down the stairs as she heard the words echoing behind herself: "Good luck, Janie!"

Jade didn't bother to correct her aunt. She was going to need all the luck she could get. Jade had no fucking idea what she was even going to wear, let alone how to act. She bypassed her office and screeched to a halt in her bedroom. She yanked her dresser open and threw T-shirts all over, decorating every available surface with random cotton rectangles.

"Somebody give me a bit of help here?" she shouted to the ceiling, hopefully communicating to the Goddess above even through the supplicant was not exactly a loyal worshipper. "What the hell does a twenty year out-of-the dating scene gal wear to her first visit to a dyke bar?"

"How about that shirt?" a cheerful voice suggested. Jade whirled. Connie was peeking into the opened doorway. She pointed to a light blue button-down shirt that managed to get caught on the back of a chair. "And if you want to be extra butch, how about that tie?"

"Sweet! Thanks Connie." Jade grabbed the shirt and froze. Ghost or not, she didn't want to strip in front of Connie. Jade cleared her throat. "Um, could you turn around for a sec?"

"Oops!" Connie put her hands over her flushed cheeks. "I wasn't trying to peep."

"Don't worry about it," Jade said while Connie obligingly faced the wall. As Jade yanked her top off, she felt herself becoming a bit warm as well. She shrugged into the shirt and quickly did up the buttons. "Okay, coast is clear. What do you think?"

"Very nice," Connie said. "The blue looks great with your eyes."

"Yeah yeah," Jade muttered, not displeased. She rummaged around and came up with some cargo pants, which Connie vetoed.

"Try jeans or those slacks."

"No to the slacks, those belonged to my mama," Jade said. "No way am I going to let some sweet young thing feel me up through my mother's crotch."

"I can see how that could make for less than an optimal experience." Connie perched on the dresser, the only clear spot in the room. She had her pointed chin balanced in her hands and looked like she was enjoying herself. For one of the lost ones, as Amber liked to call them, Connie was a pretty sweet specimen. With a sudden, wry shake of her head, Jade decided she really needed to get some action if she was stuck on how cute the ghost haunting her was. At least she was heading in the right direction by going out to Sunny's.

After a long debate and consultation with Connie, Jade settled on a pair of low-riding, boot-cut blue jeans that showed off her butt and went well with her favorite cowboy boots, and a hand-me-down wine-colored top with some understated sparkles on the front and an open neckline. As she checked herself out in the mirror, Jade wasn't entirely comfortable with how it showed a good expanse of the scarred skin at the juncture of shoulder and neck. The top hit the floor and Jade once more dug through her closet in only her sports bra and jeans combo, having discarded her modesty somewhere along the way. Finally, she found a ribbed cotton top with a high neck. The top was a present from Addie and it fit Jade almost too well. Before she could stop herself, Jade cupped her hands over the modest swell of her breasts. While she wasn't prepared to go into hardcore butch mode quite yet, she wasn't exactly all that eager to flaunt her womanly curves either.

"Don't like how it shows off my tits," Jade muttered.

"Wow, I sure do," Connie said. Jade was at once aware of the young woman standing still in front of her. Connie shook her head once, blonde hair waved about her face before she blinked and said, "Um, sorry for staring. It's just, wow Jade. You're going to cause a stampede in that. Oh my! Did someone turn up the heat in here or is it just you?" She fanned herself with one hand. Connie jumped off the dresser and made an exaggerated expression of interest as she walked slowly in a circle around Jade.

"Enough with the payback, you're making me blush." Jade swatted at the spirit, who scooted out of the way with a bright, unaffected laugh. "Quit ogling my ass too, Connie."

"Sorry," she said with a crinkle of her nose that Jade found extremely cute. "I can't decide which view I like best."

"Yeah yeah," Jade said. She studied herself in the mirror. The wide leather belt sat low on her hips and the clean lines of the top matched the close fit of the jeans. She looked long, strong, and lean.

"If you're not comfortable in just that," Connie said, back to her previous helpful mood, "How about layer it with a vest or short-sleeved shirt or something?"

"Nah, I'm cool," Jade said and aimed a cocky grin at Connie. "I wouldn't want to spoil your enjoyment." Was she actually flirting with Connie? It felt nice. There was no agenda, no traps waiting for her. Jade pulled her hair away from her face and scowled at her reflection. "You think I should slick it back? What the hell hairstyle do lesbians have nowadays?"

"You should leave it down," Connie said, studying her with an intensity Jade caught in the reflection. "It's so thick and long and the color's beautiful. Like molasses." She turned away and Jade saw a definite blush on those translucent cheeks.

"It gets in the way," Jade said. She grabbed a clip from her bag and twisted the heavy length up behind her head. With another look, she had to admit that using non-shitty shampoo and actual conditioner made a big difference from the lank rat's nest she'd gotten used to seeing falling down her back. "Okay, done. What's the final verdict then?"

"Looking good," Connie said. "Definite ten out of ten."

Jade glanced back over one shoulder. For a moment, she wished it was Connie she was meeting at Sunny's then stopped, surprised, and shut down that line of thought. Still, the way Connie looked at her had Jade feeling warm and confident. Not many women ever looked at her like that, and Jade had never felt as comfortable with anyone else as she did with Connie, even if they'd just met the night before.

"You really think I'm a ten?"

"I know so," Connie replied. She looked deep into Jade's eyes. The moment stretched out. Jade drew in a breath and wondered what it would be like to kiss those sweet pink lips. A rush of arousal filled her. Jade saw Connie's tongue dart out and wet her bottom lip before she lowered her head. The moment broken, Connie covered her cheeks with her hands and twitched as she glanced around herself.

"How about a bit of color?" Connie pointed to a little tube Jade had on her dresser.

"Oh hell no, none of that prissy girly shit. Addie got me that," Jade protested. "I don't wear lip gloss. Just chapstick."

"Why not? It's not like they'll revoke your lesbian card." Connie's head came back up. Her limpid grey-green eyes sparkled with laughter and Jade thought she saw a dimple kiss one cheek. "I think you look quite fine without, but sometimes it's kind of nice to put a bit of pretty on. You know, get yourself into the right headspace for clubbing. Your game face on. It's something I — used to do."

Jade took a long look at the young woman and wondered

about Connie and her headspace. Was it hard for someone as cute as that to get out and go clubbing? Maybe it was. From what she'd gathered, Connie wasn't very good at the whole social and going out thing, even though she seemed to have made an effort.

Still Connie had a point. Jade needed to do something to get into the right mood for the evening. Hopefully she wouldn't fuck up too badly and make an ass of herself. Instead of gloss, Jade spritzed herself with a bit of sandalwood cologne Benny re-gifted to her after he declared it "too butch" for his delicate sensibilities.

She checked herself out in the mirror one last time and decided she was as ready as she was going to be. Jade grabbed her messenger bag and strutted through the living room. She poked her head up the stairway and gave her aunt a brief good-bye before she headed out. As Jade was getting into her car, parked illegally on the sidewalk, she looked up to see both her aunt and Connie leaning out of the third floor window, giving her twin thumbs up signs.

Giddy from the encouragement, Jade rolled down her window, reached out, and returned the gesture with a triumphant fist-pump.

Chapter Four

JADE FOUND THE restaurant without too much trouble. She hesitated in front of the door.

"Cock-wielding turdfucker," Jade growled as she shoved the door open. And to think, her counselor praised her for becoming a bit more normal recently.

She hovered in the entrance until she saw a familiar face. Given the slightly pre-dinner hour, there weren't too many people in the restaurant. Jade crossed the room and slid into the chair opposite Vickie.

"Hey," she said, not exactly sure what the hell to do with her hands. "Sorry for being late. Traffic was bad." Jade cringed. Her voice sounded fake even to her own ears.

"That's okay." Vickie smiled and looked quite delicious in her own right in a skintight top that had cutouts on the shoulders and dipped low enough in the front that Jade understood Vickie wasn't wearing a bra. She made herself focus on Vickie's face and blinked. It must have been a trick of the light, but the young woman's eyelashes looked like they'd grown a couple centimeters since the last time they'd met and gotten really curled up too. Jade wondered uneasily if there were some futuristic advances in eyelash technology that she was unaware of. More to distract herself than anything else, Jade picked up the menu and studied the endless choices within. She furrowed her brow. How the fuck were you supposed to know all the shit you wanted?

"I'm glad you could come out on such short notice," Vickie said. She let loose with a hundred-watt smile full of pink sparkles. She leaned over and the curves of her breasts pressed against each other, nearly falling out of her top.

Her mind went blank and Jade was temporarily unable to reply. She scowled at herself and fought the urge to start punching the wall. The last thing she wanted to do was get caught perving over the girl in front of her. They were going to a bar, nothing more. Vickie hadn't dressed that way for her and Jade was pretty sure she'd get a slap for her troubles if she tried anything. Jade wondered if girls still slapped. Maybe they just made scathing updates to their blogs or something. It was beyond her.

After a moment, Vickie lowered her menu. "Okay, I've decided." She turned around and called the slim, tuxedoed waitress over. Jade tried her best not to gape as Vickie once more gave her a show, this time her bare back, crisscrossed by a few thin straps. In a clear, confident voice, Vickie ordered a bunch of things, most of which sounded delicious.

"Uh, yeah, Make that two," Jade said with her best nonchalant face.

"Everything here is so good, you won't regret your choice."

"I'm sure I won't, if it's recommended by you." Jade let her voice and body language venture into flirtatious territory. She was willing to start a bit of harmless flirting if it kept Vickie's interest up and guard down. Jade still felt electrified after hanging out with Connie, although the spark was dying every second she spent in that restaurant. There were too many unknown factors. She was out of her comfort zone and ill at ease. As Vickie tittered across the table at her, Jade put on what she hoped was a suitably friendly and interested expression and asked, "So what's a cutie like you doing in a fire extinguisher factory?"

"Not much." Vickie took a sip of her water and shrugged one bare shoulder. "I thought about going into chemical engineering or pharmacy but school was too expensive. I guess you could say I settled. But I don't do that in my private life. I go for the best, which is maybe why I'm still single."

"Don't worry," Jade said without thinking. "I'm sure you'll find someone. You're young, no need to rush."

Vickie made a sad pout that had Jade wondering if she'd missed something.

The food arrived and Jade fell into her bowl. She shoveled everything within reach into herself, pausing only to chug down her glass of water and snag a bunch of rolls from the basket on the table. She kept her head down and concentrated on her food. After a while, she became aware of someone speaking to her and unwillingly glanced up. Vickie stared at her from across the table with naked fear across her pretty face.

With a mental curse, Jade swallowed the mass of spaghetti and bread she had in her mouth.

"I'm really hungry," she stammered.

For a long heartbeat Vickie's face crumpled, then her smile was back, only a little dimmer than before. "That's all right. I can imagine you don't get regular mealtimes being a private investigator and all."

"You can say that again," Jade said, relieved that she'd defused the situation. The check came and Jade wondered if she was butch enough to offer to pay, but was headed off as Vickie expertly pulled out her exact fifty percent of the bill. They went across the street and down a rickety set of stairs into a dance club/bar setup. The one gay bar back when Jade was in her brief going out phase was small, smoky, and rather illicit. Sunny's was, like its name suggested, bright, clean-aired, and filled with glitter and bubblegum-inspired pop remixes.

The girls hanging off each other at the bar looked barely old enough to vote and could easily have been Jade's daughters. Hopefully not all at the same time, because that would make for fairly awkward Thanksgiving dinners. Already Jade felt slightly drunk off the fumes from the bar. She allowed Vickie to order them matching drinks of an alarming green hue.

One sip from the slim glass and Jade had to admit the green shit was nice. The room started to take on a fuzzy, friendly air. The spark of possibility drove Jade to the brink of insanity.

"Do you like it here?" Vickie leaned in close to be heard over the pounding beat and Jade got a sudden urge to flee.

"It's all right," Jade drawled as if she did the out-and-proud-dyke thing every day.

As the music rippled around them, Jade downed half of her drink in a show of bravado and leaned back against the bar. The dance floor was full of young kids, all rubbing up against each other, happy and shouting and not caring. Two pool tables took up space over to one side of the room where Jade's generation congregated. Vickie must have seen her gaze lingering, because she pressed up to Jade again and something impossibly soft brushed against Jade's arm.

"Do you play?" she asked with her mouth a few scant inches from Jade's ear.

"Uh, what?" Jade stammered and clutched reflexively at the bowl of peanuts she'd found.

"Pool."

"A little. I'm better at table tennis, actually. But I can play. I used to have my own cue." Jade didn't feel like mentioning that was more than twenty years ago.

"Really? That's great!" Vickie jumped to her feet and grabbed Jade by the cuff of her shirt. "Let's go over and play, then."

Jade allowed Vickie to pull her to one of the tables. A burly, flannel-wearing woman of about Jade's age had just finished sinking a bank shot when they came over. Her attention immediately went to the two of them. Jade shouldered in front of Vickie, sensing the territorial posturing was about to begin.

"You new here?" the woman asked. She stood, feet apart and shoulders squared. The cue was held loosely in one hand in a nonthreatening way, but Jade still kept a close eye on it.

"Nah. I go back a long way," Jade said. She straightened up to her full height and let her arms hang with the slightest amount of tension, brushing the sides of her body. "Just haven't been around for a while. It's good to be back at the old watering hole."

Casually, she rolled up her sleeves. Jade made sure to tense the corded muscles of her forearms, glad she was still pumped from lifting earlier. The woman's eyes flicked down and Jade felt a slight change in the air. She won the posing contest and was tacitly accepted into the tribe of Sunny's bar. The other woman grabbed the chalk and nodded over to the rack of cues. As Jade selected one, Vickie scampered over to the blackboard on the wall.

"How about I keep score?" She posed, showing a little too much cleavage to be accidental.

"Sounds good," Jade said. She went to the pool table with a swagger she hadn't been able to use for twenty years.

The flannel-wearing woman extended a meaty hand. "Reno. Nice to meetcha."

"Jade." She took the offered hand warily, wondering if it was a trick to get her into a fight or at least sucker punch her. It wasn't.

Jade lost the coin toss and watched Reno's powerful stroke break the balls into an explosion across the worn green felt. As if they were on a guided course, two balls thunked into pockets. Reno missed the next shot with a lukewarm curse that Jade mentally scoffed at. Then it was her turn. As she bent over the table, Jade felt a breath of air across her lower back where her top had pulled out of her waistband. She sank the three ball in a stroke of absolute dumb luck.

"I haven't seen you around here. Where you been hiding out?" Reno asked with her eyes fixed on the table as Jade lined up her next shot.

Jade hesitated for a moment before she said, "Dorvelle Federal Women's Pen."

"For what?"

The balls clicked, unimpressed.

"I'd rather not say," Jade told Reno as she stepped back. She didn't dare glance over at Vickie. She didn't want to see her pretty face contorted in fear again.

"As long as it ain't doing bad stuff to kids we're cool." Reno leaned one hip against the table and got off a three-ball shot that ricocheted around the table.

"No," Jade spat. "I'm no fucking pervert."

"Good."

The game progressed and Jade lost with Vickie keeping perfect score. Jade hoped for a referee error in her favor but that didn't happen. She turned down the offer of a rematch, racked her cue and resumed her position at the bar with another drink in her hand, this time a beer courtesy of Reno who was, if nothing else, a gracious winner.

With a nod of thanks in Reno's direction, Jade took a swig from the bottle and fought the reflexive grimace. The drink was just as nasty as the last time she'd tried it, on her nineteenth birthday—incidentally her last birthday on the outside of a cell.

"I'm sorry you lost. I wanted you to win." Vickie joined Jade after she erased the evidence of the game from the scoreboard. Instead of sitting on a stool, she nestled in between Jade's legs and pressed her full length against her. Jade's mind went blank and she froze. Vickie continued blithely, "Reno's a bitch to anyone unless you're a girly piece of fresh meat."

"I guess you went through that phase," Jade said. Against her will, a hot tension rose up in her that was not entirely pleasant. There was something that Vickie wanted from her. Jade realized that much as the younger woman pulled her onto the dance floor and used the excuse of the beat to get further wedged up in Jade's personal space. Not protection or leverage. It wasn't even sex. The way Vickie's limpid eyes were lingering on Reno told her something else was on her agenda.

Stay

She wanted revenge.

Jade was not unfamiliar with the concept of being used for things, but usually it wasn't completely to her own detriment. She wondered if she should continue to play the game Vickie started, even though she was lacking the weapons of this new age. The music and unfamiliar alcohol pounded through her and Jade figured that bowing out was the better option. Jade excused herself from the dancing and returned to the bar. She sat down next to Reno and ordered another drink, a cola this time. The beer she'd abandoned in the move to the dance floor had vanished somewhere. Just as well. Jade knew better than to drink something that had been out of her line of sight—at least she knew it *now*.

She could feel the heat of Vickie's sulky gaze on her back. Soon the girl flounced over and perched on a stool next to Jade. She draped an arm casually over Jade's shoulder and pouted at them both. Jade noticed how Vickie carefully avoided her scarred side.

Reno took a pull of her own beer before she turned her attention to Jade. "How long you been out?"

"Since I was seventeen. Got caught kissing the pool guy's daughter and figured there wasn't much point in hiding after that."

"Huh? I meant out, as in you know, free."

"Oh. That would be eleven months, two weeks, and three days. But who's counting?"

"So you know a lot of people in town? I could introduce you around."

"You do that Reno," Vickie spat. "Show off the newbie and then drop them when they're not cool enough for you."

"What's your problem there, girl?" Reno leaned over the bar. She rubbed a hand through her graying crew-cut. "I'm pretty mellow to everyone."

"That's not what Connie said." Vickie pulled herself up and crossed her arms, which made the V of her neckline a whole lot more interesting; however, the display didn't hold Jade's attention for a second. She was focused on Reno.

"You know Connie?" Jade asked.

"Yeah," Reno said. "Everybody does. She keeps to herself, though. Haven't seen her around for a while, but people come and go around here. Maybe she found someone nice to spend time with."

Vickie snapped, "No she didn't. Not after what you did to her."

"I didn't do anything."

"Yes you did. And you're going to tell Jade what it was."

"Fuck that shit. I'm outta here." Reno stood up and slung her bag over her shoulder.

Suddenly Jade was on her feet. "You do not walk away from me."

"Says who?" Reno looked her up and down, lip curled. "I'm done here."

"You're done when I say you're done." Jade acted without thinking and grabbed the other woman by her shirt collar. She flung her against the bar and bent her over backward. "What did you do to Connie?" she growled, nose-to-nose with Reno. Jade was not going to lose this fight.

"Jezzus!" Reno gasped and flailed around. Stuff fell off the bar and scattered over the floor. One elbow came up and, through either luck or excellent aim, caught Jade square on the side of the face, just underneath her eye. Her head snapped to one side but her hands gripped even harder. She didn't let go of Reno even as they both came crashing down on a bar stool. Jade resisted the urge to curse. Her eye was already tearing up and her nose was running.

"Stop! Just stop!" The voice froze Jade. It wasn't Vickie who shouted, but Connie. Jade whirled and stared. Connie was standing in the middle of the room, halfway through the pool table. Her form flickered like the first night she appeared. Around her people were having a polite game of eight-ball. Connie's face was wracked with pain. She looked like she could cry at any moment. Jade blinked, and the vision was gone. The room's noise flooded her ears.

"We don't allow fighting in here." The bartender came over, cocktail glass in hand, paused in mid-wipe. "Why don't you gals take your discussion outside?"

"Yeah, why don't we do that?" Jade said. She released Reno, who straightened her shirt, breathing heavily.

"You have to promise not to fight." Vickie tugged at Jade's arm even though she seemed to be taking a predatory interest in the proceedings. "Not over me."

"This isn't about you, Vickie," Jade glowered. "I'm here for Connie, but I won't fight as long as Reno doesn't give me a reason to."

On their way out, Jade snagged her cola. The three of them ended up in the damp and narrow alley between the bar and a Turkish eatery. The air reeked of fryer grease and urine. A lovely location. Vickie stood behind Jade and pressed herself against Jade's good arm, which had Jade twitching in discomfort. She'd never liked having someone she didn't completely trust behind her where she couldn't keep a close eye on them. Still, she figured the larger threat was in front of her, and she stared down Reno with careful nonchalance. Jade took a leisurely swig of her drink as if she had all day to hang out and chat.

"So what did you do to Connie Mason? Out with it."

"First, why the hell do you care so much? She your lady or something?"

"Let's just say I have an interest."

"Fuck." Reno dug a pack of menthol cigarettes out of her pocket. "Mind if I smoke?"

"Do whatever the hell you want." Jade shrugged. "But I'm still waiting."

Reno dug out an aluminum-plated lighter and lit herself up. Jade noticed her hands shaking. She was apparently not the brawl veteran Jade was. Then again, not many people were.

"I guess Vickie was talking about the first time Connie came out here." Reno released a stream of smoke as she talked. "That's the only thing I can think of, honestly."

"That's it," Vickie said. "Tell Jade how terribly you treated Connie."

"It wasn't that bad," Reno said. She threw her butt to the ground and stomped on it. "See, I like to show the new girls around you know, introduce them and get them known."

"Yeah, to show yourself off," Vickie spat. "And then you throw them away like garbage."

"It's not like that." Reno turned to Jade, hands out in appeal. "Look, Connie messaged me first. See this bar's got a public online account and sometimes it's tough for new people to come out alone, especially if they haven't got any friends or connections in the community. This was all like a couple years ago, so I don't see what the fucking big deal is bringing it up now. Anyway, Connie messaged me saying she wanted to go to a bar but didn't know any. So I offered to bring her here. Nothing special. It wasn't even a date or anything."

"But what did Connie think?" Vickie peered out from behind Jade. Her hands clutched onto Jade's shirt in order to get leverage to shout at Reno. "She sure as hell thought it was a date and you just sat on your fat ass texting people all night. And then when nobody showed up to meet her and see your newest find, you just left her here to get home on her own."

"What the fuck, you her mom or something?"

"No, but I'm her friend," Vickie spat. "And she told me all about it."

"Look, it's not my fault," Reno said. "Besides, I saw her back here after that and she seemed none the worse for wear. At least I never heard anything from her about it. Connie was always all right to me."

"Let's go, Jade." Vickie pulled at Jade's sleeve. They left Reno standing alone in the alley behind them. "You see what kind of people are here? You see how they treat people like Connie? New girls. Fresh meat."

"It's a tough scene," Jade said as if she had any idea what she was talking about.

"I don't want to be out here anymore. Will you drive me back?" Vickie fluttered her long lashes at Jade.

"Sure thing," Jade said. "If your friends don't mind. I thought they were showing up later."

"It's okay," Vickie said with a wave of one hand. She shook back her golden curls. "I'll catch up with them later or something."

"I'm parked over here." Jade pitched her half-drunk bottle of cola into a recycling bin and stuffed her hands into her pockets. As they walked side-by-side, Jade wondered what would happen if she reached out and took Vickie's hand. She didn't.

"I'm so sorry you had to get into a fight," Vickie said. "Reno is such a nasty piece of work. I can't believe you didn't beat her up. She deserved it."

Something about the way she spoke gave Jade a chill. Instead of answering, Jade just shrugged. A few things were becoming clear.

When they were in Jade's car, she glanced over at Vickie and said, "I guess Reno pulled something like what she did to Connie with you too?"

Vickie sank into the passenger's seat and nodded. Tears glistened in her eyes and Jade was at a loss at what to do if they started to spill over. She glanced at the sun-wilted box on the dash. Would lunging in with a Kleenex be considered too forward?

Vickie solved that problem by leaning over and grabbing a tissue herself. "I've only been out in the community here for a couple months. I thought Reno and them were all so welcoming but they were just being fake. I'm sorry you had to get involved in all this."

"No, it's been very enlightening." Jade paused as Vickie got herself back together and noted that somehow her mascara survived the ordeal intact. "So where do you live?"

"Actually, I've got some stuff I left at the office," Vickie said and Jade was relieved to notice all traces of tears were gone. "You can drop me off there."

"Are you sure? Do you have a way home? It's getting dark."

"It's okay. My car's there so I'd have to go back anyway."

"All right."

Jade started the car and pulled into the sparse evening traffic. They drove for a while in silence. Jade wondered if Vickie engineered the incident at the club. Maybe she was trying to tell Jade something.

They didn't speak again until Jade pulled into the parking lot of the office building.

"I'm sorry if this makes things rough with the bar crowd."

"That's all right, most people are nice to me." Vickie paused with her purse on her lap. She fell silent and Jade wondered if there was something Vickie was waiting for. "So you were in prison?" she asked in a small voice.

"Yup." Jade said. "Does that bother you?"

"Not really," Vickie said with a little shrug. "It would freak a lot of people out, but lucky for you, I'm not a lot of people."

"That's good to hear," Jade said. She fought the flash of anger at the insinuation that she had to be grateful for simply being herself.

"Don't take this the wrong way," Vickie said, "But you're

not, um, sick or anything are you?"

Jade ground her teeth together before she said, "I'm clean."

"Good." With a giggle, Vickie unsnapped her seatbelt and scooted over to Jade's side. Vickie was getting very close and Jade wondered if she should be excited or worried. She still hadn't decided when Vickie closed the distance between them and kissed Jade full on the mouth. She hadn't expected that and made a sound of surprise. A moment passed. Vickie's body was soft, pressed against her. Just as Jade's brain-stall broke, Vickie pulled away and got out of the car. She closed the door and looked in through the window.

"I had a great time tonight, thank you."

"Uh huh, me too," Jade managed to stammer out. As the girl vanished into the office building, Jade unconsciously rubbed at the spot on her cheekbone where Reno hit her.

Chapter Five

ON THE DRIVE home, Jade couldn't stop thinking about Vickie. Dancing with her, kissing her. She knew she should have been excited, ecstatic even, but all she felt was unease.

Even so, Jade couldn't help the lingering buzz of arousal that swelled between her legs as she remembered the generic softness of a woman's body against hers. It had been a long time. A really long time. No matter what those over-eighteen movies said, real women's penitentiary was not a panty-snapping free-for-all. Far from it, in fact. Especially for those like Jade who were into women on the outside as well. Prison was a minefield.

"So that's the vibrant bar scene of our little town." Connie was back in the passenger's seat.

Jade jumped and swerved. "Swinging bitchtits, I gotta get used to this."

"Sorry," Connie said. "Was I just here? Time and places seem to jump around strangely. Sometimes it's just all dark and then I'm somewhere. I see all sorts of strange visions." She smiled somewhat apologetically. "In fact, I'm not even sure if you're real."

"That makes two of us," Jade said with a wry grin. The tension eased from her shoulders as a softly happy feeling started up in her belly. It was nice having Connie with her. For an uncomfortable moment, Jade wondered if Connie witnessed the end of Jade's outing with Vickie.

To take her mind off things she couldn't change, Jade decided to take a detour before she went home. Her hand went into her bag and came out with a crumpled envelope and a mint. The candy went into her mouth and the envelope into her lap.

In a minty cloud, Jade said, "So what have you been doing to keep yourself busy?"

"I've been hanging out at your bookstore. Today is lesfic day and Benny put on an audiobook sample for everyone." Connie looked at Jade with a sweet, mischievous look on her face. "*A Taste of her Honey* by Delicia Sawyer. The balcony scene."

"Ooh, nice. That's one of my favorites," Jade said. She stopped at a red light and looked over at Connie. At once Jade imagined instead of Vickie, it was Connie in her arms, Connie's lips on hers. A jolt of pure fire flared to life deep in her belly. Jade squashed the thought and turned her attention back to the road. She cleared her throat and said, "And it's actually Benny's shop. I own the building, but he runs the place."

"I like it there," Connie said. She curled up on the passenger's seat as she spoke, her voice soft as rain. "I wish I'd had the nerve to go in there when I—when I had more time. It's weird, but I really feel comfortable there. It's easy for me to be there. I don't feel—pulled away." She shivered and hugged her arms to her chest. In an uneasy moment, Jade wondered where Connie went when she sometimes flickered out. It didn't seem like a very nice place.

"Don't tell Ben," Jade said, "but I like it there too. Not when it gets crowded, but in the morning when he's getting stuff ready or at night after closing."

Connie let out a small hum of understanding. "I don't like crowds either."

"But you showed up at Sunny's tonight. Thanks for that, actually. You saved me from doing something I'd probably regret. Now that I'm out, I'm doing my best to keep my nose clean."

"I'm glad. I hate fighting and I didn't want to see you or Reno get hurt." Connie looked up. "It was all I could do to be there for even a second. The more people in a place, the harder it is for me to go there. I get—I don't know, I feel like there's a barrier shutting me out. That's a lot like how my life has always been." Her head went down as if under a heavy weight. Her gently waving hair covered her face.

Jade wanted to say something to reassure Connie, but there wasn't really anything she could think of. The silence stretched out before Jade asked, "So did Reno really do that to you? Just walk out and leave you there?"

"I'd forgotten." Her voice was distant. "I've forgotten so many things. But yeah, she did. I remember now, walking home alone through that bad neighborhood. There were all sorts of guys standing around, coming out of clubs for a smoke and they catcalled me. A bunch of them started following me and I jumped into a cab."

"It doesn't sound like a place where a woman should walk alone."

"No, it isn't. But Reno didn't do that on purpose. She didn't know what a naive freshie I was. At least I hope she didn't." Connie looked resigned. "I didn't expect Reno to take me home with her or anything, but the way she just dropped me, I felt worthless."

Jade growled in sudden anger, "People can treat you like you're worthless, but don't ever let them make you feel that way. You are unique and worthwhile and stronger than you think, Connie. Don't ever forget that."

"When you say it like that, I believe you," Connie said. Something genuine rang through her words, nothing over the top or put on. Just truth. Incomplete, but truth just the same. Connie shook back her hair, which seemed to be blowing slower than the wind. She said, "After that, I went back even though it was really hard. There wasn't much else for me to do. Not that it made much difference. I didn't really have anyone to talk to so I passed the time by keeping score of the pool games. The blackboard? I bought it especially for that. Anyway, everybody seemed to like it. And I admit I liked having something to do. It was nice to have a place in that bar. A place in the community, I guess."

"Did you ever meet anyone interesting?"

"Sure, lots. Just not anyone who had an interest in me," she said, laughing a bit bitterly. "I went to that bar every week, plus a whole bunch of singles events. I got a few numbers and stuff, but nothing ever lasted more than a text or two. I guess I was too desperate or too picky or not picky enough. Who knows? Maybe I was just destined to be alone."

"Some people are," Jade said. "It's no problem unless it bugged you. Did it?"

"Not until I started hanging out with Vickie," Connie said. She twisted her hands together. "It was so easy for her. She'd go out once and everyone would fall all over themselves buying her drinks, getting her stuff, and showing off in front of her. She started to go without me more and more and I had to stop reading her updates, they made me feel so bad. I know I shouldn't compare, but it just made me feel so useless. Every time I went out was like another helping of failure."

"And then someone offed you," Jade said before she could stop herself.

"Yeah," Connie said. She turned to Jade. "What do they say? Life's a bitch and then you die."

"We'll find out what happened," Jade said. "I promise."

There was no answer. Connie wasn't with her anymore. The car seemed colder and darker without the ghost in it. An ironic chuckle slipped out of her mouth. Jade looked at the address on the envelope when she was waiting for the light to change. She followed the directions provided by her GPS and found Connie's apartment building in a suburban area that Jade had never been in.

She parked in one of the visitors' parking spaces and went right up to the custodian's door, which she banged on in a businesslike fashion. The plaque on the door had "Walter Baldesare" written on it in black felt-tip pen. No answer. She could hear canned laughter from some TV show through the door.

Jade pounded again. "Mr. Baldesare, this is not a courtesy visit. Open up."

"What the hell do you want?" A gravelly voice came from the other side of the door. "Is the laundry room flooded again?"

"Open the door. I need some information. Open it *now*," Jade said in her best commanding voice. The guards had used that not-to-be-fucked-with tone on her often enough in the past two decades for Jade to get it down pat. When the door creaked open to reveal a balding man in a ripped T-shirt and faded cotton pants that had seen better days, Jade gave what she hoped was a friendly smile.

"You a cop?"

Jade breathed a meaty oath before she said, "Private investigator."

She thought about flashing her ID but decided against it. Detective Young was always bitching at her to quit that anyway. But what was the use of having that damned card if she wasn't allowed to show it to anybody? Jade seethed quietly. And she'd even gotten a cool leather holder for it and everything.

The door closed abruptly and she heard the scrabble of a chain being drawn back before it opened fully.

"What's this about? Nothing's happened here."

"I need the keys to apartment 6B."

"Why?"

"Connie Mason's missing, that's why. High possibility she was taken out by someone. You know, murdered. You want to get in the way of me now?"

"But—what the hell?" The man sagged into the newspaper basket next to the door. "When was this? I didn't see no police around here and aren't they usually the first to come around about this kind of thing?" His stubbly face was set. "Come back in the morning with a warrant or something. That's all I got to say to you." He tried to slam the door, but Jade was too fast and stuck her booted foot into the rapidly closing space. She shoved and the door banged open. With a determined step forward, Jade was in the tiled entrance hall.

The older man tumbled into the living room and fell into a crumpled pile with his hands up and head down. "Look lady, I ain't got no money or anything here. What do you want?"

"I'm not trying to rob you." Jade felt like a complete heel for scaring the guy like that. "Look, just let me see the apartment. Here, check out the license."

Jade gave into the urge as she dug into her pocket and pulled out the little black holder. She squatted down and showed her ID. The man blinked and looked at her with total fear on his face, which had Jade feeling even worse.

Jade let out a sigh. "Okay, I know I have to work on my people skills but I need to see that room, Mr. Baldesare."

"Call me Wally," the man said as Jade reached down to haul him to his feet. "Quite a grip on you there, gal." He rotated his shoulder.

"I watched Terminator 2," Jade said, satisfied that she'd explained herself. She added on as an afterthought, "My good man, Wally!"

Dutifully, the good man named Wally retrieved a key from the lockbox on the wall and led Jade toward the elevator. Jade looked around, fully expecting to see Connie show up but she didn't make an appearance. In the elevator, Jade tried her best to make topical small talk, mentioning the weather, upcoming election, plus a few sports facts she jovially threw in for effect. Wally kept his body pressed against the doors and gave only the slightest of answers.

"Not very sociable, are you?" Jade muttered to herself as she followed the older man down a hallway. The place was classy, she had to admit. Discreetly numbered rooms lined the hallway, each equipped with a letter slot Jade guessed was for in-house communication as there was a bank of mailboxes on the first floor. The carpet was understated and they had those lights that went on and off as a person walked down the hall.

"This is like walking around on the Enterprise," Jade said and pointed upward.

"What?" Wally jumped and looked at her with terror on his face.

"I told you I'm not a criminal." Jade stopped in her tracks. "Okay, I'm not an angel or anything, but God dammit I'm not a bad person."

"Where'd you come from anyway?"

"Right here, Traynor's Port," Jade said. She leaned against the wall as he fiddled with the lock of apartment 6B. "Just been out of town for a while. Anyway, I'm giving up my valuable time to be here with you right now, so don't make me regret it."

Jade thought she heard Wally mutter, "I certainly do," to himself but then dismissed it as an auditory hallucination. He opened the door for her and gestured inside. Jade stepped into the room and something metallic crunched under her foot. Puzzled, Jade bent down and picked up a single key on a key ring.

She kept it in her hand as she walked around. Her footsteps on the hardwood floor echoed around the room. The kitchen was white and natural wood, open plan like a high-end deli. Jade strolled over and stood behind the kitchen island. She ran her hands over it and looked around herself in awe. The white and pink streaked marble counter felt amazing, cool and sleek. She sprawled across the counter and looked up at the ceiling. There was some kind of plasterwork going on up there that was both hypnotizing and technically fascinating. It looked like someone had taken a trowel to the wet spackle and patted it down all over, making a ton of little stalactites all over the place.

"Holy shit, this place is better than anywhere I ever lived in my whole goddamned life," Jade said in awe. "I never thought a fire extinguisher jockey made so much money."

"Fire extinguisher jockey? Is that some kind of euphemism?" Wally asked. He threw up his hands and used them to smooth down the few hairs he had left. "Actually I don't want to know."

Jade remembered the key in her hand and looked at it curiously. The keychain sported a plastic dolphin charm filled with glitter and tiny metallic stars. The surface was scarred and it looked like a souvenir from somewhere. Experimentally, she went over to the door and tried it in the lock. It fit.

"I'll take that." Wally's voice beside her startled Jade and she nearly dropped the key. He had a hand out. Jade handed over the key and he stuck it in his pocket with a disagreeable frown. "Must be her spare key. She's not supposed to make copies without telling me. We got a policy."

"Better safe than sorry, you can never have too many spares," Jade said, but a nagging thought prodded at her. It didn't look like a spare key. It was far too well-used. She crossed her arms and knit her brow.

"Just look around and let's get out of here. I shouldn't even be letting you in here. Ms. Mason's paid up until November."

"Why the hell would anyone pay three months' rent in advance? That's just bullshit. What if you have to get out in a hurry?"

"Only my opinion," Wally said. He eased his body heavily into one of the chairs around the kitchen table. "But I figger law-abiding people don't need to think about disappearing into the night so much. Just my two cents is all."

"When's the last time you saw Connie?" Jade asked from her post at the door.

Wally rubbed at his forehead. "Musta been a couple weeks ago. Wait, no, she came around last Thursday morning and gave me a bunch of records."

"Records?"

"Yeah, real vinyl ones. Said they were her dad's or something." Wally's face crumbled. "Connie's always been a good, polite kid. Never bitched when things broke, kept her place clean and didn't have wild parties. Plus her old man's got great taste in music."

While she wondered if that might be relevant, Jade couldn't stay still. She wandered around the room uneasily. It didn't feel right.

"There's something strange about this place," she said, more to herself than Wally. "It's freakishly clean. There's nothing here. It's like nobody lives here."

"She did say she was going on a trip."

Agitated, Jade stalked around the apartment, opening drawers and yanking doors open. She found a small bathroom and a bedroom, both were just as empty as the main living area.

"No, that's not it. This place is spotless. Antiseptic and sterilized. I could freaking eat off the floor without a plate and not get as much as a speck of dirt in my mouth. And there's nothing in any of these drawers. The place has been completely emptied. It's like—" Jade stopped. She didn't want to say any more.

"No, look over here." Wally had his fat fingers working for him as he pointed to a little pile of papers on the table in front of himself. "She left a bunch of mail and stuff here. I bet it's those stupid letters that said you won some shit. My mother's a sucker for those. Never won anything yet."

Jade pounced and got them all in her hands at once. She read one after the other with growing alarm. Her legs gave out and she sank into a chair.

"Wally, how about you leave me alone for a minute here? I need some time to think."

"Yeah, okay." He hauled his bulk to his feet, breathing heavily with the exertion. "But don't steal anything. We got security cameras in the hallway."

"Cameras?" Jade's mind raced. "Mind if I take a look at the footage from last Thursday onward? It could really help me out."

For a moment, Wally was still. He rubbed a hand across his forehead in a uncomfortable way that didn't bode well for Jade and her plan.

"Sorry, I can't do that," he said and spread his hands in appeal as Jade advanced on him. "We don't keep the footage here. Between you and me, I could be convinced to let you have a strictly off-the-record look-see, but the company that owns this place would fire my ass if I let you see them without a warrant. I want to help Connie, but..." Wally trailed off and looked as if he'd swallowed a handful of burrs.

"Hey it's cool, don't sweat it," Jade said. "I appreciate the thought anyway."

Wally deflated a little. He said, "Give me a knock when you leave. I'll lock up after you. Ms. Mason'd have my ass if she knew I left her place open with all these crazy people wandering around."

Jade stared at the documents, too absorbed in her thoughts to take offence. The door eased shut behind Wally, but Jade wasn't aware of anything except the meaning of the papers in her hands. Driver's license. Social Insurance card. Passport. Birth certificate. GST claim forms. She raised her head and looked around at the scrubbed and sterilized apartment. Not an iota of personality was left behind.

She scanned the bankbook and the last piece of information clicked into place. The last page listed a column of transactions with a bunch of places with names like Fran's Used Furniture, Vintage Wear Emporium, and Super Lime Used Car Dealership. A long series of small deposits, culminating in one large transfer to the humane society. The date: last Thursday. Connie's last day, in more ways than one.

"You weren't planning to come back," Jade whispered. Her voice was loud in the empty apartment. "My God, Connie, you weren't planning on ever coming back here."

She felt a sudden, inexplicable sadness. While Jade had faith, she'd never been overly religious, except for that one strange and uncomfortable period around the eighth year of her incarceration. However, she did believe in God and the preciousness of life. There was nothing worse than taking a life, no matter how objectively good or bad the person was. Jade had always believed that and repeated visits with the prison chaplain helped her to get that idea out in words.

She'd never believed she could command the spirits she saw, and never even thought it was her right but at that moment she needed to. Jade stood up and turned around in the empty room.

"Connie!" she called out.

Connie. Jade let the whisper echo in her mind. It carried farther than her voice could. She focused inside herself. To Jade's eyes, the lights dimmed and the spread-out streetlights outside the window flickered. *I need you, Connie. Constance Mason.* Jade invoked her whole name. *Please. I need you here now.*

The air froze. A woman appeared in front of Jade. She was not the cute, funny person Jade had gotten to know but a screaming figure wracked with pain. Everything around Jade turned to frozen glass. It choked her and burned her eyes, but she forced herself to stare through it.

In front of Jade, Connie's hair waved in slow whorls, as it

always did, but this time it was Jade who was in Connie's element. A stream of bubbles vomited from her mouth and nose.

Jade's lungs shrieked with the need to breathe. She was freezing, crushed under an unbelievable pressure. Everything around herself was fishy. They were underwater. There was nothing in her memory except for the lurch of the floor dropping out from underneath her feet and the rush of air around her body before the impact.

Connie's body writhed in front of her. Her movements were strangely sluggish. Her wrists were bound with plastic strips. A cinderblock hung from them. The weight dragged her down and Jade reached out with all of her strength. She cried out into the murk as it started to swallow her weakly struggling form.

Suddenly Connie's head came up and her eyes snapped open. She looked around herself. Her limbs came alive as she thrashed against the weight at her wrists. Her movements kicked up a shimmer of bubbles. Their eyes locked for an instant before Connie opened her mouth and Jade screamed along with her. Her entire body burned worse than when she'd been engulfed in flames.

Something shifted and Jade was seeing through another set of eyes.

One thought roared through her mind. She had to get free. She was not going to die like that! Feet kicked out, hands pushed desperately at the weight. She strained against the flimsy zip cords with every last ounce of fight she had left. The scrape of the ties being forced open jerked Jade back into herself.

Freed, Connie's limbs flailed as she sought the surface. Lights beckoned above them and Jade kicked herself toward them, needing air like a lover needed touch. Above her, starlight and steel beams swam overhead. Connie's wounded dolphin motions brought the young woman's body up beside Jade. The surface broke over her head and life rushed into her lungs along with a fierce desire to live.

Live, goddammit! There was something she was put here to do and she hadn't done it yet. There was some meaning in her life. There had to be!

The room spun around her. Jade found herself on her butt in the middle of that terrible, impersonal, devoid-of-life apartment with envelopes and Government of Canada stationary scattered around her. She gasped, sucking in delicious air.

"Why did you do it?" Jade whispered, her voice broken and raspy. "Connie, why did you jump off that bridge?"

Chapter Six

THE SHADOWS IN the room seemed to grow fainter, as if reality were fading out to white. Jade stumbled away from the table toward the living area. Nothing personal remained there either, no pictures or books. Not a trace of the sweet, shy soul who lived there. The only comforting thing was the sofa. Jade slung herself onto it and lay there for a while with her palms pressed against her eyes.

"Tell me why, Connie," Jade asked aloud, not sure if anyone was there to hear her. "Look at this place. You have a great apartment in a nice area, a decent job even if your boss is an ass and one of your coworkers is a creep. What the hell's wrong with that? Lots of people have it a ton worse."

"That's exactly it." The cracked, airy answer came. Connie was sitting in a window seat Jade hadn't noticed before. She was partially hidden behind the sheer curtains and they waved about her as if the window were open. The breeze that crept through the room was cold and damp. Jade suppressed a shiver. Connie hugged her knees to her chest as she said, "I had so much, but with no one to share it with, it was all meaningless. All the soul-searching I did in school, coming out, leaving my home and my family and moving to this city, finding my job, and then to end up with nobody, there was no point. I wasn't even helping anyone. There was no reason for me to continue, I was just taking up space."

"What the fuck are you talking about?" Jade spat. "When you don't get something you want, it's not because you don't deserve it. You figure out a way to get it and don't give up. You especially don't tie yourself to a brick and throw your fool self off a bridge. I should quit this case right this second. Dammit Connie. Why the fuck did you come to me in the first place? You already know the answers, don't you? You killed your own goddamn self."

There was no answer. Connie grew fainter along with the faraway sound of traffic. She was curled up, head on her knees.

"Vickie told you what happened to me, didn't she?" The words were soft and sad.

"Yeah," Jade said. She knew immediately what Connie was talking about. "Look, Connie, there's nothing to be ashamed about. What happened wasn't your fault. The lowlife asswipe who did it is one hundred percent to blame." Jade fell silent in an agony of indecision before she said, "Shit like that and worse happens to people all the time. You're not a victim, you're a survivor."

"I know," Connie said. She dragged a hand across her face and Jade wondered if ghosts could cry. She gave a hollow, humorless laugh. "The funny thing is, nothing happened to me other than, you know, the way I was found. They couldn't find a single piece of evidence on me. It's possible I stripped myself or someone was playing a joke on me. I don't remember anything at all of that night, but the bartender said I only had two drinks."

She hugged her knees and rocked back and forth. "If Vickie hadn't called everyone out to take care of me, I might have even laughed it off as a stupid drunk thing I did. But everyone was there and I couldn't ignore it. The stuff I had to go through afterward was the horrible part. The police report, the rape kit, waiting for all the tests to come back. The worst thing was the way everyone looked at me." She nestled her head in her arms. "They all saw me like that. Everyone at work. I was suddenly that girl who got roofied and dumped bare-assed in Gord's car. It didn't matter what actually happened or didn't. It killed me every day just to keep going there but I did. I wish none of them knew."

"Aw honey," Jade said. She wished there was some way she could hold Connie and comfort her. She only had words and she used them. "Look, I'm an ex-con. I was in prison for twenty years and it makes no fucking difference if I did the crime or not, but you can tell a lot about people by the way they react. You're not suddenly afraid of me now that you know, right?"

"Of course not." Connie said. She raised her head and Jade was encouraged by the hopeful expression on her face.

"Same here. This doesn't change anything about how I feel about you. In fact, I have more respect for you than ever."

"Respect? For me?" Connie squeaked.

"Sure," Jade said. "It takes a lot of courage to hold your head up in front of everyone like that. You could have run away but you didn't."

"Until I killed myself," Connie said in a small voice.

"Yeah, until that." Jade stomped around and cursed under

her breath. Her movements slowed. She stopped. Sat down. Buried her face in her hands. "There's something not right about this whole thing. But you do agree." She looked up and addressed Connie directly, "That you did jump off a bridge."

"Yes."

"Okay, then where the hell's the body?" Jade wanted to know. "There aren't any piranhas in the harbor that I know of. Something's got to come bobbing up pretty soon."

"You got me there," Connie said. "I took a bunch of pills before I jumped, you know to relax me and because I'm a pretty good swimmer. I don't remember anything before I hit the water and only a bit after that. I was pretty far gone. I just know — not a whole lot, but I just know something happened to me after that. Something bad."

"All right, we're going to get to the bottom of this." Jade wanted to go back to her place and look at her suspect wall again, but before she could do that, it was time to pay a visit to her friendly neighborhood morgue.

"BUT FIRST I'VE got to get some food," Jade said as she started up her car. The pasta she'd had with Vickie was still keeping her stomach happy, but she needed ammunition and didn't want to brave the morgue empty-handed. "Mind if we swing by the grocery store?"

"Not at all." Connie grinned. Her spirit was a bit faded and rumpled, but she looked a lot better than a few minutes ago, and Jade was glad of it.

"Good. I saw you got a Fresh-Mart near here. I like their produce section. They always have lots of different shit I never tried before."

"I always went there. I like their deli section," Connie said. "I'm a terrible cook, so don't let me give you any tips. You'd just end up with either Kraft Dinner or some kind of sandwich-like concoction."

"I'm no Iron Chef myself." Jade pulled into the parking lot and swiped a spot in the expectant mothers' area. She hauled herself out of the car and as she was stomping her boots back into place, two older ladies pulling little wheeled carts glared at her.

"What are you looking at?" Jade asked as she leveled a steely glare of her own back at them. Without another glance, they hurried on their way.

"I could have a bun in the oven," Jade muttered as she wrestled a cart through the ancient automatic doors. "You can't fucking tell from the outside who likes cock and who doesn't. And even then there's always the old turkey-baster." She swore quietly to herself for a while, which made her feel better.

The vegetable aisle yielded a bunch of different colored peppers and onions. Jade wasn't sure if her aunt had gone grocery shopping lately, but she only bought ham and old people's fiber cereal, so Jade decided to get plenty, just in case. She was busy looking at plastic-wrapped packs of chicken when Connie drifted over to her.

"I used to come here all the time after work to get my dinner," she said and gazed around in wonder. "It's so familiar. Things are coming back to me a lot better now. I understand a lot of things."

"That's good." Jade tossed a giant pack of chicken drumsticks into her cart. "You care to tell me how your spirit became separated from your mortal form?"

"I don't think I can do that." Connie shook her head. "I wish I could, but it all goes black at some point. I feel a lot stronger now though." She was silent for a while and drifted through things in an unnerving way. Jade found a box of yummy-looking pretzel snacks that way, so she couldn't complain.

Jade pushed her cart with a steady hand and wandered up and down the aisle, barely able to contain her excitement. There were so many things. So many choices, and free samples, too. One swoop and Jade's mouth was full of juicy sausage rolls and the sample lady had a shocked look on her face.

"You're enjoying yourself," Connie said with a grin. She hovered over the cart like an otherworldly hitchhiker.

"Yeah, I got to admit, it's fun going shopping, picking out my own food and actually putting veggies in stuff. I still make way too much every time I cook. Ooh, Arugula! Man, I wanna try that." With a gleeful sweep, the whole bunch went into the cart. Jade looked at the growing pile. "Aw, shitehawk cumbuckets. I bet I'll end up with a ton of stuff I don't need. I worked in the kitchen on and off for the whole time I was at Dorvelle and I still can't get the hang of making food for less than a whole roomful of people. At least I'm not mixing up fake mashed potatoes for two hundred anymore." She put back two of the six boxes of granola she'd thrown into the cart.

They shopped in silence for a while. Suddenly Connie said, "Jade, I'm sorry."

Jade stopped in her tracks. It was the first time Connie called her by name. Up until that point, it was debatable how aware Connie actually was about her surroundings. And the people around her. Jade fought the surge of happiness sparked into life by the sound of her name on Connie's lips.

"Sorry about what, sweetie?" Jade felt someone watching her and she bristled. A quick glance behind her revealed a guy pushing a cart filled with breakfast cereal. He had a predatory grin as he tried his best to make eye contact. With one hand, he eased his cart up against hers to block Jade in.

"Hey gorgeous, you talking to me?" He smarmed, "Come here often?"

"Sorry, you're in the wrong place. The Get the Fuck Away From Me Section's over there." Not missing a beat, Jade rammed his cart into a giant pyramid of individually-wrapped toilet paper rolls and flipped him the bird.

"Dyke," the guy muttered as he scrambled after the hundreds of rolls that were escaping all over the store.

"Turd-burglar," Jade called gleefully after him. She reached behind herself and palmed a can of tomatoes. "Cock fondling, toilet humping bag of dog-shit! Ass yodeler!"

Fortunately for his bodily autonomy, the guy decided that discretion was the better part of valor and scooted his cart over to the self-checkouts. Satisfied, Jade started to return the can of tomatoes to the shelf, but thought better of it and tossed the can into her cart.

"I'm sorry for dragging you into my messed-up life," Connie said.

"Well it's your messed-up death now." Jade grinned at her. People around her were staring and edging away. Jade knew it wasn't necessary to speak aloud, but she liked to do it anyway. It kept her grounded and the spookies out of her head. Jade ignored the strange looks as she hauled her cart over to the checkouts. She selected one with a tall and lanky brunette working at it. Her nametag identified her as Chelsea and she had silver bangles on both wrists that jingled merrily with her movements. Connie hovered at Jade's elbow. She looked interested in the proceedings as Jade continued, "After I get some of this chicken into me, how about we go down to the morgue and look for your body?"

"Is that some kind of Goth date?" The cashier named Chelsea stopped scanning items and stared. "Cause it's kinda hot the way you said that. And also making me feel like this is going to turn into an episode of CSI."

"Aw shit, no," Jade said as she fumbled out her wallet. "I was talking to, um, nobody."

"Too bad, cause I kinda go for chicks like you," Chelsea said. She swiped Jade's card and bent down unnecessarily low to grab two bags from under the register.

Flustered by the attention, Jade cursed steadily to herself as she wrestled the shopping bags into her car and soon was back on the road. Since when had the supermarket become the hottest place in both the straight and queer dating scene?

"I'm certainly increasing my vocabulary with you around." Connie's voice interrupted the monologue of swears.

"Just consider it one of the many services I offer." Jade was frustrated and not in such a great mood anymore. She slammed her hand against the steering wheel and spat one last epithet. "I gotta find how the hell Gaydar works nowadays. Seems like every fine young thing I meet's into chicks."

"They are," Connie said with a little smile that turned her into the cutest thing Jade had ever seen. "At least until they aren't."

"That's a help," Jade bitched even though her bad mood was evaporating in the face of Connie's cheerfulness. "Back in my day, dykes shaved their heads and wore flannel. That's the way it should be."

"You'd look pretty good in flannel," Connie told her thoughtfully with a tilt of her head. "Can't say about the shaved head though. I like your long hair."

"I was fucking hot with a buzz-cut." Jade paused to rake a hand back through her hair, yanking strands out of the clip in the process. "Being on the inside I learned not to flaunt though. The gals don't treat you very well if they think you're that way on the outside." Jade's face twisted and her gut lurched but she didn't elaborate.

Chapter Seven

CONNIE WAS SO silent for a while that Jade started singing along to the radio. She was busy thumping on the steering wheel so she didn't notice the truck pull up beside her until the horn blasted right in her ear. Jade jerked back and whirled to look. The driver of the truck was the guy from the supermarket and it looked like he wasn't going to let them go their separate ways without some kind of payback.

"Perfect, we get to meet up with that dickwhistle cock-pirate again," Jade spat. She rolled down her window and hollered out, "Nice to see you, panty-sucking ass-butler!"

The light turned green. The guy shouted and made rude gestures as the truck lurched forward. He cut Jade off, honking incessantly. Jade swerved and nearly hit a fire hydrant. She went into defense-mode and slammed on the brakes. The truck shot off down the road but Jade wasn't optimistic that he'd just keep going.

"No bad deed goes unpunished." She swore quietly to herself then switched to creative cursing, never repeating an oath in the time it took the truck to pull a U-turn and come charging back at them.

With a raw shot of adrenaline, Jade slammed the car into reverse and took off backward down the street. "I just fucking got my driver's license reinstated last month," she crowed as Connie twisted in her seat to look out of the back window, "And I'm already in car chases! This is awesome! Hang on sweetheart!" Jade flashed Connie a triumphant grin and gave her a wink just because she could. "You can't get any deader than you already are."

Jade leaned on her own horn and floored the accelerator, still in reverse. She streamed backward down a narrow alley, one that the wider truck couldn't follow. The car exploded out the other side. She hauled on the steering wheel and punched the brakes. With a screech of tires, the car spun into a fast 180 degree turn. As the scenery whirled around them, Jade let out a hoot and wished the roof was removable so she could enjoy the breeze. She mowed down a row of garbage cans and was suddenly glad of the roof as sloppy bits of trash rained down over the windshield. The truck screeched around a corner and filled her rear-view mirror.

"Jesus Christ on a cuntwaffle!" Jade threw the car into drive as she gunned the engine.

With the truck hard on her tail, the sedan roared into maximum overdrive. The car hit a rise in the road and achieved air for a full three seconds before they landed with a juddering jolt. Jade clutched the steering wheel for dear life as the battered sedan careened into another, impossibly narrow alley. Brick walls skimmed the car on either side with only a hairsbreadth of clearance. All four tires bounced up and down as they mowed over things Jade fervently prayed weren't alive. Something caught and the steering wheel jerked out of Jade's hands.

The car swerved and the side-view mirror on Jade's side sheared off in a screech of metal. Sparks flew as the brick wall shaved the entire driver's side before she got the car back under control. Daylight burst into the car as they cleared the alley. With her heart thundering in her throat, Jade looked around. The truck was nowhere in sight. She pulled into the parking lot of a dental clinic and cut the engine. Jade rubbed the sweat from her palms onto her jeans.

"Did you go to stunt driving school instead of Driver's Ed by accident?" Connie hollered up from the floor where she'd taken refuge sometime during the wild ride. "How on earth did you learn to drive like that?"

"Pretty cool, huh? I pulled that whole last bit out of my ass," Jade said. "I bet your heart is pounding and you're all a-shaking. Feeling pretty exhilarated myself." She patted herself on the chest and unleashed a wild grin of pure glee at Connie, who pulled herself into the passenger's seat. Jade could tell Connie was trying to look angry, but little twitches at the corners of her lips gave her away.

"God, Jade, you could have killed both of us! Okay, one of us."

"Nah, I'm a good driver."

"Yes, if you were driving a tank in an action movie."

"Aw shucks, Connie." Jade was very pleased. "Now you're just trying to flatter me. Which isn't all that bad, actually. You know, you're really cute when you're scared."

"You're wasting your time and effort on me."

"Am I?" Drunk on adrenaline, Jade started the car up like a maestro summoning an orchestra. It coughed and rolled over. A few warning lights that hadn't been there before shone brightly on the dashboard and there was a worrying rattling sound coming from the engine. As well, the muffler had come half off and dragged on the road, resulting in an unholy noise as Jade pulled back into traffic. She had to holler to be heard over the din, "There's no harm in giving a fast heartbeat to the prettiest girl who's ever been in my car."

"How many girls have you had in your car? Zero?"

"Don't sell yourself short. You're pretty. More than pretty," Jade said. She paused and met Connie's eyes. "You're the most beautiful person I've ever met," Jade said, almost under her breath. Her heart pounded. She wished she could reach out and smooth that worried look from Connie's face, tease the soft fullness of her lips with her thumb. God, she wanted to do a lot to those gorgeous lips.

With a guilty wince, Jade forced her attention back to the road as she remembered Vickie and what she'd done to Jade in that very front seat. Jesus Christ, what the hell was wrong with her? Jade gnawed at the inside of her cheek. She'd had a real-live woman in the car, one who she could hold and even kiss and here she was getting all emotional about a ghost. And her client, no less. Jade broke more propriety rules than she thought existed. She was in a whole lot of trouble and didn't know what to do, or even if she wanted to do anything about it.

Even dead, Connie had more personality than a lot of alive people Jade met. And Jade was becoming increasingly reluctant to see her move on.

Still, the case needed solving. She had a duty not only to Connie, but to justice in general. Whatever happened to extinguish such a bright light, Jade was going to find out what it was. And deal a nice round of butt-kicking to whoever was responsible.

BACK AT HER place, Jade cooked up the chicken with a bunch of veggies plus the can of tomatoes she nearly chucked at the guy in the supermarket. After she ate, the leftovers went into a massive, boat-like Tupperware container.

Full and happy, Jade stood in front of her case wall as she absently hefted a five kilo weight in one hand. The facts scattered about painted a thoroughly depressing picture. A boss who was both incompetent and corrupt. How far would he go to cover up the faulty equipment he'd been ordering?

Murel was also a nasty piece of work, and in a way so was Nathalie. The nervous, silent ones held massive grudges, Jade learned. Guys had it easy; slug it out and you were good. Women waited, putting on friendly faces and when you least expected it, you ended up with a shiv in your kidney. Not always figuratively.

The unsolved mystery of Connie's assault nagged at Jade. What kind of sick fuck would do something like that? Jade scowled. She knew only too well, but the facts didn't add up.

While Jade was more grateful than words or thoughts could express, the way Connie hadn't been fully assaulted was the most puzzling thing about it. Maybe the perp had been interrupted, or what if the act itself hadn't been the goal? After all, the main result was Connie's humiliation in front of all her colleagues. Maybe someone wanted the incident to break Connie and when she'd proven to be made of stronger stuff than they reckoned they took her out. Jade blew out a breath and shifted the weights to her other hand.

The engineers were good people. Jade couldn't see them having anything to gain from harming Connie. They, like Vickie, were valuable allies, showing her bits of the case that she otherwise wouldn't have thought to look for. Gord was creepy and seemed fixated on Connie, which meant Jade would keep a special eye on him.

And then there was Connie's job itself. Just by looking at it, Jade wouldn't want to work there, spending every day apologizing for fuckups she had no control over. Fuckups that cost people's safety and even their lives. That kind of thing wore down your will to live for sure.

Jade turned her attention to the "bar" section. It was a lot less detailed than the "work" section. Reno was probably harmless but dealt Connie's confidence a staggering blow. The whole scene was pretty rough. Things had changed a whole hell of a lot in the twenty years Jade had been in prison.

They had marriage equality now and that sketchy mobile-phone app Benny was always trying to make her get that matched chicks with chicks. Even though Jade kept out of the whole dating scene, she understood how incredibly easy it was to hook up. However, Connie hadn't been able to find anyone. Even with all the social networking available, there were still people out there who were perfectly nice, layable gals but fell through the cracks and stayed single way longer than they wanted.

Not being an expert on interpersonal relations, Jade didn't know exactly why. Personality? Maybe nobody took the time to look close enough to see Connie for the sweet, funny girl she was. Maybe she was too shy to approach anyone, or her normal, kind demeanor got her put into the dreaded friend zone.

The section labeled "family" was blank. Did the young woman even have parents? The answers Jade thought she'd get from visiting the apartment hadn't materialized. If the morgue didn't turn up any new information, Jade would go to her contact inside the police department. As much as she hated to draw attention to herself in that area, maybe someone missed Connie enough to file a missing person's report, or even call in for a safety check.

Then what? Jade hoped she'd find some answers. The world lost something precious with Connie, and Jade wouldn't let her go without a fight. She added some information from the apartment to the wall, but it was still aggravatingly incomplete. Jade went into the kitchen and put the leftover chicken's Tupperware into a bag and slung it over her shoulder.

It took some convincing, but Jade managed to get her car started and onto the road. Even though there was nothing Jade could do about her demolished side mirror or the almost complete lack of paint on the driver's side, the muffler sort of fixed itself when she accidentally hit a speed-bump at full throttle and wasn't quite so noisy. Stealth was good, Jade gloated. She pulled into the morgue's parking lot.

Traynor's Port wasn't big enough to warrant the facility for its exclusive use, so it serviced the entire county. The stone-faced building wasn't all that far from the downtown area, located close to the police station, the biggest hospital in the area, plus a number of convenience stores and a takeout falafel place. Quite convenient for someone like Jade who often had to venture into the domain of the no-longer-living and also appreciated a good falafel.

In the freedom of the empty parking lot, Jade parked haphazardly and wandered into the dark building. Her footsteps echoed against the industrial green tiled floor. The long hallway had that same disinfectant smell the dentist did, but something dark and ripe hung under it, not inviting deep sniffs. A male-looking figure stood at the end of the hallway, almost part of the shadows. He melted away as Jade got closer. She wondered if he was a new addition, or just passing through. The office was easy to find, the only lit corner in the whole place. If Jade worked there she'd leave the lights on all the time. But then again, not everybody could see what she did.

"Hey there." A broadly smiling woman stood up as Jade poked her head into the room. Her teeth shone white against her dark skin and her hair was tied up in a cheerful scarf. "Haven't seen you around here for a while. How's business?"

"Not too bad, Fanny. Hit a bit of a roadblock in my investigation, though," Jade said. She produced the container of chicken. "I made too much so I thought I'd use it as a bribe. Seems like every time I get in front of that stove I come away with enough to feed an army. I already stuffed my face and my aunt won't eat anything with tomatoes in it."

"Smells great. Holy cow, Jade, there's enough for a Catholic family here," Fanny said as she peeked into the container. The name plate on her desk was inscribed with *Fantasy Starr, MD* but she'd cheerfully told Jade anybody who called her that ended up as a new addition to the morgue's collection. Jade didn't know how much of that was a joke, so she obliged.

"I bought one of those family packs that have like a whole flock of chickens in there," Jade told her.

"No problem. I have an intern working here right now, Kam Thambiah. Good kid. He's living on campus and let me tell you, their cafeteria sucks, so I'm sure he'll be glad to help me make short work of this. Your cooking is excellent bribe material." She sat down at her desk and gestured to a chair. Jade slung herself into it and twirled around once. It was an ancient wooden armchair, the kind her school principal used to have. Fanny picked up her glasses from where they were hanging around her neck and slipped them on, suddenly all business. "So what can I help you with tonight?"

"I need to know..." Jade stopped as she got a cold dash of nerves. Her elbows prickled. "Um, I need to know if there's been anyone fished out of the river in the last couple of days. Like, around the Angwin Bridge to start."

"You got a name?" Fanny was busy at her computer, tilting her head to look under her glasses.

"Connie—Constance Mason. I don't think she'd be an easy ID. Left all her papers and stuff behind."

For an agonizing few minutes Fanny clicked at her keyboard and made noncommittal "hmm" noises to herself. Finally she pushed her chair back with a sigh.

"Well?" Jade asked more harshly than she intended.

"Sorry, I got nothing. It's been a slow week. I checked the other municipalities in case she'd drifted down a ways, but nothing. Are you sure of the place and time frame?"

"Pretty solid on both. How about any Jane Does? Not necessarily from the water, but the harbor area in general."

"That opens up the possibilities a bit. I got one this morning, pretty early. Mid-twenties, found behind a container in the loading dock. TOD about two days ago."

"Sounds like a possibility," Jade heard herself saying.

"We still don't have an ID, so maybe if you'd care to have a look?"

"Yeah, I could do that." Jade stood up.

The walls felt very far away. She followed Fanny's generous rear into the freezer with an involuntary shiver that had nothing to do with the sudden cold. Normally, Jade didn't particularly dislike the morgue. At least it was quiet there. She hated hospitals more. They stopped in front of a stainless steel cart, the only occupied one in the room.

"You ready?" Fanny asked as she grasped the closure of the body bag.

"No." Jade felt faint. "Hang on." She concentrated on getting herself under control. Fanny's gaze on her didn't waver until Jade had taken a few good, deep breaths.

"Want me to count to three? Honey, you're not usually nervous like this." Fanny's brow furrowed in concern.

"Fuck. Okay, do it, Fan." Jade steeled herself. She needed to know. With a practiced yank, the body bag opened and Jade gazed down at the waxy face. Suddenly her knees buckled and, embarrassingly, her legs gave out and she sank to the floor.

"So she's your girl?"

"Not her," Jade choked, shocked to find tears streaming down her face. The corpse on the cart was someone else's girl. Someone else's missing daughter or sister or girlfriend. Someone else was desperately wondering what happened to her, maybe even calling her cell phone a whole bunch of times, not knowing the worst had already come to pass. Jade hugged her arms to her chest and cursed quietly. Fanny's warm hand came down on her shoulder.

"I gotta get out of here." Jade hauled herself to her feet and charged back into Fanny's office. She fell into the chair and put her head down into her hands. The feeling of relief punched her in the gut.

The guilt hit only a second later.

A paper cup of water appeared next to her and Jade sucked it down.

"You okay?"

"Yeah." Jade took a long breath and shook her head. "That girl in there's Cherie Kobal."

"You know her?"

"Nope," Jade said. She rummaged in her bag and came up with a plastic clip, which she used to drag her hair back. "She told me."

"Well, that helps me out a lot. Thanks." Anyone else might have said the words sarcastically, but Fanny had dealt with Jade for long enough that she understood. "Why don't you hang out here for a while until you feel better? I've got some business with Ms. Kobal in the next room."

Jade nodded. A few moments later she heard the door close behind Fanny. In the silence, Jade gazed up at the ceiling. What on earth had she been hoping for? It was too late for Connie already. There was no hope for her except to put her spirit to rest. The best possible outcome was that Jade would solve the case and Connie would pass over to the other side. Jade knew that. She'd helped others that way and knew the gate only worked one way. Staying behind past their time was unnatural and out of balance. She had a mission to put things back in order.

But this time, Jade didn't want to right the balance. She didn't want to say goodbye to the cute, sweetly sad, and sometimes funny person she'd just met. Jade pounded her fist on the desk, hoping the physical pain would overpower the mental.

"Hey, are you all right?" It was Connie.

"I wasn't, but I'm getting better by the second," Jade said. The rush of happiness at seeing the familiar young woman startled her. "I'm glad to see you, but Connie, why weren't you there? In the morgue, I mean, your body anyway. What the hell's happening here anyway? Why the hell are we even having this conversation?"

The young woman looked taken aback. Then she grinned, an impish light to her face. She made a pose with her hands over her head in little fists, making panda ears. "Maybe I'm your guardian angel. I've come to give you driving lessons and fashion advice."

Jade batted at her with a rolled-up magazine. "I know my fashion sucks, but I drive perfectly fine. I don't recall running over anybody. Or breaking any traffic laws—okay, maybe I did a few. But I didn't get caught."

"No, that you didn't." Connie perched on the desk. She smiled through her unearthly pallor and waving hair.

"You are a mystery." Jade leaned back in her chair and studied Connie. "Where the hell's your body? It's got to be somewhere. You think it really did get eaten by piranhas? Or sharks? Maybe it got sucked into a sewer or some crazy scientist-type's got a hold of it and is doing experiments on it. Okay, that last one's pretty low on the possibility list." Jade mulled over the information she'd learned so far and chewed furiously on the cuff of her sleeve. "I guess the next place for us to check out is either the bridge or the police station. I'm so not in the mood to be called Spooky right now by Officer Tightass so how about we check out your bridge? I think my car's up for another spin around town, if you are."

"I'm up for anything with you. Jade, I really appreciate all you're doing for me," Connie said. "If there's anything I can do, let me know."

"Really?"

"Sure."

"All right then, tell all the other spookies you see that my bathroom's off limits," Jade said. "I'm getting tired of seeing extra people every time I close the mirror."

"Will do," Connie said and saluted with a happy flourish.

Chapter Eight

CONNIE WAS QUIET during the car ride and gradually faded until Jade wasn't sure if she was even there anymore. In the silence, Jade parked her car in the empty Park 'n Ride then clambered out and made her way over to the Maria Louisa Angwin Bridge that stretched between Traynor's Port and Portsmouth. Jade took a deep breath and edged onto the pedestrian walkway that ran the length of the bridge. Even at the best of times, Jade was not a big fan of heights. It wasn't the falling she hated as much as the landing. The grating under her feet was unhelpfully thin and she could feel the bridge moving in a deep, sluggish undulation punctuated by shivering rumbles.

As she reached the mid-way point, Jade looked up and down the bridge. She saw at least two figures, possibly three. Echoes, she determined. Without consciousness or awareness, they were energy imprints of the last moments of someone's life. There was nothing Jade could do for them. A short caravan of trucks rumbled past and one of the figures flickered out.

Jade held onto the railing and pretended there was nothing scary and far away beneath her feet. She wasn't sure if she was supposed to be looking for anything in particular. Connie wasn't there to give her hints and Jade hadn't been able to find out the location of Connie's jump. The vision Connie shared with her back at the apartment gave her few clues. Luckily there was only one bridge in town so Jade didn't have to haul her ass up and down a bunch of different bridges all night. Good thing too, as she was already running on fumes.

The cold cut through her tired fog and Jade hugged her arms to herself. The wind off the harbor was strong and biting. Her ribbed top didn't even slow it down. It had been a pretty nice summer so far, but Jade wished she'd thought to chuck a windbreaker in her bag before going out.

She gave a bitter laugh about how soft she'd gotten. Twenty years of shivering through Canadian winters in those shitty, thin prison-issue sweatshirts should have given her enough practice at being cold. But she hated it. Jade would rather be too hot than too cold. Being cold just sucked. If you were too hot you could always strip down, but too cold and you were out of luck. She had never gotten used to it but learned to suffer through it. There was no way they'd have let her wander around all day wrapped in her blanket anyway.

Jade crossed her arms on the chin-high railing and looked out over the harbor. The lights from the refineries in Portsmouth turned the water into a shimmering wonderland. Much different from the dingy industrial behemoths in daylight.

She thought about the process someone would have to go through in order to get over that railing to the open scaffolding on the other side. It wouldn't be easy. After heaving yourself over the first railing, you'd have to get over another railing before you could get to the side of the bridge. There was a gap between the two railings and they were only connected by metal beams every meter or so. It was more likely a person would fall through the gaps than make a jump. Jade mulled that option and found it made sense. Someone slim and petite like Connie would be able to pass through easily.

However, there was the problem of getting to the gap in the first place. Although Jade was taller than the average woman, even she would have trouble climbing over both railings. Not to mention the fact the place was pretty dark and swayed gently along with the wind and the few cars that passed.

Then there was the fact that Connie's hands were bound at the time. Jade frowned into the bitter night wind. She must have gotten herself at least over one railing before she put the ties on her wrists and bound the cinderblock to them. There was no way she could climb over already weighted down. It must have taken an iron will and then some.

Having seen enough of Connie's life, Jade determined she was in a seriously dark place mentally. But how could such a sweet, wonderful, and funny person get to that point? Apparently she'd had second thoughts. Somewhat too late, but second thoughts nonetheless.

A chill, damp feeling seeped through her. Jade wasn't alone any more. Connie was beside her, but she wasn't the slightly strange and cutely quirky person Jade had gotten used to. Connie had dead eyes that were staring out over the river. She was faded and her form flickered and stuttered like an old movie.

"Hey, are you all right?" Jade asked before she could stop herself. There was no answer. Connie was an echo. Jade was witnessing the memory of that night. It was a raw, personal thing she was seeing and Jade didn't want to be there. She didn't want to have any part of the last moments of Connie's life. However, it was important that Jade see it. She wished with all her being that Connie knew she wasn't alone. If she could transcend time and space, Jade would be there beside Connie. She would have stopped her. She would have pulled her back and held the young woman in her arms, telling her how precious and unique she was. But Jade could only watch.

Her questions about the how and what were answered. Connie was calm and composed, intelligent and lethally logical. She'd brought along a step-stool and she used that to get over the first railing. There, she took out a plastic bottle and shook it. The bottle was half-empty and Jade wondered if Connie had already been drinking whatever was in it. In the diffuse light from the bridge supports, Jade saw a bunch of half-dissolved pills swirl up into the liquid.

With no emotion on her face, Connie hauled the stool up after herself, using a string tied to it and then dropped the stool down into the black river, following it with her jacket and shoes. She stood in her sock feet on that freezing steel support and gulped down the murky cocktail before she also dropped the empty bottle into the river. If Jade were more on her head, she'd have been upset for the amount of littering that was going on. As a devoted river cleanup-crew member, Jade was offended by anyone messing up nature. However, she didn't have the luxury of offence right now.

Connie weaved, her head slumped and jerked upright again, and it took several agonizing minutes for her to dig a cinderblock and a pack of plastic ties out of the backpack. By the time she was securing them around her wrists, using her teeth to pull them tight, Jade was in tears. She knew it was no use, but she shouted at the apparition. She begged Connie to stop, look around and see she wasn't alone. To think for a minute about those left behind. Not her nasty boss and Gord the creep, of course, but the other people. The group of engineers, even her landlord, and Vickie, who obviously looked up to Connie.

And Jade.

"Don't do it, Connie!"

Her cries spiraled away into the black night air. The echo stepped between the beams of the bridge and vanished into the blackness below.

Jade lunged after her. She dropped to her knees and stretched her arms out as far as she could, wedged uncomfortably between the iron slats. The keening of the wind between the steel beams was the only response she got. Minutes passed. Once more the echo appeared.

She couldn't watch. Jade threw herself away from the railing. She landed on her butt in the relative safety of the pedestrian walkway and sat there until she got her head on straight. She was aware of the echo struggling over the railing, replaying that night in an endless loop. She had to get out of there. Blinded by tears, Jade shook as she stumbled to the end of the bridge.

The ringing steel under her feet changed to the comforting thud of concrete sidewalk. Back on safe ground, Jade stuffed her hands into her pockets and just breathed. The vision's hold on her ebbed and Jade was glad of it. She scuffed through the gravelly scrub and looked around underneath the bridge. If Connie had survived the initial jump, where would she have come up? Around the bridge the riverbanks were steep and artificial. They didn't look as if they'd be easy to climb up normally, let alone in a drugged and half-drowned haze.

A cluster of industrial lights around a sunken area caught her attention and Jade went over to investigate. She ended up over-looking a square concrete pit about four meters deep and big enough to park a couple cars in. The pit was dug into the slope of the banks and open on one side where the greasy line of water met the land. The area looked like it had something to do with maintenance. Jade's intuition prickled. She had to get down there.

The concrete platform was accessible by a long iron ladder that led from the gravel path. A chain-link fence around the top of the enclosure demonstrated it wasn't a public area, but the fence was only chest-high and Jade got over it without even breaking a sweat. Before she realized it, Jade had the rungs of the ladder under her feet. The cold metal was gritty against her palms as she clambered down.

Her vision got increasingly blacker as she lowered herself

into the concrete pit. When she reached the bottom, her legs gave out. Overcome by a strange, murky lethargy, Jade sprawled onto the cold ground. While she couldn't see it, she felt something horrible and sickly spread over the concrete. It seeped into her limbs and robbed them of strength. Above her, the grey clouds scudded across the night sky. Jade wanted to close her eyes forever and sleep.

"Get up! Get up and get out of here!"

"Five more minutes," Jade mumbled, the words were difficult to form. She was tired. So tired. She didn't want to fight anymore. The darkness was warm. Jade wanted to sink into it.

"Do it *now*, Jade! So help me I'm not going to leave you here!"

A sudden, stinging thwack across her face shocked her awake. Jade struggled to sit up and fell back onto her elbows as a wave of dizziness came over her.

"Jade, come back to me." Connie's voice broke the spell.

Still somewhat stunned, Jade looked around. She tried to locate Connie and found the young woman's figure hovering about halfway up the ladder. Jade held one hand on her cheek as an amazed smile pulled at her lips. "Did you — did you just slap me?"

"I might have." The thin voice filtered down to her. "I don't know what I did. I just had to get you back. You need to get out of there. Please."

"Connie, sweetie, I have to tell you, you are one remarkable, uh, presence." Finally Jade was able to haul herself to her feet. She grabbed the rusty iron ladder and climbed back up to ground level. Her head swam as she staggered back out to the street. The artificial orange lights bathed her in their wan glow. Life flooded back into her.

"Thanks for getting me out of there, Connie," Jade said. "That was pretty intense."

"You shouldn't be here." Connie's face was drawn. "This is not a good place."

"Something happened here. I have to find out what it was."

"That may be the case but I'm already gone. It does nobody any good if you go down here too."

"Yeah, okay," Jade had to admit.

Connie shouted directions and egged her on until Jade made it back to her car and collapsed into the driver's seat.

"Go home and rest," Connie said from the passenger seat. "You can't solve this case in a day. I'll do what I can to try and remember, but this isn't the place for you. I'm sorry I led you to something like this. I can feel it too." The specter shivered. "There's a gravity well of sorrow here. It's not good for anybody." She turned back to Jade. "You need light and warmth and your room. Come on, put the key into the ignition. How about I turn on the radio to that country station you always like to listen to?"

Music filled the car. Jade wasn't sure who'd actually turned the radio on, but it grounded her and brought her back to the present. She couldn't bring herself to take the wheel. Not yet.

"You need to get out of here. The longer you stay, the closer this *something* comes."

"I'm all right." Lethargic spell broken, Jade flapped a hand at Connie, who hovered at her elbow with a concerned expression. "I just got a bit in over my head, if you'll pardon the expression."

"No problem. And you're not running any red lights on the way home, do you understand?"

"Yes ma'am." Jade put the car into reverse and got out of the parking spot, then tooled out to the main road.

"Good. I'd feel awful if you went back to jail, or at least traffic court on my account. Your parole officer would have my head, I'm sure."

"That's all right," Jade said. She carefully signaled before she made a turn. "I don't have one of those. I do have a counselor though."

"Why not?"

"Turns out I was able to prove without a doubt that I didn't do the crime. The so-called murder victim was living quite happily in the Bahamas on the money he embezzled from the company. He set me, the dumbass intern, up to take the fall for it and the company I'd been working for was only too happy to comply," Jade said. "My first client as a P.I. was myself."

Connie looked impressed. "It looks like I chose the right private investigator for my case, then."

"You sure did," Jade said. For the first time in years, Jade found herself talking about her own history. "He was a manager in another department in the company where I worked," she said. Jade's voice was soft and blended in with the song on the radio.

"Cormick Breamer. I maybe said two words total to the guy but he picked me to take the fall for him." She glanced over to the passenger seat. Connie had her full attention on Jade. "We were at this company function and he offered to give me a ride home. He made sure everybody saw us leave together. He'd put something in my drink and I passed out in his car. He made it look like I killed him and tossed his body into the harbor. Made it look like I was embezzling from the company and he found out about it and I was trying to cover it up."

The car shuddered to a stop at a deserted intersection. Red light filtered down through the windshield. Jade crossed her arms over the steering wheel and rested her forehead on her wrists. Weariness dragged at her. She sat up with a slight groan.

"We had a warehouse down by the docks and he set the place on fire, like I was trying to get rid of the evidence. I woke up right in the middle of that. That's how I got all this." Jade freed a hand from the steering wheel as she gestured to her scarred left arm. "The trial was delayed while I was busy trying not to die. Then for the next twenty years I wished I had."

"Oh Jade." Connie's voice was full of sorrow. "Nobody should have to deal with that."

Jade shook her head and drew a cuff across her face before she continued, "I know why he picked me. I was young, gay, and proud of it. It was a different time. There wasn't a lot of sympathy for me." The light changed. Jade stomped on the gas. The road blurred in front of her. "And the rest, as they say, is history."

"I didn't know." Connie looked very young in the flashing streetlights.

"That's all right. I'm glad you missed all the hype when I was on trial. That was a fucking crazy circus of bullshit. For the span of a couple months, I was the most famous person in Canada." Jade mustered up a carefree grin that faltered as she did a bit of mental math. Holy shit, the same year she'd been in the hospital burned to shit and under arrest, Connie was in the hospital being born. Her life ended about the same time as Connie's had started. The grin vanished.

"Still, I wish I had been there. I would have stood by you. And I'll stand with you now."

"Thanks, that means a lot."

Jade saw her building in the distance and was suddenly very

soft and sleepy. It had been quite the day and she was more than ready for some downtime. She also wanted a shower, and if Connie's word was to be trusted, she wouldn't have any uninvited visitors that night in the bathroom, something Jade considered a good thing. She didn't mind the other rooms so much, but there were some places a gal just wanted to have to herself. After twenty years of not being able to take a shit without at least ten people hearing, Jade thought she deserved that much at least.

Chapter Nine

JADE WAS ALONE by the time she got back to her place. She dropped her bag as soon as she cleared the doorway. As she walked through her rooms, she shrugged out of her shirt and pulled her sports bra over her head. Those too fell in a pool onto the floor. Her head echoed with details. She could hear a hundred people speaking in her mind and just wanted to shut them out. She ached all over, drunk with fatigue. She needed a bit of time to get used to all the strange shit that was going on. Jade never felt so alone in her life. She ached to hear Connie's voice. To see her.

Jade considered, very seriously, that she'd fallen for a ghost.

She didn't want to laugh at herself, but she couldn't help it. Jade cackled as she stumbled toward her bathroom. She shook out her hair and kicked off the rest of her clothes before she padded through the doorway.

Her bathroom was small and simple, with a narrow sink and commode next to the shower stall. If Jade wanted a full bath, she could go up to her aunt's place on the third floor. So far, she'd only been up there twice. Both times she'd gotten bored and felt the whole affair with those gross bath beads a waste of time.

Jade turned on a hot cascade of water and waited until it was a good temperature before she stepped under it. She grabbed her sponge and put an absolutely inordinate amount of nice-smelling soap on it. She made huge, luxurious mounds of bubbles and rubbed them all over herself. The suds and water coursed down over the hard lines of her body, smoothing the fossilized waves from the numerous skin grafts that ran down her arm and shoulder.

Jade found herself introspective. Talking to Connie brought back memories and for once, Jade didn't try to shove them back where they belonged in the bottom drawer of the bureau of her subconscious. When she'd first set foot in prison, she'd been scared as hell and super defensive as a result. She didn't let anyone get close to her, just as fearful of allies as she was of enemies.

After hope that she'd magically get sprung died, Jade relaxed quite a bit and the place started to be something like home. True, some really bad shit happened there, but she'd gotten used to being in prison. She'd even had a good time occasionally and found some real friends.

Jade let the hot water course over her wry grin.

She went through a lot of phases during her twenty-year incarceration. The phase where she swore she'd read every single goddamned book in the library, another one where she got religion. Fortunately that hadn't lasted overly long and she went back to her somewhat salad-bar Protestant-ism without much fuss.

One phase she pumped iron until she could arm-wrestle even the warden. One she memorized all the trivia they watched on Jeopardy and outguessed the best contestants. Lots of phases.

And now it was over.

Jade hung her head and breathed the steam in. She basked in the comfort of having her own space where nobody would intrude. Nobody was watching her, checking to make sure she stayed within the absolute confines of the rules or waiting until she let her guard down enough to strike in a sick mixture of sex and violence. Jade could close her eyes under the hot spray without fear.

Privacy was not a right. It was a privilege, one that could be taken away so easily. Privacy was one thing, but being alone was another.

People who knew about Jade's incarceration sometimes asked how she could have survived twenty years without a place to call her own. It was a valid question. When she was inside, Jade wanted her own space more than anything, but once she actually found herself alone, she realized she didn't want it as much as she'd thought.

As soon as she got out, Jade bought the building that housed Benny's bookstore, renovated the upper two floors, and acquired Adelaide Rodgers as a housemate, her mother's older sister and Jade's only living relative.

Jade lost the desire to be alone as soon as she'd found herself that way. Even now, she could barely stand it. Privacy was great, but being alone with only silence and nobody to listen to the funny comments and off-color jokes she came up with left her with an ache in the pit of her belly. Jade squeezed her eyes shut.

Maybe Connie was right. Jade let the hot water course over her body as rivers of suds pooled wastefully around her feet. She didn't deserve what she had, even though it cost Jade twenty years of her life, her name, her family, and most likely her mental stability.

The bigwigs on the company's side during the farce that was Jade's trial had thrown a ton of money around hiring one of the most famous cutthroat criminal lawyers in the country, along with sketchy journalists who dug up everything from who Jade took to her prom (Amy Goldman) to how many times she'd lied about her age to get into the one gay bar in town (twice). It took almost three years from her initial arrest to her sentencing and over that time, Jade was vilified, stripped bare, and exhibited like a freak show attraction. The media latched onto her case like a rabid wolf and the entire country went crazy over the weeks of her trial.

The final slamming of the prison door had almost been a relief.

When Jade got out, it was an entirely different matter. In return for keeping things quiet and not starting a huge shit-slinging lawsuit, Jade was offered a payoff by the same bigwigs who put her through hell. And Jade took it.

That payoff left her with a fat wad of mutual funds and investments that guaranteed she wouldn't have to work a day in her life if she didn't want to. She was a property owner, she had an private investigator's license that let her poke around and get away with stuff normal people couldn't, and she had a couple people close to her who she could call friends. Maybe one person didn't deserve so much.

Jade leaned back into the warm spray. The darkness she was usually able to keep at bay welled up within herself.

"I don't deserve any of this," Jade whispered aloud.

"Yes, you do."

Jade felt the words more than heard them. She kept her eyes closed and raised her head slightly to tune into the faint sound. There was something light but unmistakably there at her back. She leaned into it, needing the contact more than she'd dare to admit. She stayed like that for a moment, until the presence left. Jade wondered if she'd imagined it, then thought better of it. She never imagined things like that. Not since she woke up from her coma. Sometimes the walls between worlds blurred, especially when Jade got really fucking tired like she was that night.

She opened her eyes and shook herself awake in a spray of water. Over her shoulder, Jade glanced through the frosted doors of the shower stall and a jolt of surprise electrified her body. Someone was there. With a pounding heart, Jade eased the door open and peered out. It was Connie.

"Hello!" Connie waved. In the steamy air, she looked more solid than ever and Jade caught her breath. God, she was cute.

"How the hell did you get so cute?" Jade asked, only half-joking. "And how did you get in here? Not that I mind, I mean, you know. As long as it's only you."

"Yup! Only me. I'm keeping my promise and being the guardian angel of the bathroom," Connie said and tilted her head. "I hope that's okay. Don't mind me being here. I'll blend into the background. I'm good at that." She twisted her hands together. The happy smile faded from her face. "I'm sorry, maybe I should have waited somewhere else, but it seemed like a good idea at the time. How about I just go now?"

Jade yanked the shower door fully open and didn't realize she was standing there completely exposed until she saw Connie's cheeks flare pink and her eyes go somewhere else. Something naughty and needful bloomed within Jade, and she wasn't sure if she could stop herself. "It's okay Connie. I want you to be here," Jade heard herself saying. "I'd—I'd like you to stay."

She let the door stay wide open and didn't care if she flooded the bathroom. Connie raised her head. Their eyes met once more with the breathless intensity that called up nameless desires in Jade's mind. She needed Connie so fucking bad she couldn't even move.

"It's not enough," Jade breathed. She didn't know what those words would bring but she knew what she wanted. Finally, she broke the contact and leaned forward with both hands pressed against the cold tiles of the shower stall. Her entire body shook. This was not what she'd dreamed of or asked for. But it would have to do.

She needed to move. Jade twisted the shower off and grabbed a towel to rub herself down. The towel smelled heavenly. She buried her face in it and almost lost herself into the softness. There was danger in letting her guard down, but Jade didn't care.

She felt a cool breath upon her shoulder.

"Connie," Jade whimpered. She felt as if she was falling into somewhere cold and dark. "I wish you were here."

"I am," came the answer. "As long as you want me."

Jade allowed herself to believe it. She smiled against the good softness of the towel.

"Stay with me for a moment."

"I will. I want to be here. With you."

There was need in Connie's voice. Jade hadn't been sure of anything before that moment, but at least she knew she was not alone. All the loneliness and fear she'd been fighting came to a head. Twenty years took what little innocence she'd had and left a deep and costly knowledge.

Jade passed her office and its rickety cot in the closet. She padded on bare feet to her bedroom. The sheets of her bed against her skin were unbelievably soft. Supple, clean, and unstarched. She arched her back against them. Her wet hair trailed over her pillow, dampening the pillowcase and making the cotton cold against her skin. Jade was no stranger to keeping to herself. Sharing an intimate moment with someone, letting the action mean more than just raw release, was not something she'd chosen to become overly familiar with. Loving someone, opening herself to harm, the risk was too great. Jade was not the kind of person to let things get out of control. But now, she felt that control falling away, and she welcomed it.

The cool heaviness at her side didn't leave. She hoped it wouldn't. Finally free to let desire guide her, Jade wondered if she was making the wrong decision and inviting disaster. She dismissed the pinched worry. Whatever came next, she would have the memory and it would be hers forever. Whatever happened from that point was not important. The world would keep turning and Jade would see a thousand more sunrises with it. Even if she didn't, the sun wouldn't stop rising. People wouldn't stop waking up and eating muffins and spilling coffee on themselves and cursing at slow traffic lights, a million tedious moments and annoyances that made up life. Jade leaned back and let her body sink into the hovering semi-aware state that waited on the other side of complete mental and physical exhaustion.

She felt herself drop. Everything went dark, as if Jade was blindfolded.

"Connie, I want you here with me," Jade said into the darkness. The room was so black, Jade didn't know if her eyes were open or closed. Not even the streetlights peered in from outside. Jade wanted it that way. She didn't want to trust her eyes. She didn't want to see things for the unearthly pallor and translucency they were. She only wanted to feel. And that was what she did. The blanket slipped down her arm and Jade felt Connie beside her, breathing over her.

"Come here," Jade whispered. She was lost in a dream as she reached out. Gentle fingers stroked down her arms. They didn't shy from Jade's scars but caressed and kissed feeling and life back into them.

"You're beautiful, Jade." Connie's voice was as gentle as her touch. "I never knew anyone so beautiful."

"You're just sweet talking me," Jade said into the blackness. She raised her arms over her head and draped them over her pillow. The soft wisps traced down over her body and found her breasts and nipples. Against her better judgment, Jade gasped. She arched up against the soft, cool pressure.

"This is not happening," Jade breathed. She pressed her face against one upraised arm. "Tell me it's a dream."

"It's a dream," Connie said.

"Good," Jade said. She felt her thighs being moved open with a soft, searching touch and willingly yielded to it. "I hope you respect me in the morning."

"I will. I always have," the voice came again in her ear. A shift, a soft whisper. Jade felt hot breath against her neck. The softest kiss teased her skin. Jade moaned.

"It's okay, I won't hurt you," Connie said. "Don't be afraid."

She wasn't. Jade made an involuntary sound, once again arching her back as gentle fingers found a secret place. She hadn't meant to be so passive, but the spell was delicate and she didn't want to risk breaking it. She held herself still, like a butterfly had chanced to land on her finger.

Jade hardly dared breathe, but she did manage a "Sweet Jesus!" when she felt a spear of pleasure stab up from between her legs straight to her heart. The slow motions didn't relent. The touches built in strength and confidence as they drew more ragged breaths from Jade. She was unaware she'd kicked off the blankets until she was fully exposed on top of the bed. The presence over her was tangible and grew heavier and stronger with the quickening motions.

Warm fingers traced a path up her belly and Jade felt arms come around her, lips pressed against her own. She melted into the embrace as she was kissed and loved and sucked into a vast maelstrom. Sprawled back over the pillows, Jade cried out as a tentative touch filled her then moved from within herself to the aching nub. Shocks of pleasure jabbed through her as the motions increased in pressure. Jade panted into the darkness, hungry for more.

"I'm almost there," Jade said. She couldn't help the moan that escaped her lips, her head thrown back in pleasure. She arched her body and splayed herself open. "Finish me," she begged, not able to bear any more. "Connie, finish me!"

And she did. A white hot spasm broke her body into thousands of pieces. Jade gasped as she lost her ability to breathe and think. At that moment, clear as daylight, she saw Connie's tousled, flushed face inches from her own. The young woman's eyes were half closed, mouth open in a cry of pure release. At that moment, the words came bubbling out of Jade's mouth.

"It would be so fucking easy to love you."

The confession burned in Jade's throat. She felt relief greater than tears shake her. She didn't care if there was an answer. Actually, she hoped there wasn't. The darkness faded into a dusky hue. Jade was aware for the first time of the reflections from passing cars on the ceiling, the fluorescent light above her that still held the slightest glow. The clock radio at her bedside shone red, the numbers indicating 3:23 a.m.

Jade fully expected to find herself suddenly and irreversibly alone after that moment, but Connie's cool heaviness was still beside her. Jade didn't turn to look but she felt the young woman's slumber against her back. That was enough. Connie had been nothing but cold when Jade first met her. The even breaths against her shoulder were so warm and natural that Jade wondered for a second what was a dream and what was reality.

The next morning would dawn with its annoyances and frustrations, stupid paperwork and dumb rules and the tedious people who enforced it with their narrow-minded self-absorption. The world would keep turning with all its injustices and misunderstandings, but Jade would have a moment that was hers alone.

She wanted with all of her being to keep it in a crystallized fossil in her mind. That moment Connie was her entire world. Jade's words of confession. She didn't want to think about what was right or wrong and all the grey areas in between. The heaviness at her back gave her all the answer she needed. If tomorrow never came for either of them, Jade would still have her moment.

She would keep it in her mind and heart for all eternity. Or at least until she woke up and had a good long think about reality and face the fact that a dead girl just got her off.

Chapter Ten

JADE WOKE UP on her cot, still weary and unsure how she'd gotten there before she remembered stumbling into it by pure habit on her way back from getting a glass of water. The disorientation only added to the unreal feeling Jade carried around with her.

In the course of the night, some of the Post-it notes she'd failed to stick on well enough came off and decorated her blanket and floor.

"Tit-licking piss buckets," Jade hissed as she scooped them up and put them back in place. She didn't know why she bothered. The case seemed to have solved itself. She paused and scratched her chin as she studied the notes. Something wasn't right. Jade didn't feel the completion she normally did when she solved a case. It wasn't over. There was something more Jade needed to find.

Jade dredged up a T-shirt and some new underwear from the unfolded pile at the end of the cot and shrugged into them before she grabbed at the spill of discarded clothes on the floor. As she shook out her jeans from the previous day, the crystal Amber had given her and her cell phone both fell out.

A bunch of new alerts crowded her phone's screen. Jade missed three calls the night before from a number she recognized as Vickie's. She stared at the phone for a long moment. She wanted nothing more than to throw it out the window; however, Vickie was her best source of information and Jade couldn't ignore her. As much as it galled Jade, keeping on Vickie's good side was a smart strategic move.

Jade stalled for time. She knotted her hair at the base of her neck and secured it with a plain elastic band she found on her wrist. She stuffed the crystal and its somewhat battered paper wrapper into her bag. Reluctantly, she managed to get her phone to redial the number on the first try.

"Hello?" Vickie sounded groggy. Jade glanced at her watch and cringed. It was only a little past five. No wonder she was still tired as fuck.

"Uh, sorry for missing your calls last night." With her phone at her ear, Jade yanked at the elastic in her hair, which snapped with the sharp motion. Long strands fell into her face. She blew them out, pleased she managed not to blow out curses along with her hair. "I was busy looking for clues and stuff."

"Did you find anything new?"

"I can't really say for sure," Jade said in a carefully casual tone. "But I had a good time with you last night." She hoped the words didn't sound as fake as she felt.

"Yeah, me too. It's not every day I get to witness a bar fight."

"That was no fight," Jade protested. "Hell, that was hardly a disagreement at all. I thought the whole thing was very civil." Jade paused. She steeled herself and continued, "If you're not busy, I'd like to see you again soon. This time without the brawling."

"I'd like that too." Vickie's sickly sweet giggle filled her ear and Jade pulled the phone away with a grimace. "How about meeting up for lunch? Do you like Thai?"

"Not really," Jade said. She actually had no idea if she did or not, but she did know where she wanted to go. "How about that place across the street from your work? You know, the diner."

"Are you sure? It's not exactly what I would call a nice place. It's so grubby and old. The food sucks too."

"Hey, I like retro stuff like that." Jade forced her face to smile. "You know, it brings back memories of the good ol' days."

"Okay, whatever you want." Vickie drew the words out in a doubtful drawl like a spoiled child being forced to humor her elderly relative.

"Great. What time works for you?"

"I've scheduled my lunch break from twelve thirty, so how about meeting at the restaurant then?"

"I'll be there." By the time Jade ended the call, the band of her sports bra was soaked with sweat.

She found the top she'd worn the night before. It had a bunch of scuff marks on the elbows and some kind of rusty stain on the back. Definitely unwearable. She didn't have a whole lot of clothes, so Jade just threw on a clean pair of chinos and a cotton button-down shirt over her T-shirt, and left it at that. She hesitated before fastening a thin gold chain around her neck. The cross pendant glistened in the morning sunlight. Jade glanced down. She liked the way it peeked out from her collar. Any help was welcome, after all.

Jade ducked into the bathroom to brush her teeth.

"Clit-teasing bastard," Jade barked at the mirror. She had a noticeable bruise on her face just under her left eye. Obviously Reno had landed well with that lucky elbow. Jade rummaged around in the drawer and came up with a cake of theater makeup. She leaned forward and stared into the mirror as she swiped on a thick layer of foundation.

Jade located a bagel and chewed on it while clomping out to her car. In daylight, the sedan looked in a lot worse shape than she remembered from the night before. Jade wished she had a buddy in the auto repair business who could slap some sense back into the vehicle, but the only people Jade knew besides Amber and Ross were those related to the judicial system. Both sides.

She'd exhausted her other options so Jade decided to pay Detective Young a visit. Jade started the car and rolled into the sparse pre-rush-hour traffic. Even though her criminal record was expunged when she was released from prison, Jade still felt a natural uneasiness when facing the police. She made sure to park extra carefully in the visitors' lot in front of the station. Jade sat in the car for a few minutes and took several of what her counselor called "deep, cleansing breaths."

She thought about the lunch date with Vickie and hoped she could get through it without screwing up too badly. After all, when had such a pretty and cute young thing taken such an interest in her? Never. That's when. A guilty feeling buzzed like a mosquito in her ear and Jade brushed it away. No matter what happened between herself and Connie, Jade had to face the reality that one of them was a ghost and that wasn't conducive for a proper relationship. She wasn't dating Vickie either, they were just having lunch and hopefully Jade could get some more information relevant to the case.

Once she was mentally ready, Jade pocketed her keys and went into the station.

The place smelled like over-boiled coffee and sweat. A couple guys were sleeping in the waiting room, both reeking of booze. Behind the front desk, the office buzzed with rustling papers and ringing phones.

"Hey there, Spooky."

Jade turned at the voice and saw the officer, a young guy named Lance Becker who liked to give Jade a hard time. She gritted her teeth and forced a smile. There was no need to antagonize the locals, not even a tight-ass like him.

"Let me guess," Becker said. "You're here to see Detective Young."

"Yup." Jade leaned on the front desk in what she hoped was a suitably respectable and non-suspicious pose. "Could you let him know I'm here?"

"Go ahead and tell him yourself. He's over there."

Becker moved back and gestured to the main office where Detective Irving Young was at his desk. As Jade approached, he waved her over with a look of tired resignation.

There was nothing especially different about him, no new-age and woo-woo aura, but out of all the other people on the force, he was the only one who listened to her and didn't question why she knew the things she did.

Jade heard the other guys ribbing him mercilessly about her and was content to put up with being called Spooky because she knew he was there for her. As much as Jade became used to being put down and harried by the right side of the law, she was on Young's side and he was on hers. She came to that conclusion a long time ago back when he first visited her in prison.

Now approaching retirement, Young mostly piloted a desk instead of being out and active in the pursuit of justice, but he managed to make up for that by working longer hours than anyone else. The fact that he had a record for solving cold cases also kept him buried in paperwork and old files.

Jade wandered between paper-covered desks and dodged a couple of "Morning Spooky" calls in the process. Young's crumpled suit looked just as bad as Jade's bar-going outfit had that morning. He was fifteen years Jade's senior and his light brown hair was thinning, but his bushy moustache made up for it. He had a habit of standing at his desk with one knee on his chair, leaning over it to answer the phone or tap away at his computer. He was doing just that as Jade reached him. His face sported a night's worth of beard and his scalp gleamed at her under the fluorescent lights. He looked up from his computer screen and acknowledged Jade with a grunt.

"How're you doing, Young?" Jade let a big grin split her face. She grabbed a chair and spun it around under her hand before she straddled it and leaned her arms over the back of it.

Instead of answering Jade's question, he harrumphed. "What can I do ya for, Mayflower? Got any more ghosts with leads for me?"

"Kind of. I'm looking for somebody. Actually, more like someone's body."

"You tried the morgue?" Young had a toothpick in his mouth and waggled it at her.

"Not sure if that's sarcastic, but yeah I have." Someone came by with a tray of paper cups of coffee and two of them landed on Young's desk. They both paused to slurp some brew. Jade fought the grimace as the bitter taste hit her like a kick in the face, but she didn't feel like she had enough clout with the police to ask for sugar.

"Got a name?" Young was never one to waste time or words.

"Constance Mason." Jade put her cup down and pushed it away from herself. "Time of death, I've narrowed down to last weekend, give or take. Thursday was her last day at work, and the last time anyone saw her that I know of. She was already, um, gone by Monday night." Jade quickly summarized the facts she had. Young scribbled notes as she spoke.

"Description?"

Jade fought the slight warmth that came to her face as she said, "She's got short blonde hair, kind of wavy. Slim build, small, I'd say about five-four or thereabouts. Green eyes. Twenty-four years old." And she's sweet, sexy, funny, and damn good in bed. She didn't regret it, but Jade wasn't quite sure yet how she felt about what happened the previous night.

"How soon you need this info?"

"ASAP," Jade said. "She's standing right behind you."

He jumped and twisted to look. "Shit, Mayflower. You know I hate when you do that." Young actually used his chair the way it was intended as he plopped back down. He let out a sigh as his shoulders settled under the dull suit jacket. The lapels were shiny from repeated trips to the dry cleaners. "I'll see what I can dig up and let you know. Gimme a minute, okay?"

"Sure thing."

Dismissed, Jade wandered back into the main office with her cooling coffee in her hand. She didn't think she could finish it, but she didn't want to just abandon it on Young's desk.

"Hey Spooky," Becker called as she passed his desk. He had his feet up on it and was leafing through a file folder. "How's Elvis?"

"Pretty good. He says hi." Jade made a gun from her fingers and aimed it at him.

"What happened to your face?" Becker asked. He put his feet down and peered at Jade in a way that made her want to beat him, but she didn't, just because she was that much into social justice and harmony. And not getting arrested in the middle of a police station. "Get into a fight?"

Jade put a hand up to the spot on her face where there was still a nagging ache. Obviously her makeup-applying skills weren't exactly runway-worthy. "Nope. Your mom closed her legs before I was done." Jade decided against the urge to punctuate the sentence with an explanatory gesture. She did have manners, after all.

"Oh, ice burn!" Becker said as a bunch of other cops hooted at him. "Nice try, but my mom's way too classy for you."

"Not last night she wasn't."

Jade sidestepped until she was out of Becker's line of fire. She found a free chair and slouched into it. She sipped moodily at her coffee and surveyed the room as people bustled around her. Most of them glanced at her as they passed, but nobody spoke to her. Besides being Spooky, Jade didn't know what they thought of her.

They may not have made the connection between Janebeth Trescott and Jade Mayflower, especially the younger ones who wouldn't remember the original trial and had most likely overlooked the small news her release made a year ago. Some of the older guys looked at her like they knew, but for the most part nobody got on her case about her story, which was fine because Jade enjoyed living quietly. However, she wasn't the kind of person to sit around and get fat. She hadn't gotten her P.I. license for nothing, and even though she knew she wasn't supposed to do it, she got the clitoral equivalent of a hard-on when she flashed it about.

After a while, Detective Young came over to Jade's

impromptu campsite with a printout in his meaty hands. "I have good news and bad news. Which do you wanna hear first?" He didn't bother sitting down, even though his feet looked like they hurt.

"Gimme the bad first," Jade said. Her fingers clenched around her cup.

"Okay, the bad news is nobody's pulled anything dead from the river since those kids went over in their daddy's Beemer last spring and we got nothing on Constance Mason except for a certain incident a month ago down at The Old Deck Tavern that maybe you already know about."

"Yeah, I do," Jade said in a hard voice. "All right, and the good news?"

"If you get your ass down to Victoria General, there's a Jane Doe in ICU that matches the profile of your vic. Admitted early on Friday and nobody's been in to see her except the guy who did her fingerprints, which, by the way, didn't get a hit. That's all we got for the moment."

Jade jumped to her feet, breathless and dizzy. She was out of the door and in her car before she was aware of what she was doing. The coffee cup ended up scrunched between the driver's seat and the door.

Her heart raced.

She could barely allow herself to hope. There were tons of women who matched Connie's description, but the timing was spot-on and Traynor's Port wasn't all that big. What if it really was Connie in ICU? What did that mean?

After she left the police station's parking lot, Jade tried hard not to break any major traffic laws on her way to the hospital. She was shaking and breathing hard by the time she slammed through the parking gate and threw her car haphazardly across two parking spots in the hospital's lot. She had better things to do than carefully perfect her parking technique.

A flash of her P.I. license got her past the reception desk. A young orderly gave her a room number in ICU and Jade impatiently pounded the call button of the elevator.

"Jesus Christ, take fucking forever," Jade muttered. She jumped from one foot to the other until the elevator finally arrived. She rushed through the opening doors, not daring to think, not even daring to breathe until nature made her suck in a lungful of oxygen at around the third floor.

She didn't even try to affect an appearance of decorum as she slammed down the squeaky-tiled hallway. Jade nearly shoved a nurse with an armful of little plastic-wrapped boxes out of the way and didn't even pause until her frantic forward motion brought her to a long Plexiglas window that separated the hallway from a row of beds.

One of them was occupied.

The door gave under her frantic hands and Jade stumbled into the sterile, disinfectant-reeking room. Tubes and beeping monitors huddled around a swaddled figure whose hands were unnaturally still on top of a hospital-issue waffle blanket.

It was Connie.

For the second time in as many days, Jade fell to her knees.

Chapter Eleven

STILL LIGHTHEADED WITH disbelief, Jade hauled herself to her feet and leaned over Connie's unresponsive form. She looked like she'd been through a zombie apocalypse. Her head and both hands were wrapped in bandages, a ventilator obscured the lower half of her face. She was hooked up to a number of machines and an IV steadily dripped above her. Jade's fingers twitched, she ached to reach out to the young woman lying so still, save for the hissing, regular breaths that rose and fell under the blanket.

At the sound of the door opening, Jade whirled. A slim, bespectacled man in brightly patterned scrubs stood in the doorway. He came into the room and fixed her with a searching expression.

"Do you know her?" he asked, his voice soft and calm. Immediately, Jade relaxed a notch.

"Yeah, I do," she said. She shifted her weight from one foot to the other, worried that he was going to ask her to leave. The opposite happened.

"That's great," he said. He reached out both hands and grabbed Jade's. "All of us in nursing have been rooting for this young lady since they brought her in. I know this must be hard for you, but do you have time to fill out some forms?"

"Sure," Jade said. The nurse, who introduced himself as Alan Walsh, rushed off and soon Jade was parked on a molded plastic chair in a tiny waiting room, in possession of an admissions form and a pen bearing the hospital's logo, which she was told she could keep. After she filled in as much information as she knew, Jade handed the documents back. She couldn't wait any longer. She had to know. "Okay, I did my bit," she said. "Now it's your turn. Tell me about Connie. What happened to her? When was she admitted? Is she going to be okay?"

Alan adjusted his glasses on his nose before he spoke. "Are you family?"

"No, I'm..." Jade trailed off. What the hell was she? Stalling for time, she took off her clip and shook back her hair. She came to a decision and said, "I'm a friend."

With a hum of understanding, Alan gave her a long look before he sat down opposite Jade. He loosely clasped his hands in front of himself. "Ms. Mason was brought here by ambulance and admitted in critical condition early Friday morning. She lost vitals on the way in and was resuscitated. As of now, her condition is stable, but it's still touch and go."

Jade pressed a hand to her face as she pictured the scene. She cleared her throat. "What happened to her?"

Alan shook his head. "I can't give you those details. I'm sorry."

Jade let out a long breath. She was disappointed but not surprised. "Look, I'm not family, but is it okay if I visit?" She was not above using her P.I. status as leverage, but she couldn't hide the fact that she was much more than just an investigator to Connie.

"Of course it is," Alan said. "I'm really glad there's someone here for her. She needs someone to call her back, make sure she knows there's life out here and give her hope. She's already crashed twice and there's not much more her body can take. A person can only die so many times before they just don't have the ability to come back anymore. I don't want to see that happen, not to someone who's been through so much already and who has so much of her life left to live."

Jade froze. "She crashed twice? When was the second time?" Her words were a sick croak.

"Last night. About a quarter past three."

A shard of ice stabbed into Jade's chest. She remembered what was going on at about that time. It had to be a coincidence.

"Oh and by the way," Alan's eyes danced and his voice slipped into a lilting singsong worthy of Benny, "You, my dear, *are* family. Feel free to come by and visit your friend anytime."

With that he rose and swished out of the room. Jade gaped at his retreating back for a second before she bolted for the elevator.

BACK IN HER car, Jade slammed her hands against the steering wheel.

"Is everything okay?" Connie was in the passenger seat.

Nearly crying with relief, Jade was shocked at how happy she was to see the young woman. "Just fine," Jade said. The words spilled out of her mouth in a jumbled rush. "Connie, sweetheart, we found you. Your body that is. You're alive. I'm not gonna lie, you're in a coma and it looks pretty grim, but you're alive."

"I am?" Connie squeaked. She scooted closer to Jade and said, "That's good because I'd hate to think I made you into a necrophile."

Jade froze with a sick feeling in her gut.

"It's okay, Jade. I was just teasing and I'm not going to make this weird." Connie became serious as she said, "I know this doesn't make us girlfriends or whatever, but you were so sad and alone. I've been there—it was practically my default setting. For once, I could actually help someone, and so I did." She flushed and bit her lip before she said, "For the record, I've never done anything like that before, you know, take charge, and I really liked it."

Connie's words and calm, accepting manner erased the unease that was eating at Jade. In return, Jade gave her a slow smile and said, "For the record, I did too." She chewed her lip for a moment before she continued, "But I don't think we should do anything like that again."

"Why?" Connie looked small and taken aback. "Was it that bad?"

"Not at all," Jade said. She had to force the next words out. "It's just, at that exact time you, um, your body, well, died. I don't know if it was related—"

"I know," Connie interrupted. "It was but not in the way you think."

Jade looked over in surprise and met Connie's eyes. The connection between them felt like a splash of hot, electric water over Jade's chest.

"You didn't kill me," Connie said. "I was ready to go. Going to the bridge did something to me. I felt myself leaving. You brought me back."

Jade couldn't speak. Connie's frank words filled her with light. She put her hands on the steering wheel. The apparition in the passenger's seat was flushed and glowing, more relaxed than Jade had ever seen her.

"Wow, okay then," Jade said. "So, if we're not girlfriends,

then what are we?"

"Hmm," Connie said as she tapped one finger to her lower lip and Jade fought the urge to put her own lips right where Connie's finger was. "How about friends? Really good friends." She wriggled in her seat and looked adorable.

"Sounds good to me," Jade said. She took a breath and said, "Connie, I need to find your family."

Her happy mood vanished in an instant. Connie started fading out. "Why?"

"Come back to me, honey." Jade reached a hand out but her fingers passed through Connie as if nothing was there. Of course. "Is there anyone who'd be good for you? This is your one chance. Let me know who you'd like to be contacted. Parents? Brothers or sisters?"

Connie barked an unpleasant laugh. "My brother wouldn't care if I died in front of his house. He'd just be pissed that my carcass messed up his perfect lawn."

"Well he can be a little shit and fuck right off then," Jade said. "How about parents? You got any aunts or uncles?"

With her arms hugged to her chest, Connie looked very small and alone. "Maybe my mom I guess. I don't remember where she is. Maybe I don't want to." Her face fell into her hands, hair spilled through her fingers. Jade hated seeing her like that, so upset and incomplete. "I don't miss her. Maybe she doesn't miss me either," she whispered. Her form flickered.

"Stay with me, come on, sweetheart."

Slowly, Connie raised her head and leaned back in her seat. "I wish we could choose our families," she said.

"We can," Jade said. "Ben's not related to me but he's just as much my family as Addie is. Ross and Amber and Sky too. In my head, I call them the family of my heart." Jade winced. She'd never said that aloud and the words sounded just as corny as when she thought them. However, Connie uncurled herself and nodded.

"I like that idea. The family of my heart." Connie spoke cautiously, as if she was trying the words out for size. "I know who I'd pick."

"Who?"

Connie just clasped her hands in her lap and gave Jade a mischievous grin. "It's a secret."

"Okay, you're allowed to have those," Jade said as she turned her attention to putting her key into the ignition.

"I'd choose you," Connie said to the dashboard, eyes down. She straightened up and leaned over. Jade felt the tiniest brush of air and chill against her cheek. As soon as she realized what was happening, it was over. Jade twisted in her seat to look at the young woman, but she'd already vanished.

Connie kissed her. Jade's lips spread in a crooked grin.

Energized, Jade stomped her car into life and roared out of the parking lot. She ended up back at the police station, sprawled over Detective Young's desk, sweating and impatient. Where the hell was that man? She seethed to herself at how inconsiderate he was to have something else better to do than wait around for her.

"What's the hurry now? Something on fire?" A jolly voice roused Jade and she looked up to see a cheerful officer standing beside the desk. He wasn't all that young, about fifty Jade guessed from his graying hair. She hadn't seen him before, she didn't think, but maybe she had. There was something familiar about him but she couldn't place him.

"Hi there Officer," Jade looked at his nametag, "Chapel. Sorry, I was just waiting for Detective Young."

"He'll be along shortly I expect." He rocked back on his heels and folded his arms over his chest. "Hope he can help you. Looks like you're in a bit of a bind."

"I've been in worse. And thanks."

"Who are you talking to?" Jade whirled to see Becker.

"Officer Chapel — hey where'd he go?"

"Nice one. Frank Chapel hasn't been here since 1998." His thumb indicated a row of framed photos on the wall. Memorial photos. Well, that explained it. Jade liked Officer Chapel. He seemed like a nice fellow. Maybe he'd be back and she could get some info on people. Especially that smart-mouthed Becker who was always getting up her gears about stuff.

"Okay." Jade found a twirly chair and threw herself into it as Becker drifted off toward the break room.

"You again." Jade looked up to see Detective Young standing over her. "What, the morgue kick you out for chatting up the stiffs?"

"Haha. No. I got the ID on the Jane Doe. You were right. It was Connie," Jade said. "And I need you to get someone in her family to come down, like right fucking now. I gotta find out what happened to her."

"Okay okay, calm down," Young said. He propped one knee on his chair and leaned over his desk. Suddenly Jade was on her feet.

"No I will not calm down! I need answers and I need them now." Jade felt tears come to her eyes. Fuck, this was not a good time to get emotional. Maybe it was getting to be that time of the month. She swallowed hard and said, "I'm sick and tired of Connie being ignored and treated like she's of no importance. That stops right now."

"What the heck is going on with you, Mayflower?" Young asked. A few passing officers looked at them curiously before they moved off.

"This is important. Time is running out," Jade said. "I need to find Connie's mother or else there'll be hell to pay. I have to find out what happened to her. She could be in danger."

"There's an incident report with your name on it," Young warned.

"That's just wonderful. As long as it gets me answers do what you have to do," Jade said. "I need to find out how she got injured. The hospital gave me the basics, but not everything."

"I gather your, uh, *source* is not being helpful about that aspect of the case?"

"Yeah, you could say that." Jade muttered a bad word and gave up her annoyance. She felt hollow without it.

"Hey, you gonna sit there all day or what?" Young's voice cut through her brain-stall. "A bunch of us are going to Sal's for lunch. Want to come with?"

"Lunch? Shit!" Both feet landed on the floor as Jade heaved herself upright.

"I take it that's a no?"

"Nothing personal, got a…date." Jade tried to hide the guilty pang the word brought.

With a frantic glance at her watch, Jade pelted out of the office.

SHE CAREENED THROUGH traffic and ditched her car down a side-street. Just as the clock struck twelve-thirty, Jade barreled up to the door and didn't even pause before she blew into the diner. Vickie was already seated and she waved Jade over.

Jade sat down across from Vickie in the booth and tried to shut down the part of her brain that insisted on replaying the scene where Vickie kissed her.

"Hey." Jade couldn't think of anything else to say. She pointed at the menu. "So, what's good here?"

"It's all the same tasteless, unhealthy crap," Vickie said in a loud voice.

From behind the counter, a sturdy and graying waitress frowned at them. She came over with her notepad in her hand and said in a pointed way, "Our daily special's pretty popular. Today is meatloaf with mashed potatoes."

"Sounds good, I'll have that," Jade said, grateful the decision had been made for her.

"Meatloaf?" Vickie's lip curled. As if a switch flipped, she put on a smile and dipped one shoulder forward. "I'll have the chicken salad with dressing on the side. And a water. Bottled, not tap. I hope you can do that." The derision in her tone was biting.

"I'll see what our chef can do about that, hon." Unmoved, the waitress stashed her notepad. "My name's Dixie and if you gals need anything, give me a holler."

"Will do," Jade said as Vickie studied her nails.

They chatted a bit about nothing in particular until their meals arrived. Dixie made a show of plopping the bottle of water down in the middle of the table. Jade squirmed under Vickie's scrutiny as she tried not to bolt her food. She felt like she was just picking at the bits on her plate and had to fight the long-ingrained habit of keeping her head down while she ate. The conversation stuttered along until Dixie came to take their empty plates.

"Want to get dessert?" Vickie asked.

"I'm gonna pass, even though that apple pie on the counter's calling my name," Jade said wistfully.

"How about coming back another time?"

"Yeah, sure," Jade replied without thinking.

"Great. Clear your Friday evening for coffee and pie with me then." Vickie aimed a satisfied smile across the table.

Jade nearly choked on her sip of coffee when she realized

she'd made another date with Vickie.

"So what's on your schedule for the rest of the day?"

Jade put her cup down and said, "Actually, I was wondering if I could follow you back to your office."

"That's fine," Vickie said. With both elbows on the table, she leaned forward and Jade tried not to notice what was peeking out at her from the unbuttoned front of Vickie's blouse. "Have you got anything? New leads?"

"I got something all right. I want to see everyone at once," Jade said. "You know, make sure the information doesn't get jumbled."

"Okay," Vickie said. She put some money down on the table and rose.

Jade followed her into the office and stood at reception like the mannerly visitor she was. While Jade was aware she could go there on her own, it was beneficial to have the clout of Vickie's presence. The place was warm from the afternoon sunlight. A few people were finishing off their lunches at their desks and the air held the scent of bologna sandwiches and reheated fish.

"What now?" Murel looked up from her Tupperware of lasagna.

"It's nice to see you too," Jade said. She leaned one elbow on the reception desk counter and leveled her best charming smile at Murel. "I'd like to call a meeting of all the staff."

"Right now?" Murel lifted one penciled-in eyebrow. "Folks is still at lunch."

"When everyone comes back," Jade said. "It's important."

"You should listen to her, Murel," Vickie piped up in a loud, bright voice. "Jade's been in prison so she can kick your butt if you get in her way."

At once all noise in the office stopped. Jade pressed her lips together. She fixed Vickie with an exasperated look.

"Oh sorry," Vickie clapped both hands over her mouth. "Was I not supposed to say anything about that?"

"It's fine," Jade said through the headache that was gathering between her eyes. She turned back to Murel who had frozen mid-chew. "Anyway about that meeting?"

"I'll, uh see what I kin do."

AN HOUR LATER, Jade was back in the hallway, scowling at the elevator. After getting the okay from both Murel and Mr. Butters, she commandeered the meeting room and got alibis for the entire staff for the night Connie was found. Mr. Butters insisted on being present and Jade didn't particularly mind. It would save people bleating about shit afterward if she had a chaperone during the interviews. Given the fact she was asking about a span of time in the middle of the night on a weeknight, most of the alibis consisted of variations on the theme of "asleep at home," with Gord's being a slimy allusion to being serviced by a trio of ladies to which Jade cracked in reply that she hoped he'd used protection so his hand didn't get a virus.

All in all, it was a huge waste of time. Jade huffed out a breath and poked the elevator call button a few more times.

"Um, Jade?" Vickie said from behind her and Jade turned around. Vickie had her phone in her hands and looked nervous. "Can I talk to you for a minute?"

"Sure." Jade fought the urge to twitch away as Vickie took her by the sleeve and led her into the private washroom at the end of the hall. When Vickie locked the door behind them, Jade got a bad feeling.

"What's this about?" she asked in a harsh voice. Jade's nerves jumped as she pressed herself back against the wall. Nothing good had ever happened to her in a locked room.

"I just wanted to tell you my alibi," Vickie said in a small voice. "My real alibi."

Jade's curiosity overrode her unease.

"I couldn't say this in front of Mr. Butters but I was, um." Vickie's face flushed as she said, "Well, look for yourself." She turned her head and held out her phone. Her hand trembled. It took Jade a moment to understand what she was looking at. The time stamps which started at around 9:30 on the night of Connie's accident. Vickie started scrolling and Jade sucked in a hard breath.

Jade knew what texting looked like from being subjected to Benny's phone screen numerous times but this was different. One participant communicated in words while Vickie replied with pictures. They started out pretty tame, but soon Jade's eyes bugged out and her breath quickened in her throat in spite of herself. She felt dirty and used by the end of the conversation, if it could be called that. Jade thanked God Benny had never subjected her to the gay boy version of that.

"You're not very good at taking orders," Jade said in a croak with one hand over her face. "I mean, whoever that was asked for your hand in your panties and you sent a butt shot. Nice, uh, composition by the way."

Vickie snatched her phone away and stuffed it into her back pocket. Her eyes blazed. "They were only suggestions. I do what I want." Suddenly she simpered and pursed her sparkly pink lips. She fluttered her eyelashes. "You don't think I'm cheap and slutty, do you? Because I'm not. I was just lonely. I wanted someone to be with me and that was the only way I could get it."

"Don't sell yourself short, Vickie," Jade said. She had seen that sort of thing many times, although not in such a graphic way. "You don't need to give away the goods for companionship. If someone's, uh, company comes with a price then you don't need them. You're better off alone."

"How about you?" Vickie asked in a soft, breathy voice that gave Jade an uncomfortable jolt. She took a step toward Jade, who realized she had nowhere left to go. "Did you feel something when you looked at those pictures? When you looked at me?"

"Vickie, I don't think we should go there." Jade fought the urge to put her hands out and steer Vickie away from her. She couldn't show aggression. It would only escalate the situation.

Her heart pounded and her body began to shake.

Jade did not want to be in that position. She thought she never would be again. The next time Jade saw her counselor, she knew she'd be dredging up some deep history. Jade bit off a shocked curse as Vickie pulled up her shirt and flopped one breast out. A single, pink nipple regarded Jade like a sullen Cyclops.

"Come on, you know you want it," Vickie purred. "I'm here. Take it."

Jade swallowed a fist of panic as she considered her options. Girls tended to get vicious when they got turned down, but Jade didn't want what Vickie was offering her. In fact, Jade had never received such an unsexy or unappealing proposition, even in prison.

With a rush of unpleasant memories, Jade was back in hell, edged into a corner with only one way out. She steeled herself and reached out. It was not going to be fun, but Jade had no choice. She leaned forward and was going in for a kiss when Vickie turned her face away.

"Not there," she said and thrust her chest out one more time. "Come on, get it over with."

The tone of Vickie's order snapped Jade back to the present. Nobody was holding a knife to her throat. Jade had a choice. The choice to refuse. And she took it. She eased Vickie's shirt back down, taking care not to brush against her bare skin. The look of venom Vickie shot her disappeared so quickly Jade wasn't sure if she'd imagined it or not.

"Not here, okay?" Jade said in the gentlest voice she could muster. "Not like this."

At once, Vickie turned around and frantically righted herself. "Oh my god, you probably think I'm such a whore."

"Not at all. I don't judge women for the sexual choices they make," Jade said. She brushed a hand over her forehead, sloughing off a layer of cold sweat. "I just think somewhere we got our communication lines crossed. Don't take it personally, it's just not the right time." And it never fucking would be.

"That's fine," Vickie said. She gave her head a little toss. "As long as you still let me call you sometime."

Jade let out a long breath. She got off easy. "Okay, I wouldn't mind that."

She escaped from the washroom and was back in her car when her phone rang. It was Young.

"Talk to me," Jade said to the phone. She felt very smooth.

"I got some info for you. Connie's mother's on a cruise to Alaska. They're out of contact with the mainland, but I left a message with the coastguard. This better be legit. I owe a bunch of guys favors now."

"Wow, you found her, holy shit," Jade said. "But Alaska? How did she get way the hell up there?"

"The whole thing was booked by Brian Mason, the vic's brother. Looks like the mother's divorced. Dad's been out of the picture since both of the kids were real small."

"Okay. Thanks, Young."

"No prob. Take care, kid."

"Yeah yeah, you too big guy," Jade said with a grin.

Jade sat in her car for a while, deep in thought. It looked

more and more like Connie had planned her own disappearance, down to her family being out of contact. How long would it have taken for anyone to even notice she'd gone? Jade got a chill. She had to find out what happened after Connie jumped. Something had gone wrong. Something derailed the perfect plan.

Jade needed to find out who did it.

As she pulled into traffic, Jade remembered what the next day was. Connie's investigation was going to have to wait.

Chapter Twelve

"HOW DO I look?" Benny twirled around in front of the full-length mirror in the café corner. His usual colorful jeans and cute T-shirt combo gave way to dark corduroy trousers and a collared shirt. He had a sweater vest in one hand and flipped it over his shoulder. "Upstanding enough?"

"Yeah, perfect," Jade said.

"And your butt looks super cute in those pants," another young man piped up from where he was sitting on one of the stools at the counter. He held up his cell phone and took a picture of Benny. "I'm almost jealous."

"Jordan!" Benny went over to his boyfriend and got some hugs as they looked at the photo together. "Don't be jealous. I'm going to see my mom. There are like only three guys in the whole place."

"Yeah, but how about in the parking lot? And how about sex-starved ladies?"

"Don't worry about Ben," Jade said. She swirled her cup to get the last dregs of hot cocoa. "I'll protect his virtue for you."

"Are you sure you don't want to come?" Benny leaned his tousled head against Jordan's shoulder. "I want to introduce you to my mom."

"Maybe next time. I'm not so into meeting the 'rents right away."

"Okay." Benny didn't look too upset as he struggled into his sweater vest. It clung to the clean lines of his young figure and sat just right on his slim hips. Jade wasn't looking but she thought Jordan picked a pretty cute guy to be his boyfriend. He probably was rightfully worried about Benny getting too much attention—from women as the case may be.

"Bus moves out in five minutes." Jade grabbed the key ring from the counter.

"Borrow your aunt's car," Benny whined as he hung off Jordan's arm. "I don't know what you did to yours, but it looks and sounds like it could fall apart at any moment. I don't wanna get stranded anywhere. Jordan's making me dinner tonight."

"It won't fall apart." Jade was offended. Her car was in perfectly good condition, aside from a few new scrapes and bumps and the fact that the muffler was currently being held on by duct tape and wishes.

"Pleeeease? If you don't I'll sing the whole way there."

"You have a cute singing voice," Jade said, and Jordan glared at her. She held up her hands. "No need to get territorial. Benny's like a brother to me."

"Yeah, and so is Luke to Leia," Jordan huffed. "Don't even get me started on those *Game of Thrones* people."

"Oh God," Jade said. "Not that again. Not getting into that. But you know I'm not into guys, right? Even ones as cute as Benny. Besides, Deb would punch me in the throat if I ever laid an impure finger on her kid."

"Tee hee," Benny said as he twirled. "My mom is kind of scary, but she takes good care of me."

"Yeah, another reason to stay home for the day." Jordan looked worried.

"Hey, Deb's harmless," Jade said, enjoying herself. "Except to people who get between her and Benny. Anyway, I'll go see if Aunt Addie needs her car, just for you, Ben."

"Thank yooou," he called.

Jade bounded up the stairs just as Benny grabbed Jordan and disappeared behind the café counter with him. Jade found her aunt in the kitchen, up to her wrists in ground beef.

"I'm making Swedish meatballs," she said. "If you're not going to be around for dinner, I'll put some in a Tupperware for you."

"That'd be great," Jade said, already hungry for her aunt's meatballs. "I might be late coming back tonight."

"Just nuke them and they'll be fine."

"Sure thing. I wanted to see if you needed your car today. I'm taking Ben up to see his mom and my car's not in such good shape."

"What did you do to it?" Addie grabbed a cloth and wiped her hands on it, the better to assume an annoyed pose. "Tell me you didn't sideswipe the fence again. I'm not paying for another paint job on that clunker."

"No, I didn't," Jade said in a tight voice. "You don't have to pay for anything. Jeez! Sorry for asking."

"Fill it up before you bring it back," Addie said as she turned back to her cooking.

"You serious? Thanks!"

Before Addie could think of more conditions or change her mind, Jade snatched up the key ring from its dish where it resided anytime her aunt was home. She dashed downstairs and herded Benny into the land shark of a car. Jade drove extra carefully and didn't pass half the cars and trucks she could have. She kept the seat pulled uncomfortably close to the steering wheel because her aunt was a noisy bitch about her car. If anything was changed in the slightest, Jade would never hear the end of it. She barked at Benny for moving his own seat but he just smiled and turned up the radio.

After an hour and a half of putting up with Benny reading the syrupy texts from his boyfriend out loud and making Jade an accomplice in photo documenting the Esso where they stopped for gas and snacks, the tall fence of the Dorvelle Women's Penitentiary loomed up in front of them.

Beside Benny, Jade went through the outer security gate with the mindless precision born of a year of practice. Jade didn't speak much, just a few polite sentences to the guards and kept her hands in clear view. She fell into the familiar ritual of waiting for the guards to open doors for her. Shoulder-to-shoulder with other visitors, she unloaded her pockets into the tray.

"Hey there, Benny." A burly female guard came over. Her short hair was in a tiny ponytail. "You're looking cute today. Hey, isn't that the sweater vest your mom knitted for you?"

"It sure is," he said, showing it off.

"Looks good on ya," she said. "Maybe I need to frisk you, I'm thinking."

Jade immediately tensed and got ready to get in the way of anything untoward happening, but Benny just laughed and did a little dance. They were joking around. Jade let out a breath. She wasn't used to lightheartedness on the inside of those barbed-wire topped concrete walls.

Benny greeted a few more of the guards and got a pat on the butt from one of them. After the security procedures, they went into the mess hall, which was converted into a visiting area for the day. Female prisoners were low enough on the government's list of priorities that the facility was poorly-equipped and the level of security extremely broad. Tax evaders were housed beside murderers, weed-growers ate and showered with arsonists. In her time there, Jade saw a lot of people come and go, some more than once.

Jade exchanged nods and fist-bumped a few of the inmates as they passed to get to the table where Deb Kennard was sitting. She looked good, short hair trimmed and neat, if showing a lot of grey. Her hands were folded on the table, grey standard-issue sweatshirt sleeves rolled up slightly over her big wrists, nails short and tiny. Her face was lined and looked older than her years until she caught sight of them. Deb gave them a big grin as she jumped to her feet and grabbed Benny in a hug.

"Hey you." She held him at arms' length while she looked him up and down. "Well if it isn't the vest I made. It fits!" Her voice was gravelly from years as a dedicated smoker. She'd been in the process of quitting when Jade was released. From the sound of her wheezing cough as she got back into her chair, she wasn't being all that successful.

For the next few minutes, Benny and his mother chatted about normal things, how the bookstore was doing, thanks for the latest care package they'd put together for Deb, the local sports team. While Benny went on at length about Jordan, Jade leaned back against the wall.

The first time she'd come back for a visit, the guards ribbed her mercilessly, and it took all the guts she had not to turn back. Over the past year, Jade had gotten used to being able to leave at the end of the hour. It was nice seeing her old prison-mates too. Some of them, anyway. Jade made sure to keep a safe distance between herself and a broad, grizzled inmate. The woman blew Jade a kiss, then made an obscene gesture. One of the guards gave her a sharp word of admonishment.

"Thanks for taking care of my boy," Deb said to Jade as Benny wandered off. His bright voice rang through the room as he greeted a few of the other inmates. "I mean it."

"No problem," Jade said. She slipped into the now-empty chair across from Deb. "You took care of me enough when I was here. It's the least I can do."

"Yeah," she sighed. Her fingers looked like they wanted to light up a smoke.

"Any word on your release date?"

"Nothing. The in-laws got some hotshot lawyer up every-one's ass about everything," Deb said. She stretched. "Maybe I shoulda pleaded guilty right away all those years ago, but I thought I could get away with it if I just held out. Nobody helped us when I asked and only came pounding on my door after I helped myself. The fucking system, eh?" Her pale eyes went over to where Benny was showing a guard a new dance move he'd been practicing.

"He's a good kid," Jade said. She'd watched him grow up in monthly installments, and it was the most natural thing in the world to twine her life with his.

"He turned out all right, huh?"

"Yeah he did," Jade said. She leaned forward and dropped her voice. "Deb, maybe you can help me out here. I'm looking into a suicide. Maybe it is and maybe it isn't."

"Huh, I'm betting on *isn't*. It's the best thing in the world if you can make it look like a suicide. Better than framing someone that's for sure. How'd they do it?"

"Jumping off a bridge."

"Dumb idea," Deb said. She waved her hand expansively. "You got to hang around to see if it stuck. And there's lots of ground to cover just looking for the body to make sure. Poison or hanging's the way to do it. Not that I know anything about that." Deb let out a fake hearty laugh as a guard began to pay attention to their conversation. She lowered her head and continued in a quiet voice, "If I were going to do someone in like that, I'd wait my ass under the bridge and make sure they didn't come up for air, maybe hold their head under if they needed it. You'd still need another person involved at the top, chucking them off so bad idea there. Team shit is too risky. Whoever bleats first gets off easy. You don't want to give anyone that kind of leverage over you."

"Good point," Jade said. "How about if they knew the person was going to jump?"

Deb thought for a while. "I guess if someone was already depressed or something, they could make them more freaked out and stressed out about stuff. Give them ideas of a way out. Some-times people reach out when in need of a bit of support."

"And if that support pushes them in the wrong direction,"

Jade said. "Or the right one, depending on your point of view."

"But you know, the worst thing is when they wake up," Deb said. Her eyes were haunted. "It's like they get this hard-on for life that's not even funny. That's why I waited with a tire-iron in my hand in case that lush piece of shit turned out to be immune to antifreeze." Deb folded her arms over her chest and glared triumphantly around the room. "Which he was. Damn near ripped my arm off, that fucker. And I'd do it again in a heartbeat. I took his beatings like the fucking doormat I was, but the second he lay into Benny, I knew he had to go."

"Nobody's going to hurt Benny ever again," Jade said. "Not as long as I'm around. You have my word, Deb."

Jade reached across the table and clasped both of the older woman's hands in her own. She held on for as long as she could before the guard flicked them a warning glance.

"Hey, I'm back," Benny trotted over with his hair all tousled from being patted. He was a favorite with the older set especially, because he was so cute and chatty. Benny couldn't be mean even if he had to.

Jade handed over the chair to Benny. After a while, a guard led them out. Oddly, Jade felt Connie's familiar presence as they walked down the hallway back to freedom. They picked up their stuff from the security gate and Jade was busy for a while putting everything back in her pockets. She really liked having lots of pockets.

They rode back in more or less silence. Benny napped, looking like a little gay angel. While the young man slept the sleep of the innocent, Jade listened to a comedy show on the radio. It was a musical about the Department of Fisheries, which featured an impersonator of their Prime Minister singing a duet with the leader of the opposition. Jade tended to follow politics pretty closely and found a whole lot of funny parts in it. She was trying not to laugh too loudly when she saw Connie sitting comfortably in the back seat.

"Welcome back, stranger." Jade aimed a smile into the rear-view mirror. "I'm glad to see I didn't chase you off."

"I went back home," Connie said suddenly. "To where I used to live in Willow River."

"Oh God, why? I mean, I guess sentimental but oh jeez, you're from good old Willow? My condolences."

"It's not all that bad. If you like NASCAR and shooing deer off your lawn and raccoons out of your garbage. There's also this guy with a chip wagon out by the strip mall and you can get a really good poutine there. He also does a mean chips, peas, and gravy too."

"Nice. I haven't had a heart-attack on a plate in ages." Jade turned the radio down. "For some reason they don't serve it in the big house. Guess that's because we got rid of the death penalty. But I can't really say anything. My folks are from Caper Cove. All they have out there is one big-ass lighthouse."

"Promise me you'll take me out there? I sold my car."

"And pretty much everything else in your apartment and gave all your money to the humane society," Jade said. "Sorry, but I looked in your bank book."

"That's all right. But will you? It doesn't have to be anything special. I just, well, I just think it would be kind of nice, seeing the ocean with you."

"Sure, I wouldn't mind that," Jade said.

Jade focused on the road as she didn't want to think a whole lot, especially not about their nineteen-year age gap and the fact that for most of Connie's life, Jade was behind bars. There was also the problem that only one of them was conscious, at least in the legal sense.

"Thanks. Now I have something to look forward to."

"Did you find what you were looking for? Back home, I mean."

"I don't know what I was looking for. But I did meet my grampa. That was kind of cool. He was in the kitchen and we had a nice chat. I guess he really is keeping an eye on the family." Connie's face was peaceful. "I miss my gramps. He used to have this little iron skillet and whenever we went over to his house he'd make us any kind of eggs in it. Seriously, any kind at all! Grampa's like me, we both suck at any kind of cooking except breakfast. He said I could have the skillet after he died. It was the only thing I wanted of his and I always wished I could have gotten it."

"What happened to it?"

"Lost. Thrown out. I don't know. My mom chucked out everything she didn't want of his after he moved to assisted living. She said she didn't want to have to deal with his stuff after he died. I guess it was easier for everyone that way."

"I'd like to meet him," Jade said. "He sounds like a good fellow."

"He was." Connie raised her head and met Jade's eyes in the mirror. Her elfin grin got a positively naughty twist. "When I wake up, I promise I'll make you a breakfast that'll knock your socks off."

That look sent a thrill to right where it counted and Jade wondered if Connie was flirting. Deciding she was, Jade returned the look. "I'd like that. I hope you know I'm a big eater. It's been said my appetite is rather," she cocked an eyebrow, "voracious."

Connie rewarded her with a bright laugh. Jade glanced over at Benny, who was still asleep.

"So did you see the inside of the prison?" Jade asked her.

"Yes, it doesn't seem too bad," she said.

"Well, after twenty years of staring at those same walls, I got pretty sick of it. I was crazy to get out of there. It nearly got the better of me."

"You seem to be doing all right."

"I am," Jade said. "I do what I can. Trying to make the world better place."

"I want to do that," Connie said. She leaned forward on her hands.

"Do what?"

"If—if things don't work out for me, physically I mean, I'd like to stay around here. You know, protecting you and making sure nothing bad happens. Helping you from my side. If that's even possible. I want to do what I can." She straightened up with a cute little smile on her face. "I can be your spooky sidekick."

The thought of Connie's spirit being trapped in eternal limbo stabbed Jade in the chest and she nearly pulled the car over. "Don't say that," Jade rasped through the pain. "Please don't. Don't give up. I certainly haven't. We're going to get you out of this, got it?"

"Thanks, Jade. I believe you," Connie said.

"Good. Because you should." Jade swallowed and focused on the road. "I guess I should tell you the police got in contact with your mother."

Connie shrank back into herself. Just then, Benny returned to the land of the awake with a yawn and a stretch.

"Sorry for falling asleep. Jordan kept me up late last night," Benny said and looked quite satisfied with himself. "Can we stop for some snacks?"

"Okay, I guess so," Jade said. "Want to get something for Jordan as a souvenir?"

"I got him an official Dorvelle Women's Penitentiary T-shirt last time," Benny said with a pout. "But he won't wear it."

"Wonder why," Jade muttered.

"Is that a tone?" Benny asked. He turned and shot a grin across the front seat. "Maybe I'll just have to make Jordan an offer or," he drawled out the words as he laced his fingers behind his head, "withhold a certain act he likes until he complies. Oh yes, Jordan, let's see how long you can survive without your favorite thing, hmmm?"

"Ben," Jade said, eyes on the road, "you scare me sometimes."

In the backseat, Connie laughed and Jade had never heard a more beautiful sound.

Chapter Thirteen

JADE SPENT A restless night at home and slipped into the ICU of the Victoria General as soon as she could the next morning. True to Alan's word, nobody stopped or questioned Jade. That almost made up for the fact that Jade hated hospitals. The place was full of whispers and the angry hum of lives that ended too soon.

Jade made a mental note to get Benny to help her with a few of them when he came up for air — although he probably wouldn't for a good, long while. After being away from Jordan for the grand total of one day, Benny refused to come to work that morning and left the running of the bookstore and café to the part-timer, Jim. Jade was certain Benny was making up to Jordan for lost time and then some. At least she'd managed to get him to look up and print a bunch of pictures of the maintenance pit under the bridge before succumbing to his boyfriend's charms.

For the first time, Jade wished she had a real partner. Someone she could count on and who she could support in turn. Someone like Connie. Jade's breath caught painfully in her throat as she remembered Connie's offer to become her spooky sidekick.

Jade's steps slowed as she entered the long room where Connie lay.

"Hey girl," Jade's voice cracked as she whispered into the still air. She swallowed and tried again. "It's me, Connie. I'm right here with you, sweetheart."

Wires and monitors crowded around her still form, tubes came out of just about every place a tube could come out of. Jade stifled a wince. It pained her to see Connie all trussed up like that, but there was still a spark of life in her. That alone made Jade happier than anything else. She ignored the faint, confused mutters echoing from the far corner as she dragged over a chair and got comfy. Jade was certain there were at least six other places she should be, but she couldn't let another day pass without seeing Connie.

The room suddenly felt less empty and Jade looked up to see

Connie standing over her own prone form, looking fairly concerned.

"This is so surreal," she said.

"You're telling me."

"Do you think I'll remember anything when I wake up?"

"Can't say for sure. When I was in the hospital, I think I dreamed half of the shit I remembered."

"I hope I remember," Connie said. "I don't want to forget what's going on between us. I don't want to forget you." She ground her hands into her eyes and Jade fought the urge to reach out to her.

"If you do maybe it's for the best."

"What do you mean?" Connie looked on the verge of either tears or anger.

"It's just, Connie look at me," Jade said. "I'm a forty-three year old ex-con who sees ghosts. Not exactly the best girlfriend material. You deserve better than that."

Connie fixed her with a long look.

"Do you think you deserve better than me?" she asked in a small voice.

"Oh hell no," Jade said in a rush. "If I had a girlfriend half as cute and fun as you, I'd be the luckiest person on earth."

"You could have me," she said. "As a girlfriend. I'd go in a heartbeat if you asked me." Before Jade could even come up with a response, Connie broke the moment by giving Jade her signature mischievous grin. "And of course if I was awake and not some kind of ghost. Although I guess one benefit of not needing to eat is I'm a cheap date."

"Nothing about you is cheap, sweetheart," Jade said. She took a deep breath and made a decision. "When you do wake up, I'll be there. That's a promise, Connie. What happens next is up to you."

At Jade's words, Connie's face flamed red. She was still for a moment before she leaned over her own prone form. Jade was at once struck by the oddness of the situation.

Connie said, "Do you think it would help if I gave myself a shake? Or how about I try and go back in?"

"Oh jeez, I don't know. I'm not really an expert at stuff like that from this side."

"Did I mention how weird this is?"

"Yup. I suppose you'll boomerang back into yourself when you're ready," Jade said. "Hopefully soon. You don't want to have to do a whole lot of physio when you get up. Muscles atrophy if you sleep for too long."

"That's true." Connie came over and faced Jade. She looked very serious. "I have to ask you something that's hard for me to ask, and maybe even harder for you to answer. But I have to know."

Jade tensed up.

There was a long pause as Connie gathered her thoughts. Her head came up. With determination on her face, she asked, "How do I go to the bathroom?"

Jade nearly laughed with relief. She said, "It's no big deal. Look, here's your pee tube and the nurses take care of the other stuff. You've probably got a diaper on under there. I've been there. Not fun, but business as usual for hospitals."

"That's good to know, I guess." Connie clasped her hands in front of herself and regarded her body. "This is all very interesting. It would be a good learning experience even if it weren't me down there. Although I guess it is fair enough. Most people don't get to visit themselves in the hospital."

"That's for sure."

"You have to find out who did this to me," Connie said. "I wish I could be more help."

"Honey, it looks to me like you did it to yourself. Unless you have a way to convince me otherwise?"

"I'll do my best. I know some things look very suspicious. I know it looks bad for me," Connie said in a soft voice. "Okay, I admit to jumping. I was serious about ending it all at that moment. I really couldn't see any way to make things better. But the weights came off. I took them off. Some things are coming back to me about that night. Probably going out to the bridge again helped. I remember not drowning. I remember the water being so cold and the way the air smelled. Like fish and poop."

"Romantic," Jade said. She held herself very still as if she could will Connie to remember.

Connie raked her hands through her hair as she strode up and down the room. "I was so afraid then."

"Afraid of death?"

"Afraid of life." Connie looked straight at Jade for a moment before she resumed her pacing. "I remember surfacing, breathing and choking and coughing on that gross water. I felt like puking. Then I got pissed off, like how could I die when I hadn't lived yet? I know, kind of late to realize that. But maybe I had to do something big in order to get the message through my thick head." She came back to Jade's side. Jade guiltily put down the bag of peanuts she'd been shoveling into her mouth.

"Don't be too hard on yourself," Jade said between crunches. "We all do stupid things. Luckily you've got another chance to do things better."

"I really, really hope I don't die."

"Me too."

"Take my hand." Connie's voice was a thin whisper. She stared down at her comatose form with a look of intense concentration on her face. She whispered again, with more urgency, "Jade, I need you to take my hand. Look at me."

"All right, sweetie." Jade slipped her fingers around Connie-the-human's hand. Between the wads of gauze and bandages, her fingers were cool and slightly damp. They felt like limp sausages in her grip.

That was the first time she'd actually touched Connie. She tightened her grip but not too much. Emotion welled up in her throat and she had to swallow a couple times before she spoke. "You're going to be okay. You won't die, Connie. I won't let you."

"Thank you."

Jade held Connie's hand for a moment longer. Connie was so insistent, it was like she tried to give her a message. Jade released Connie's hand and looked across at her spirit.

"Would it be okay if I examined you a bit?" Jade asked. "Nobody will tell me anything, but there's no rule against taking a look myself. I'm no doctor, but I know a bit."

"Sure," Connie said.

Jade started her inspection with the bits that were outside the blankets. From what she could see, Connie's slender fingers were mottled with bruises. A quick examination of the other hand revealed it was as well. Weird. Jade expected the angry red welts from the zip-ties that decorated Connie's wrists, but not that. Jade considered maybe she'd bashed up her hands climbing around on the bridge or even when she pulled herself from the water, but the wounds were on the backs of her hands only. One side of Connie's face was similarly injured. A hunk of gauze was taped to her left cheek and extended from her temple down to almost her chin. The skin under it was purple with streaks of yellow. A mesh bandage wrapped around her head held it all in place.

The damage was too contained. Too well-placed. Both hands, just the fingers not the knuckles. The side of the face. Someone did that to her. Connie survived the jump. After she came up for air, someone did their best to finish the job. If Connie were trying to climb up the ladder and someone whacked her off it, the fall would explain how and where she'd been found.

"I'm going to put my hands on you, see if you've got any other injuries," Jade said. "Is that okay? You can tell me to stop at any time."

"Go ahead, I trust you," Connie said. She hovered beside the bank of machines next to the bed.

Jade kept her expression neutral as she gently took Connie's wrists and moved her hands to either side of her body. While Jade wanted to take the blanket off, she didn't want to risk the nurses to think she was some kind of pervert and revoke her get-into-ICU-free card.

Jade pressed a hand very gently to Connie's abdomen. Under her palms, Connie's physical form was firm and solid. Jade couldn't detect any bandages or swelling.

As Jade continued her slow and careful examination, Connie got a sudden, mischievous look. "I shouldn't be jealous because it's technically me you're touching, but I kind of am."

Jade looked up with a raised brow. "I'm not getting off on this, you know."

"I know," Connie said. "But I can't help thinking I want to feel your hands on me."

Jade caught her breath with the sudden need that flared up within herself. She took a step back and said, "Okay, I'm done."

She replaced Connie's hands the way they'd been and while she tried not to draw the contact out, she was reluctant to let Connie go. The examination hadn't really yielded anything except the fact the head injury was the main one. The machines beeped and hummed, keeping score of the young woman's life.

With a heaviness in her belly, Jade rested one hip against the side of the bed and brushed the damp hair away from Connie's still face. Her skin was pale and her face looked slightly swollen. Jade wasn't sure if that was normal or not. Absently, Jade trailed a finger down the unblemished side of Connie's face. So beautiful and so fragile. She was hanging on by a thread. Jade's chest grew tight. She wished there was something she could do to call Connie back and breathe life into her slumbering body.

"Are you going to kiss me?"

Jade jerked herself upright and yanked her hand back. Her fingers burned from the contact. "Sorry. I mean, no. Not right now."

"You can if you'd like. I don't mind. It would actually be nice, in a strange metaphysical kind of way." Connie perched on the small table on the other side of the bed that held a phone and an ancient copy of the white pages. Her chin rested on her hands. She looked far too cute to be a nearly dead person.

Jade looked back at the comatose woman and seriously considered taking up Connie's offer of a kiss. The "how" was a problem, though. Jade would have to do some maneuvering, but she didn't want to move any tubes or disturb anything. She also didn't want to think about what the hospital staff would do to her if they busted her molesting the coma patient.

"You are so cute," Jade said. "God, why are you so cute?"

"Who're you talking to?" A nurse poked her head into the room.

Jade jumped back. Her face felt hot. "Just Connie," she replied.

"All right then," she backed out with a knowing look on her face. "Tell Connie all of us here all say hi."

Without thinking, Jade looked over at Connie-the-spirit and said, "Everyone says hi."

Silence fell, punctuated by only the hiss of the ventilator and the various beeps from the machines. The nurse wore an odd expression on her face and Jade wanted to slap herself on the forehead. Without another word, the nurse let the door fall closed behind her.

Connie had a hand over her mouth and her shoulders shook.

"What are you laughing at, young lady?" Jade asked. She rummaged through her pockets and found her bag of peanuts. She shoved a few of them into her mouth and crunched in a bad-natured way as she said, "That nurse thinks I'm a couple sandwiches short of a picnic now."

"Sorry," Connie said. The tip of her tongue protruded as she held in her giggles.

Jade stowed her peanuts. She settled back in her chair and asked in a soft voice, "Connie, sweetie, do you remember anything else about the night you jumped?" Jade paused as she searched for non-frightening words. "After you came up for air, was anyone with you? Did you see or hear anything?"

Connie's face went still. Her hands came up to her face. "It's like I'm there and then here and nothing moves in order. Was I dreaming? Am I dreaming now? I'm sorry." She shook her head. "It's not getting any better. I was so out of it. Nothing's coming to me except feelings. Rage. Fear. Sickness. I felt so sick. Must have been the water. Or the pills. The last thing I remember is this sound. Like, a kind of popping sound over and over. It keeps getting closer and then everything goes black." She gasped and held her head. "It hurts, Jade it hurts so much."

"Take it easy, it's okay," Jade said. Sympathetic pain resonated through her. At that moment, she would have given anything to be able to gather Connie up in her arms. "Don't sweat it. The police are looking into the incident too. At least Detective Young is. He's a good guy. And we're going find out what happened that night."

Chapter Fourteen

EVEN THOUGH SHE wanted to spend the entire day with Connie, Jade's business with Young needed to be taken care of first. She allowed herself one more long look at Connie's still form before she left the hospital and headed for the police station.

"You again," Young greeted Jade in his usual way.

She slung herself down in the chair opposite his desk and offered the bag of peanuts from her pocket.

"Nuts?"

"Yeah, I have to be, dealing with you."

"Hardy har har," Jade drawled.

The detective reached over the desk and allowed Jade to pour a generous amount into his hand, which he brought up to his moustache and hoovered into himself.

"You know," Young said when he'd finished crunching, "there's this thing people use, it's called the phone. You do have my number, Mayflower. You don't always have to come in and mess up my desk with your presence."

"But then I wouldn't be able to see your beautiful smile," Jade said. She batted her eyelashes and clasped her hands under her chin.

"Yeah, right. Anyway, I asked around and no cars were pulled from the bridge area."

"How about Connie's mother? Any contact?"

Young shook his head. "Don't worry, she'll get the message eventually. Those cruise ships check in every couple of days, and it's not like they don't have satellite communication and stuff like that."

Eventually could be too late. Jade clenched her hands into fists. As much as she wanted to go on a cursing spree, she was still in the middle of a police station where such things would most likely be frowned upon. Instead, Jade put her head down into her hands and breathed deeply until she could see straight again.

"How about the hospital?" Jade asked. "What are they doing

about security?"

"I talked to some guy in charge about the situation. She's in ICU. He said normal hospital security would be enough," Young said.

"It isn't." Jade jumped to her feet. "At least have the hospital staff put the kibosh on anyone talking about Connie to *anybody*. And have a guard at Connie's door checking IDs."

"You think that's necessary?"

"Yes, I do."

"I'll see what I can do. D'you have any idea about who the perp could be? How about a motive?"

"I have a few ideas, but nothing's really jumping out at me." Jade sank back into her chair.

Young's phone rang and he turned away to answer it. Jade considered herself dismissed. She looked around for Chapel and didn't see him, so she wandered out to the parking lot. Jade got in her car and felt a strange buzzing against her leg and after she swatted madly at herself, she came up with her cell phone. She fumbled with that fucking screen and its arrows and whatnot. Jade cursed as she tried to get the stupid thing to work.

"Cock-wielding rectum bandit's gloryhole puke factory...uh." Jade looked at the phone screen in surprise. "Hello?"

"Honey, you have got to learn how to use that phone," Benny's voice said into her ear. "I'm not asking a whole lot, not texting or tweeting or anything, but just stop swearing for a minute while you're figuring out if you've answered the phone or not. You've offended my delicate sensibilities."

"What do you want?"

"Just want to know what's happening with you and that cute li'l ghostie."

"Nothing you need to hear," Jade said. She wanted to slam the phone down but didn't know how. She settled for searing the air with every single bad word she knew. And she knew a lot.

"Honey, what I don't need to hear is all your swears," Benny said. "Here, I'm sending you some nice relaxing music. Breathe deeply and feel in touch with nature."

Trilling flutes punctuated with birdcalls started filtering through her phone.

"Aren't you supposed to be busy today?" Jade snapped. "You know, taking care of Jordan."

"Been there, done that," Benny said, blowing into the phone and Jade could imagine him miming smoking a cigarette. "But now we're at the Blue Ocean Lounge. It's the bar across the street from Sunny's. How about coming out for an early drinky-poo and some relaxation before things get crazy with Pride Weekend and all? There are a number of ladies here who seem to be single and playing for the same team if you know what I mean."

"Thanks for the info," Jade said, "but I'm fine here."

"If you change your mind, we'll be here for a while."

"Don't hold your breath," Jade said and she ended the call with her thumb. While she really wanted to go back to the hospital and maybe read some poems or some romantic shit to Connie, she decided to go see if Ross was around.

At the container village, Jade bypassed both the hotdog stand and Womyn's World and went straight into Ross's shop. The inside was spotless and uncluttered with a padded medical chair in the middle of it and a compact set of shelves that held the tools of Ross's trade along the far wall. The other walls were covered with photos and sketches ranging from butterflies to grinning sugar-skulls. The lord of the domain was lounging on a folding chair with the newspaper in his hands when Jade called out a greeting.

"Hey there," Ross said. He folded the paper and stood up. "Amber told me you'd be by. How about you have a seat and we can get to work."

"Sure," Jade said. She got herself settled and watched her old friend setting up. He gathered his long hair into a ponytail before he started getting out bottles of ink. "The beard's looking good, dude."

"You think?" Ross took a break from puttering to stroke a gloved hand over the rich chestnut growth. "I grew it out for Pride."

"Going as Rainbow Jesus again?"

"Yup."

"Nice," Jade said. She draped her arm on the padded armrest and rolled up her sleeve. Slowly, Jade drew a finger over the faded sparrow. She traced the sharp and colorful vines that spiraled up her arm, dusting over the collection of individual designs that nestled in between the leaves before stopping at one that showed an old, tattered envelope. It was sealed with a heart.

"You know what's weird? I miss writing to you."

"You still can, Jay. It's called texting."

"Nah, seeing you in person is better. And I still haven't fig-ured that damned phone out yet."

Ross gave his booming laugh. Jade lay back and let her mind go back to the letters that had spanned twenty years. Ross was her staunchest ally when the entire world turned against her and Jade liked to think she'd been his. It only made sense that he'd be the one she'd let retouch her oldest tattoo and give her the full sleeve she'd spent most of her incarceration mentally designing.

Pattering feet preceded an overall-wearing ball of energy. Jade sat up and swung her feet over the side of the chair just in time to receive a lap-full of bouncing girl. Her bright red hair was tied back in a bunch and her pink-cheeked face was all smiles.

"Hiya Jade!"

"Hey Sky," Jade said. "How's things?"

"Great!" she said as she wriggled around and got comfort-able. "Are ya gonna get a new tattoo today? Can I help pick it? Can I watch?"

"No, I'm getting an old one redone so it's already been picked, and yes, you can watch if your papa says it's okay," Jade said.

"Daddy, can I watch Jade getting redone?" Sky jumped off Jade's lap and pelted over to her father. He freed a hand from his task to pat her on the head.

"As long as you promise to be good and not bother Jade."

"Yay!"

Jade winced as Sky's sharp voice filled the shop.

"Go and tell your mother you're gonna be staying here for a while."

"'Kay." And she was off.

"Good kid," Jade remarked from her perch. "Pretty as hell. You're going to be beating off guys left, right, and center when she gets old enough to date. Girls, too."

"Heh, I'm waiting for that. She looks more like Amber every day," Ross said. "And acts like me, so maybe I won't have to chase off too many potential dates once they get a taste of her attitude."

"I think she's a great kid and has amazing parents," Jade said. She lay back down and crossed her ankles. "She'll be all right."

After a short consultation, Ross got out his gun and started working. True to her word, Sky sat quietly on the mushroom chair she'd dragged over from Amber's shop and watched the procedure with interest. She wasn't the only one. Jade caught a glimpse of waving blonde hair out of the corner of her eye and turned her head to see Connie standing shyly in the corner.

"It's okay sweetie," Jade said as she held out a hand to Connie. "You can come over next to me."

Connie's smile as she crossed the room lit up Jade's heart like a beacon.

"Who's she talking to?" Sky asked in a loud whisper.

Ross didn't glance up from his task as he answered, "Probably just a friend who's paying us a visit from somewhere far away."

That seemed to satisfy Sky and she went back to her industrious watching. Connie stood beside Jade and seemed fascinated with the procedure.

"It doesn't hurt?" Connie asked.

"Yeah, it does," Jade answered. To his credit, Ross didn't bat an eye and continued working. "But it's a good hurt. Getting inked isn't something I take lightly. I chose to get something permanent on my body, and the end result is like, a testament to the pain I went through. It shouldn't be easy."

"They're beautiful," Connie said in a soft voice. "Would it be okay if you told me about them?"

"Sure," Jade said. Normally she didn't like people asking about her tattoos, but she was glad Connie had. Jade wanted her to know. She wanted to share everything of herself with the young woman beside her. That had never happened before. Jade had never been in love. She was now. The knowledge hit her like a truck. She loved Connie. Jade was so in love with Connie she didn't know what to do with herself.

Jade forced herself to lay still instead of running around and punching the air like she wanted to. She cleared her throat and said, "My parents were hippies who did stuff like chaining themselves to trees back in the sixties and they both knew what it's like to be thrown in the slammer. Not for twenty years, mind you, but they still understood." Jade paused to gather her thoughts. Over the buzz of the gun, the only sound was the soft classical music from Ross's phone. Jade never told anyone about her sparrow before and she felt like she was giving up something very deep and secret about herself.

She continued, "When it looked like I was going to be put away and there was nothing more we could do, my folks took me to this tattoo shop downtown and told me to pick something that would remind me I was going to get out one day. Something I could keep with me always, no matter what else they took away from me in prison. So I got this sparrow." Jade glanced down at the bird that was taking delicate shape under her friend's gun.

"She kept me sane when everything else was going to shit," Jade said. "Sometimes I'd stand in the yard and hold my hands up to the sky and imagine her flying away, taking me with her. Twenty years I waited to see the open sky. Twenty fucking years." Jade was startled at the bitterness in her voice. She was usually more fatalistic than that. She closed her eyes and put her free hand over her face.

"You okay, Jay?" Ross asked in a quiet voice. "You want to tap out and take a breather?"

"Nah I'm cool, just stirred up some history," Jade said. She lowered her hand and glanced over at Connie with a shaky smile.

"I'm glad you told me," Connie said. She was so close that Jade felt the electric chill of her almost-touch.

"I wanted you to know," Jade said. "The other tats represent important people in my life and the vine is me. Twisted and imperfect but surviving." She looked down at her arm and said, "My mom's the rose because she loved to garden and my dad's the waves around it because whenever he got stressed from his job, he'd talk about ditching everything, buying a Cape Islander, and becoming a fisherman."

"Your parents sound wonderful," Connie said softly.

"Yeah. They were," Jade said with a catch in her voice.

"Let me guess one." Connie leaned over Jade with a fascinated look on her face that Jade didn't mind at all. "That rainbow heart with all those sparkles is Benny, right?"

"Yup," Jade said. Connie looked up and their eyes met. Jade was extremely aware of the depth in them. At that instant, she knew exactly what her next tattoo would be. Jade said, "And you are going to be a star because you brought light and direction to my life, and I want to make all your wishes come true."

"Jade," Connie whispered. The word held volumes. She

faded out but the look of stunned happiness on her face stayed with Jade for a long time.

"Not that I was listening on purpose," Ross said, "But if you let me use that line on Amber, your star's on the house."

"Seriously?" Jade asked. She considered the proposal for a moment before she said, "Go ahead, man. You've always had my back, it's not that often I get to have yours."

"Sweet."

Jade leaned back into the cushions and let the buzzing pain roll over her. The touchup continued without incident and soon Jade was studying the newly revitalized sparrow on the inside of her wrist, the head at the base of her hand as if she was taking flight. The new tattoo was more detailed and vibrant than the original but still retained the same overall feeling.

"Wow, that's really nice," Jade said. "Thanks Ross, you really outdid yourself."

"Anytime," he said.

Jade took one last look before she let him wrap her wrist. As he was going through the usual aftercare lecture, Amber bustled in with a tray of iced tea and Jade dutifully gulped down a cup of it.

Suddenly Jade wanted something stronger. She wondered if Benny was still at the lounge. Jade decided to take a chance and dealt out a round of goodbyes before she headed out. The fresh late summer air greeted her as she wandered out, jingling the keys in her hand.

She found Benny and Jordan sitting together on a sofa with big mugs in front of them. Jordan was wearing the prison tee over a cute rainbow-striped long sleeved shirt. Jade raised her eyebrows with a new sense of respect for Benny. He knew how to get stuff done, that boy.

"Jade honey!" Benny said as he and Jordan scooted over to make room for her on the sofa. "Glad you could make it."

"Yeah, I thought it would be kind of nice to hang out at a gay-friendly place for once."

Benny passed her the menu and Jade studied it with a confused frown. How the hell did people know what the fuck they wanted to drink? She was much more at home with something being plunked down in front of her. The cute waiter came over in his too-short apron with his notepad held at the ready. As he stood over her with an impatient huff, Jade froze. She gave up on having dignity as she looked helplessly at Benny. He popped up and ordered some kind of original concoction with a fancy name for her. Soon the waiter put a large, round mug down in front of Jade.

"Thanks," Jade muttered. She took a gulp of the drink and discovered it to be a thick, berry-tasting version of coffee. She'd just put a few lumps of brown sugar into her cup when Benny nudged her.

"See that table full of luscious lesbians over there? Anyone in particular catch your fancy? We can send her a drink or a macaron or something."

Jade didn't raise her eyes from her cup as she let out a heavy sigh. "Ben, I'm not interested."

"Not interested how?"

"I just don't want to go chasing women right now, okay?" Jade chewed her lip before she said, "Besides, I kinda have someone on my mind right now."

"You don't look so great," Benny said. "Do you need some love advice from the cupid of amour himself? You can ask me anything." He preened. "Or Jordan. He used to date women."

"Just one. When I was in my bi now, gay later phase," Jordan explained. He gave Jade a sideways glance. "You aren't going through one of those, are you?"

"No," Jade snapped.

"All right then." Jordan sipped his latte and shared an infuriatingly knowing look at Benny.

A sad song about goodbyes and unrequited love came on and Jade felt herself going fuzzy on the inside. God damn, what happened to her iron self-control? It melted as surely as the sugar in her coffee. She grabbed a napkin and blew her nose into it.

"Look, Jade." Benny was suddenly serious. "If there's something bugging you, then maybe talking about it will help."

Jade took a deep breath. Without preamble, she blurted out, "I slept with Connie."

On second thought, she probably should have eased into the topic before dropping that bomb. The two boys were looking at her like she'd just confessed to something unthinkable like molesting Chihuahuas.

"Connie?" Jordan was the first to recover his power of speech as he clutched Benny's shoulder. "The ghost? How does that work?"

Jade let out a long breath and said, "It wasn't different from, uh, you know, regular humans. I just lay back and let her do her thing."

"I don't believe it," Benny squawked out. His voice ratcheted up in pitch and volume as he said, "I do *not* believe it! You're a bottom?"

"Shut it, Ben. I made an exception," Jade said. She could hardly believe they were having that conversation. "Besides, things aren't so black and white with women. More like a rainbow of grey."

"You go girl!" Benny said and broke the tense mood with a big smile. "Damn, Jade."

"Hey, watch your mouth. If she thinks I'm rubbing off on you, your mama will have my ass on the block." Jade dropped her head into her hands. "But this Connie thing. Shit, I don't know what hit me. Maybe I've been having too long a dry spell, but I don't know. I really like her. I more than like her."

"But she's dead," Jordan said. He jumped and said, "Sorry."

"It's okay," Jade said. "That's not what's bugging me."

"So what's the problem?" Benny asked. "Is it because she doesn't have a physical form?"

"No. The problem is me." Jade rolled her mug between her hands as she spoke, "You know my history. I haven't really been in anything resembling a normal relationship. I don't know if I can do it now. Let's forget the ghost thing for a moment. Would someone as cute and amazing as Connie really be satisfied with someone like me?"

"You're not so bad," Benny said. "A little rough around the edges, but seriously, any girl would be lucky to have you. Anyway, relationships aren't that complicated. You call and text about random stuff. You get them presents and hang out. You remember their birthday. You have sleepovers and maybe even fights but you make up and life goes on." Benny fixed her with a calm gaze, "Rocket science it isn't."

"Since when did you get so smart, Ben?"

Benny just preened. Jade studied the depths of her mug.

Her only hope was that Young came through with protection for Connie. Someone had it in for Connie, and Jade was going to find out who it was and kick their ass.

Chapter Fifteen

JADE FINISHED HER coffee and left the Blue Ocean Lounge. She spent the rest of the day and evening haunting her own house. Connie showed up and simply hung out while Jade made herself dinner and watched TV. It was nice, even though Jade had to watch herself carefully and not get into any of the heavy topics that were buzzing around in her head. The last thing she wanted was to drop the L-bomb on Connie so she settled for thinking it instead.

With the words of love she couldn't say on her mind, Jade dozed off on the sofa and woke up while the sky was still dark. She slouched into her office with a coffee and divided her attention between her notebook and case wall, but unanswered questions dogged her.

Who would benefit from Connie's death? What was the motivation to kill her? Jade wracked her brain for the identity of the person who would be strong or evil enough to look Connie in the face and then smash her across it.

No inspiration came to her. Jade slammed her notebook shut. She needed answers and they certainly weren't going to show up at her door. Thinking she'd have more luck at Connie's place, Jade got into her car and gunned it down the road at full speed, stopping only to pull into a gas station and get some snack cakes. They were poison, but Jade liked the cream filling. She was not all that happy about the fact that they looked like dongs, and she was in no way into dongs. But goddamn, that filling.

Full and on a sugar high from three cakes, Jade banged on the custodian's door.

"!*Oy, Señor Wally! Arriba!*" She shouted in Spanish, with all those extra exclamation marks and everything *Señorita* Mayflower could come up with. It took him a while to answer the door and she saw he was in the middle of shaving.

"Don't you bother people at normal hours?" he asked in an annoyed voice. "The sun's not even up yet!"

"P.I.s don't run on normal people's schedules," Jade said

with a guilty glance at her watch. "I need to check out Connie's place again. Gimme the key and I'll get out of your face."

Wally hesitated before he shrugged and dug the key out of the box on the wall. "Whatever. Just don't steal anything."

"Of course not. And thanks," Jade said. She took the key and went up to Connie's floor. As Jade wandered down the hallway, she noticed another unit's door was open a crack. A dark shape lurked just inside. Someone was watching her. In two steps, she crossed the hallway and landed hard against the door. It impacted with something on the other side. Jade shouldered the door open and looked down at a man sprawled over the floor.

"Can I help you, sir?" Jade asked in a low growl.

"Thanks but I can manage." The voice was muffled but strangely familiar. He had his head down, hands over his face. Jade reached down and grabbed the guy by the collar. She threw him down on the prim flower-print upholstered sofa. It was Gord.

"What the fuck are you doing here?" She shook him with every word. He looked positively terrified. Spittle and foam flew off from him and he made a scared, whining sound. Jade stifled a curse. Over the past twenty years, she'd gotten used to tougher customers and was almost sorry for handling the guy so roughly. Almost.

"Don't kill me okay? I'm not doing anything wrong! Really!"

"The hell you are," Jade retorted. "What do you think you're doing squatting two doors down from Connie's place?"

"I'm house sitting," Gord said. Jade tightened her grip and he flinched. "Really. I found this gig on Community Helplist."

Suddenly incensed, Jade hauled Gord across the narrow room and slammed him against the wall. A number of teacups rattled in their saucers in the china cabinet next to them.

"Tell me the truth," she hissed through her teeth, "Did you drug Connie and take advantage of her?"

"No I didn't!" Gord said and snuffled. "Why would I do something like that? I love Connie, I would never hurt her like that. If I knew who did it, I'd kill them."

With a sneer, Jade let go of Gord and watched to see if he'd bolt. He tried to, but she got a boot out in front of him and kicked the door closed.

"You have to get up pretty fucking early in the morning to

get a jump on Jade Mayflower," she snapped.

"You can't do this to me. I'm calling the cops."

"Go right ahead," Jade said as she settled down on the sofa. It was hard and felt like Styrofoam under the flower-print velvet. "I don't have anything on my schedule for today. And I was actually thinking of going to see the police with your sorry carcass myself."

Gord folded onto the floor. He was crying, really bawling and shaking. Jade just sighed and shifted on the hard sofa.

"I'm not doing anything wrong," he blubbered.

"What exactly are you doing, then? I'm going to ask you this exactly once so spill it or lose it."

"I just wanted to make sure she was okay, you know, not sad or alone or anything."

"I'm sure Connie was just fine without you," Jade assured him with no small amount of acid. "Were you stalking her? Did she have enough of you so you attacked her? Tell me the truth or I swear to God I'll pop your fool head off your shit-filled carcass right now."

"I wasn't stalking her. I was just watching out for her." Gord's shoulders heaved and he wiped his nose on his sleeve.

"Not much difference from where I am. You are a pathetic excuse for a human," Jade said. "I wish I was allowed to carry firearms because your nuts would be history. And I mean that in the angry-dyke sense of the word. Totally. On your feet then. Now."

"Where are you taking me?"

Jade hauled Gord to his feet and used a well-placed elbow to encourage him to move in the direction of the door. He twisted around like a kid trying to get away from a schoolyard bully.

"I demand to talk to a lawyer," he whined.

"You aren't talking to anyone other than me and Detective Young. Right now you are suspect number one." On the short trip down the hallway, Jade used every opportunity she could to kick him about the shins. Jade slammed her hand down on the elevator call button and whirled to stare down Gord. "Were you and your 'trio of ladies' here on the night of the twenty-fourth?"

"Y-yeah."

He raised his arms as if expecting to be hit. Jade experimentally made a fist and cocked it. That seemed to be the magic pill

because Gord started talking in a wet babble, "I didn't do anything to Connie. I don't know what happened, but the last time I
saw her she was alone. She just walked out of her apartment at
about nine and never came back. I swear that's all I saw. I heard a
car pull up just before she left, but that's it."

"Who was driving that car?" Jade asked.

"I don't know," he said. "She was always alone. Nobody ever
came here. I made sure of that. I watched all the time. No boy-
friends — or girlfriends."

"So, you think she was into girls?"

The elevator came and Jade threw him into it.

"I'm sure of it," he said. "She always went to that bar,
Sunny's. I tried to get in but some huge bull dyke threw my ass
out and spat on me. Can I tell the police on her? That's assault.
And discrimination. For being a guy!"

Jade laughed, but not in a pleasant way. "So our little stalker
has an opinion. Let's bring you down to the station and see what
Detecting Young has to say about all this. Plus what you were
really doing here."

"I said I'm house-sitting. Mrs. Yun gave me a key. She really
did. I'm supposed to be here. I'm watering her plants and feeding
her fish while she's in Korea."

"What a coincidence she lives in the same building as the girl
you're stalking," Jade said. She dragged Gord's blubbering carcass through the lobby and returned the key to a shocked-looking
Wally.

"Hey, that's the kid looking after Mrs. Yun's fish," Wally
said. "If he stole anything, you make sure I get it back by tonight
or I'm calling the cops."

"That's exactly where we're going," Jade told him over her
shoulder as she opened the passenger side door and pitched Gord
into the car. She glowered down at him. "Any funny business and
your nuts are history."

"You said that already."

"That's just how much I mean it," Jade growled as she got
behind the wheel. "Buckle up, buddy."

"What if I don't want to?"

With a resigned sigh, Jade removed one hand from the steering wheel and ended Gord's rebellion by driving a fist into his
gut. The blow made him sag bonelessly against the old brown and

rust seat cushions. A groaning, retching sound came from the huddled pile next to her.

"Ruin my upholstery with your slobber and your nuts are history," Jade said vaguely aware she'd already used that threat. She twisted the key in the ignition and sent the sedan barreling down the road.

A few minutes later, she marched into the police station with Gord in a wristlock. Jade felt all eyes on them but she didn't care. After recovering his ability to breathe, Gord had spent pretty much the entire car ride bawling and was in noticeably bad shape.

"Hey, congrats on the new boyfriend." Jade heard some smartass in the background say. "When's the wedding?"

Young hurried over from his desk. "Person of interest?"

"You could say that," Jade gritted. She steered Gord around with her elbow. "Name's Gordon Holloway. He worked with Connie and at the very least is a stalker. At the most, this guy had better cough up a solid alibi or else—"

"My nuts are history," Gord supplied, head down and sobbing.

Pleased, Jade nodded and continued, "Anywhere I can stash this sack of shi—uh, garbage?"

"Interview room two's free right now. How about we continue our chat in there?"

"Good idea." Jade attempted to follow them but was invited to wait outside. "I brought him in, don't I get to at least watch?"

"Keep that lady away from me," Gord said from his hiding spot under the interview table.

"I think he'll be less upset without your presence," Young said. "You go and hang out with the guys in the break room."

Sulking, Jade did as she was told. She found a chair and looked at the TV as a few members of the force moaned about the ball game the night before when apparently their team got "slaughtered" by the fire department. Then she amused herself by hunting down Chapel and trying to get inside info about the young cop who always gave her a hard time.

"Fellow named Becker," she said. "Ever heard of him?"

"Not that I know of," Chapel said and scratched his head. "Must be one of the new fellers."

When Jade saw Young and Gord coming out of the interview

room she hurried over. For some reason, Gord wasn't in handcuffs.

"What's going on? Aren't you going to arrest him?"

"Afraid not," Young said as he headed back over to his desk. "He looks mighty fishy, but we got nothing solid at the moment. And I talked him out of pressing charges against you."

"Thanks," Jade said in a sour voice.

She scowled at Gord's hunched back as he made his exit.

Young pulled his knee off the seat of the chair and sat down with a weary sigh. He motioned to the chair opposite and Jade dropped into it.

"Besides the fiasco with Mr. Holloway, how are you doing in your investigation?"

"I've got some stuff," Jade said. She glanced over at the coffee machine in the corner. "How about I get us some coffee and I can bring you up to speed."

"Sounds good."

Jade got them two cups of coffee and a couple creams and sugars as she knew Young liked to doctor his coffee although she forgot exactly how. She sat back down and quickly went over the newest information, including her half-formed theory about what happened that night.

"So you're saying the girl jumped and then, what?" His thick fingers tugged the plastic lid off a creamer. He measured half of it into his coffee and set the remainder down on a clear spot on his desk where it left a little white dot. "Crawled her ass out of the river and then got murdered?"

"She was pretty beat up," Jade said. She swiped two of the sugars and emptied them into her cup. She'd forgotten to get stirrers and swirled her coffee around like a centrifuge as she continued, "I've been in to see her in the hospital a couple times and her face and hands are all bashed up. Can you get one of your medical examiner people down there to check? Maybe they can tell if she was fighting or something. Like, defensive wounds."

"All our 'medical examiner people' are working in the morgue and named Fanny Starr." Young took a swallow of coffee. "In case you weren't aware, this is not Vegas or Miami."

"Okay, how about this." Jade dug around in her bag. She came out with a handful of printouts. "Here's the bridge, see where I've put the red circle? That's where she jumped, and that concrete area over there is where she ended up. It's lower than the road so you can't see into it when you drive by. I've been down there, it's some kind of maintenance area. The hospital people were pretty stingy with their info, but when I was there, I got the impression that's where something bad went down"

"How'd a person get back up to the road level from there, then?" Young studied the printout. His finger poked at the grainy picture. "That some kinda ladder?"

"Yeah," Jade said. "It's about four meters straight up from there to the road."

"Maybe she was trying to climb up and just fell. You said she took something before the jump? And I can't imagine she would've been in very good shape after nearly drowning. Besides, how would anyone know she was there? Sorry, but people tend to not just murder folks they randomly find around. Specially in that place. Not a lot of foot traffic on the Angwin in the middle of the night."

"What happened to Connie wasn't an accident. I'm sure of it. What if it wasn't just somebody passing through?" Jade crossed her arms over her chest and slouched back into the chair. She bounced one knee. The desk started rattling along with it and, with a guilty twitch, she sat still.

"What, you think someone was already there?"

"Yeah. What if Connie didn't go there alone? That creepy sack of shit Gord said on the night she disappeared, Connie went off in a car that she wasn't driving. I don't know if we can believe that, but it explains a few things. Look, Young," Jade tried to look as calm and rational as she could, "I know it looks like Connie did this to herself, but I'm sure she didn't. Not all of it, anyway. Someone is getting away with attempted murder."

"Yeah, helping someone to off themselves is still murder. Killing yourself, same, but well not so much. If you do it right, the perp's gone along with the vic. Hard to prosecute."

"Convenient," Jade said. She rubbed at her neck. She must have done something to it during the car chase the other night. "I don't know what's going on. I think I gotta go back there and check out the place again. Maybe I'll get something else." She stood up to leave. "How's the security coming with Connie?"

"I'm gonna be honest, we're spread thin as it is. No way am I wasting one of our people to hang around there." Young placed his hands flat on his desk and looked up at her. "But after you left yesterday, I made a couple calls. They're not letting anyone see Connie who's not on the official list—so far you're the only one on it. They gave me an earful about messing up their records, but you know how they get. Hospitals, eh?"

"Thanks," Jade said.

"And don't make me give you the spiel again. The one about flashing your ID like you're a cop, okay?"

"Sure thing, Young." Jade tried to look repentant.

Young's phone rang. With one hand on the receiver, he said, "Now quit bugging me and go chase some spooks or something."

With a jaunty salute, Jade was on her way.

Chapter Sixteen

"I AM DEFINITELY getting too old for this."

Jade brushed off her jeans after hauling herself over the chain-link fence. Wrestling with Gord's punk ass that morning hadn't helped her overall condition.

In daylight, the maintenance area under the bridge still looked rather ominous. It could be accessed by a door on the other side of the concrete cubicle, but she'd opted for the direct route over the fence. Jade stood on the edge and peered over the side at the ladder going down to the concrete ledge. Shielded from the morning light, the concrete was cool and the air was still and dank.

There were some "no trespassing" signs courtesy of the Department of Transportation but Jade paid no attention to them. She was more concerned with being spotted and told to get out before she got any more clues. A prefab office-type building squatted a few meters behind the maintenance area, but at the moment it didn't seem to have anyone in it.

Jade quickly shimmied down the ladder. It was rusty and flaky against her palms. She tried not to think about what happened there, just the facts.

The gross, oily water of the river lapped up against the concrete bunker. More ladders led both into the river and up into the inner workings of the bridge. Through the gaps in the beams, Jade could see a couple people on bikes passing overhead. Cars rumbled by unseen. It was pure luck that someone saw Connie and called 9-1-1. Maybe that girl had her own guardian angel.

Jade dug her cell phone out and was trying to remember how to make it take pictures when she heard a voice behind her.

"Hey, you can't go down there. And you can't take pictures. This is government property."

Jade whirled and stashed her phone. The source of the warning was a scruffy man who was standing at the top of the ladder Jade had just climbed down. She tried to affect an air of both nonchalance and authority, hoping it was enough for the guy to refrain from summarily booting her out and she called out, "I'm looking into an incident that happened here about a week ago."

"Early on the twenty-fifth, right?"

"Yeah. There was a girl found down here. You know anything about that?"

"I might. Hang on a sec."

The guy quickly climbed down the ladder. Once he was on level with Jade, he pulled off his hardhat and held it under one arm. He had a pair of well-used gloves hanging casually in the vee of his safety vest.

Jade eyed him. He was pretty young, earnest-looking.

"I'm Jade Mayflower," she said with as much authority as she could dredge up and held out a hand. "Private investigator. And you are?"

"Oh sorry. Trevor Greene." He wiped a hand on his shirt before offering it. Jade gave him a hearty shake. He winced and surreptitiously flexed his fingers after she let him go.

"What can you tell me, Trev?"

Trevor rubbed a hand over his sandy stubble before he said, "This is my station here and I was just coming back to lock up when I saw the girl down on the ground. Blood all over the place. Look you can see the stain here where it seeped into the cracks. At first I thought I was looking at a dead body. Freaked me the heck out. This place still kinda does. Especially at night."

"Yeah, I can imagine. So what'd you do when you found her?"

"Just like in training," he said. "Checked for vitals, you know. Found a pulse, put her in the recovery position and put my jacket over her. Then I called for an ambulance. They came pretty fast, no traffic that time of night and all. I didn't even have time to get the first aid kit we keep up in the office. Good thing too."

Jade fought the emotion that rose in her throat as she asked, "So the girl was in pretty bad shape, huh?"

"Yeah, who knows how long she was lying there. I didn't want to leave her alone out here, so I just called from over there. Cell reception down here's shit. You gotta climb halfway up the ladder before you even get a signal."

As he spoke, Trevor's hands waved toward something behind Jade. A quick glance over one shoulder revealed a cubby where a grey plastic phone nestled under a metal awning. It was weather-beaten and looked pretty old.

"That thing still works?" Jade asked.

"Yup. Usually we use it to get touch with the main office, but you can call out on it. It was off the hook when I found it." He shrugged before continuing, "Maybe she was trying to call for help?"

"That would make sense," Jade managed to say even though her body was frozen, her brain in mid-stall. The phone call. Connie was trying to reach out for someone. She used her last breath to do it. The person who she was reaching out for was the key to the whole thing. Her muscles came alive with the need to move. Jade shoved her way past Trevor and headed for the ladder.

She called back over her shoulder, "Thanks for the info, Trev."

"Hope it helps," he said. He took a step forward and Jade paused with both hands on the ladder. "Look, did she make it?"

"I can't give you that information," Jade said. She let go of the ladder and looked the young man in the face, not disliking what she saw. "How about you give me your number and I'll give you a call if I have any news."

"Appreciate it," Trevor said. He handed over a battered business card and Jade carefully stuck it in her wallet before she bolted up the ladder.

ON HER WAY back to the police station, Jade hurled herself bodily into a convenience store. She frightened the proprietor by falling onto the counter with a bunch of snacks and bottles of pop clutched in her hands. She barely waited for her change before she dashed back out to her car. En route, she stuffed half a sandwich into her mouth.

"What now?" Young was walking down the hallway with his hands full of file folders when Jade came barreling in with her loot in a plastic bag that swung wildly from one arm.

"Here, have a bar." Jade passed one over and took one for herself.

"You brought snacks? Much obliged."

Jade's long strides took her down the hall alongside Young. "I think I got something that could break this case."

He paused in peeling his Coffee Crisp. "Huh, you don't say.

And that would be?"

"The phone," Jade said through a mouthful of chocolate. She swallowed and said, "There's a phone under the bridge. You have to get all the outgoing calls from there the night Connie was injured."

They reached Young's desk and he hurried behind it. He abandoned his candy and focused on Jade.

"Tell me more about this phone."

"I talked to the guy who found her. He said the phone was off the hook when he got there. Maybe Connie was trying to call someone."

Young shrugged, "Okay. And if she was calling 9-1-1?"

"The guy said that too, but what if..." Jade paused dramatically, "what if she was actually calling someone closer than that? Someone who was involved in helping her feel so depressed that she was thinking of ending herself. Somebody who drove her to that bridge and waited to see if she really went through with it?"

"Somebody who came down and killed her? Kind of like a second opinion. Except instead of getting better, you got dead."

"That sounds like it would be better referred to as 'insurance,'" a glasses-wearing woman leaned over from her desk to add.

"Yeah, sounds like it." Young mulled that for a while. "Thanks, Maureen."

"Anytime, Irv."

"I just think it's a solid lead." Jade felt a bit deflated now that her big reveal was out. "There are so many strange things about this case, so many dead ends that I think it's worth it to follow this one up."

"Strange case." Young's eyes scanned his computer screen as he typed. "But they all are when you're in on it, so that's nothing new."

"You're welcome," Jade said sourly. She realized her pants had been buzzing for a while and she excused herself importantly in order to dig out her phone and swipe her finger across it a bunch of times, swallowing the curses as she remembered Benny's advice.

Vickie's number appeared on the screen. Jade froze and let the phone ring itself out. With a grimace, Jade realized she was going to have to cave and call her one of these days. Even worse,

Connie hadn't been around much recently. Jade was used to having her around and felt her absence.

She returned to Young's desk. He was still on the computer.

"I'll see about getting you those phone records, but it's gonna take a bit of time, so why don't you go and do some more super sleuthing and let me call you."

"You are going to call me, right? You're not just trying to get rid of me?"

"I'm pretty sure that I'll see your sorry butt in here if I don't call, so anything to keep you happy and out of my face here. I'll let you know as soon as I know anything."

"I appreciate that." Jade said.

She got a sick, nervous feeling in her stomach as she looked at her cell phone. She ignored it until she was sitting in her car. The phone lay on the seat next to her, taunting her with its "missed call" alerts all over the screen.

She grabbed the phone and pressed redial. Vickie answered on the first ring.

"Oh Jade, I'm glad I got a hold of you. Are you okay to talk now?"

"Yeah, sorry for not getting back to you sooner." Jade felt awkward and out of practice with her woman-handling skills. On the inside, you pretty much knew where you were: top or bottom. But girls on the outside, you had to tread carefully. Jade needed to end things with Vickie before they went too far, but she wasn't good at dealing with tears or drama. She never was and losing twenty years of normal human interaction to the Department of Correction had not helped her any in that area.

"That's all right. How is everything going with the case?"

"Busy," Jade said. "Very busy with a lot of stuff right now. Look, um, I'm right in the middle of something."

"Oh," the voice on the line sounded small and sad. Jade cursed her lack of smoothness at lying. On the inside, lying did not stand you in good stead. Not unless you could bullshit off a huge one without even thinking about it. And that, Jade could not. Vickie continued, "I just wanted to make sure you didn't forget about our coffee date tonight."

"No way would I forget that," Jade told her. She tucked the phone against her shoulder as a thrill of panic raced through her. Damn! Was it Friday already?

"Great. Give me a call when you get there tonight and I can come down and meet you. The boss gave me some extra work today but I'll probably be done around five-thirty. If I'm not done yet, would you be okay to wait?"

"I can do that." Jade shook back her sleeve in order to get a glance at her watch. Not even noon yet. She could wait for Young's call anywhere, and there was someplace she was aching to go. "Anyway, thanks for your call. Um. Your call before I called you back."

Vickie laughed, tinkly and cute. "Don't worry about it. I know you're really busy and don't have a set schedule. Comes with the territory of being your own boss, I guess."

"Yeah, well, see you later on."

"Okay, bye."

Jade ended the call and wished she was a bit more eloquent. Then she thought about what Vickie said. She was her own boss. She nonchalantly swung a hand over her head in order to assume a cool and relaxed position but ended up whacking her wrist on the overhead light. After she finished cursing, Jade started the car. The muffler was behaving fairly well and she was even able to make out most of the music that was happening on the radio. She sang along with only a few furtive glances at her cell phone in case Detective Young called her.

SHE GOT TO Connie's room just as a nurse finished putting a new bandage around Connie's head. A tray next to the bed was full of used dressings and bits of surgical tape. Connie was still bandaged and tubed from neck to eyebrows with wires and more tubes snaking out from various places under her blanket.

"How's she doing?" Jade asked by way of greeting. "Any idea about a possible wakeup time?"

The nurse shook her head. "It's hard to tell, but she's getting weaker by the day. She's on full life-support and that's keeping her here for the time being, but it's only a matter of time before something happens. Infection or some complication."

Jade's voice stuck in her throat and she didn't miss the sympathetic look the nurse gave her as she left. Jade pulled over a chair and settled down in her accustomed place next to Connie. She very softly brushed back a limp strand of hair that peeked out from the bandages.

Where the hell had Connie gotten to anyway? She was almost of a mind to call Benny at the bookstore and see if the place was more haunted than usual. Jade hitched her chair forward and slid her hand over the cool, inert one on the bedcover. She gazed at the form of the woman she loved and treasured above all others, who was walking the thin line between life and death.

"Come back," Jade said. Her voice broke in the silent room. Jade cleared her throat and tried again. "Connie, come on back now. It's all right."

Only beeping and silence answered her. Jade decided to stay at the hospital for a while and, if nothing else, be something of a security guard for Connie. It was weird hanging out with Connie's body while her spirit was off somewhere doing something else.

A lot of things in Jade's life were weird. She thought she'd gotten used to the weirdness when the universe threw something new and even stranger at her. What next? Aliens? Jade hoped not.

When her stomach growled, protesting the passage of time, Jade went down the hallway in search of the vending machine she thought she'd seen earlier. She tucked a can of root beer in the crook of her arm and wandered back into Connie's hospital room. She pulled up the chair that was rapidly becoming "hers" and got comfy with the bag of leftovers from her convenience-store run that morning. After Jade finished her late lunch, she talked to Connie.

Jade told her about random stuff she thought about, things she planned to do, thoughts about distance learning, plus she threw in a couple of jokes for the hell of it. Of course Connie didn't respond, but Jade wanted to think she was listening. Even if her spirit really was floating around somewhere else, getting into things and maybe scaring Benny, it was possible her brain was saving the stuff she heard for processing later.

Jade ran out of things to say. She watched the rhythmic rise and fall of the unconscious girl's chest in front of her. In such a short time she'd become such an important part of Jade's life.

"Where are you Connie?" she asked softly.

"Right here." Jade heard the voice immediately behind her and jumped up, heart pounding.

"Don't do that." Jade turned around and gave up even pretending to be annoyed at the sight of Connie. "Long time no see, girl. Where've you been hiding? Things have been awfully quiet with you gone."

"Did you miss me?" Connie perched on the windowsill. The afternoon sunlight streamed through her and made her look angelic. She didn't say the words in a conceited way either. She seemed surprised.

"Yeah, I did." Jade shrugged and aimed a crooked grin at Connie. "You liven the place up. And I mean that not in an ironic way at all. It's true. I like talking to you."

"Thanks, Jade. That feels, well, that feeling is really nice."

"You mean as in hot and bothered in the panty area type of feeling?" Jade's mouth said before she could stop it. She slapped herself on the forehead and said, "Sorry sweetie, that was uncalled for. Got to reinstall the brain-mouth filter. Sorry."

"No, it's okay." Connie's smile was worth every second of Jade's embarrassment. "Brain-mouth filters are overrated. Sometimes I'd like to disengage mine."

Jade sat back down and gave an involuntary groan as a muscle in her back complained. At Connie's worried look, Jade rubbed at the sore spot and said, "Wrenched myself going down somewhere." Jade caught herself and froze. She held up a hand. "And I don't mean that in a perverted way."

"It's all right if you did." Connie hovered around and didn't look very angelic at the moment. She had a sly grin on her face. Her dimple added to the overall impish effect. "I think adding a little perversion to your life isn't a bad thing. Makes things fun and spicy."

"That makes two of us," Jade said. She gave Connie a quick, jaunty grin before the uncomfortable thought about how Vickie had come on to her the other day wormed into her mind. Jade had never been very concerned with monogamy, but she wasn't comfortable with where things were going with Vickie.

A relaxed silence fell. Jade reflected that it wasn't hard at all to sit there, with the clock ticking in the background and the strangely homey sounds of people coming in from the hallway mixed with the regular hisses and beeps of the machines around Connie's form. Outside, the sound of traffic filtered in very faintly.

Jade happened to be sitting in a patch of sun that warmed the arm of her shirt and leg of her jeans. She made sure her tattoo was sufficiently covered before she kicked out her legs and crossed her ankles. The series of days spent prowling around until the wee hours then getting up at the crack of dawn caught up with Jade. Her eyelids grew heavy, her awareness of the room around her softened. Her head dipped once and she righted herself with a jerk. Her eyes drifted to Connie, who was peering out the window. She was so vulnerable and yet so strong. Jade ached to touch her, to be close to her. Just being near Connie made Jade feel whole, like her life was worth something.

Another wave of sleepiness hit Jade and she *slipped*. At once on her feet, Jade looked down in alarm at her own half-transparent body. A glance behind her showed her physical form slouched in the chair. The hospital room around her was dark and a faraway wind howled. Jade was in Connie's element. Connie stood at the window and seemed absorbed in whatever was going on outside. A thread of light stretched from Connie's spirit to where her body lay on the bed. It was thin, almost nonexistent in places. Jade's own tether was strong and still, more a band than a thread. In the murky space, Jade took a step forward. Excitement electrified her limbs. She came up behind Connie and very carefully and very softly wrapped her arms around the young woman.

At the first contact, Connie jumped.

"It's only me, sweetheart," Jade said. Neither of them were completely solid so Jade felt more of a cool pressure than anything else, but after the night they'd spent together, it was the closest she'd gotten to touching Connie. And it felt unbelievably good.

"How did you—"

"Slipped," Jade said.

Wordlessly, Connie leaned back in Jade's arms with a sigh. Jade breathed out a moan of longing. She wanted to burn every moment into her brain.

"I like when you hold me." Connie closed her eyes and lifted her chin.

"Me too. I'm not going to let you go," Jade murmured. She kissed Connie lightly on the side of the neck then caught her breath. Connie's tether glowed and seemed to thicken even as Jade gazed on in wonder. She thought about how Connie told her their night together had saved her. Maybe there *was* something Jade could do.

Jade was about to say something when a horrible wrench jolted through her entire body. The impact with the floor drove the breath from her lungs.

"Are you okay?" Connie, the wavering, almost-not-there Connie Jade had gotten used to was back. She knelt down next to Jade.

"I'm good," Jade said even though her chest was on fire and her head felt like someone had kicked it. She got to her feet and took a few deep breaths. She'd forgotten how slipping really messed her up. During her long-ago hospitalization when she slipped, she always woke up in the middle of frantic activity and alarms.

"That was strange," Connie said. She looked at her own hands then back at Jade. "You hugged me."

"Yeah, was that okay?"

Connie nodded once. Her cheeks flushed and she bit her lip as a shy smile blossomed. Jade was about to say something else when Connie flickered out. Jade bit back a groan of frustration. Again. Things got good and then Connie just left. Voluntarily or not, Jade wasn't sure but she sure as hell wished she'd stuck around for a few more minutes. Then again, Jade might blab something she shouldn't so maybe it was a good thing after all.

Jade checked her phone to see if Young had called and noticed the time. It was already after five. The meeting with Vickie was coming up. She'd have to hustle. Jade jumped up and re-tucked in her shirt. She glanced around to make sure she was really alone.

Before she left, she paused to adjust the blanket over Connie's slumbering form and brush a strand of hair from her forehead. The blonde curls were greasy and stuck together, her face mottled with yellowing bruises, but she was still beautiful. It hurt her to see Connie like that, but at least she was safe, although how long her body could stand being held in electronically-induced limbo tore at Jade's mind.

Jade moved out from between the IV bags and wires slowly, reluctant to leave Connie alone. She left the hospital and went back to her car only to have it die on her.

"Oh fucking hell, don't do this to me," Jade muttered. She

twisted the key and stomped on the gas pedal, which only succeeded in flooding the engine.

"Great. Just perfect." She banged on the steering wheel and sat for a while, fuming.

She leaned over with a frustrated growl and opened the glove compartment. She shoveled her emergency Mars bars into her bag before slamming it shut. When she righted herself, she unfortunately locked eyes with a guy in a van who was obviously waiting for her spot. In an effort to communicate her apologetic feeling, Jade got out of the car and made a big show of kicking at the tires and swearing at them. She shrugged and gestured for the guy to keep looking. He answered by giving her the finger.

"Nice. Thanks a lot and you have a nice day too," Jade shouted after him. Under her breath she added, "Jizz-guzzling colon felcher."

She dashed out toward the road, searching for a bus stop. Of course the only one she could find was going in the completely wrong direction and the next one wasn't due for another fifty minutes. The diner wasn't all that far, Jade could walk. She checked the time again. Damn, she was going to be late. As she started down the street, Jade grabbed her cell phone and tried to find one of Vickie's missed calls. Of course she hadn't saved her number; what was the use? And besides, Jade wasn't exactly sure how to do that yet.

"Hello?"

"Hi Vickie? It's Jade."

"Oh hi! I was just about to head out now. Have you arrived yet?"

"No, I was just calling to say I might be a little late."

"Oh." Vickie sounded disappointed. "How late?"

"Look, my car died and I'm hoofing it. I'll be there in maybe half an hour? Sorry about that. If you've got stuff to do, we can cancel." Smooth, very smooth, Jade sighed at herself. She pressed the pedestrian button on the traffic light and waited for it to change. A vintage mustang passed her with the bass from some new techno-song pounding through the air.

"No, that's all right. I have a bunch of paperwork I need to finish. How about give me another call when you get close so I can come down and meet you."

"Okay, I can do that." Jade thumbed the phone off and concentrated on not getting lost in the maze of winding downtown streets.

Traynor's Port was one of the oldest cities in the country and the streets sprouted naturally instead of being planned, which led to a sprawling, meandering mass of roads that didn't ever lead from point A to point B.

As Jade hustled her butt down the sidewalk, she noticed a bunch of places she recognized, interspersed with new shops and buildings. The jarring overlay of her memory and the present town made her feel as if she were caught between worlds. She waited for the traffic light to change and studied the shop across the street from her. It appeared to be in mid-redecoration. A sign out front declared an opening date a few weeks in the future. Apparently it was going to be a kind of eating establishment that called itself the Kindness Café. Jade wondered how long the eatery would last. As far back as Jade could remember, that particular corner of real-estate was in a constant flux of businesses coming and going.

The other businesses around it hadn't changed from Jade's memory, even that ancient watch-repair shop that never seemed to have any customers. She idly wondered what it was about that particular corner that killed every business that sprouted up there. It could have something to do with the location or the parking situation. Jade looked up with a sudden chill. Or it could have something to do with the black figure looking out of the second floor window, no other feature visible except for glowing red eyes. Even as Jade gazed up at it, the figure raised two fists and started pounding on the glass. The dusty green awning below shook ever so slightly.

Jade didn't swear, just made a long, *Fffffff* sound with her lips. For a second, she considered walking away, then she looked up at the lone figure again and she knew the decision had already been made.

"All right, you win," Jade muttered. Finally the light changed to green and she trotted across the street. As she'd learned to do when separated by a good distance, Jade formed the words in a bubble in her head and let them go. *Hey there, dude. What's the deal?*

The answer hit her in a flat wallop.

In a hissed stream of swears, Jade clutched at her leg. It felt like spikes drove through her calf. She stumbled and lurched against a mailbox, supporting her weight on her elbows as her legs gave out.

The street vanished. Cigar smoke and kerosene fumes choked her. The smell of unwashed men filtered through the agony. Through involuntary tears of pain, Jade saw a huddle of suits. Wide ties and coarse hound's-tooth jackets. Voices buzzed around her.

Where's the money?

A harsh clatter down wooden stairs jolted through her.

Last chance, where's the goddamn money?

You got the wrong guy! I'm just a clerk!

Okay, if you wanna play it that way. Fine with me.

A flash and deafening bang. Then silence. Agony. The smell of earth clogged her nose and mouth. Her leg was pinned under an unbelievable weight. The waves wracked through her with no end. Above her, the world flickered and changed. The sounds of jazz music and stomping feet gave way to the rich, greasy air of Chinese food followed by cinnamon and the yeasty smell of baking bread. The scene changed again and again, faster than Jade could follow, faster than she could comprehend. All the way through it, a voice howled in pain.

Red stars brought her back to the sunlit street. Jade cursed and rubbed her chin, the coppery taste of blood on her tongue. She was crumpled on the sidewalk in front of the mailbox, apparently she'd whacked herself on it as she'd dropped.

Message received.

Jade got to her feet and dusted herself off. She needed to get into that cellar. She swiped Chapstick across her bleeding lip and waved off the helpful biker who asked if she was okay. The building emitted hammering sounds and Jade could hear some kind of lively Indian music along with them. Sneaking in was going to be pretty much impossible.

Jade steeled herself to lie her ass off. She dragged off her clip and shook her hair out. She arranged it over her shoulders and put on a friendly, harmless façade.

One of the windows peering from the cellar was in front of a storm drain. It had filled with leaves and overflowed enough to partially rot away the wooden frame. The glass looked mossy and diseased. With a coin from the stash at the bottom of her bag, Jade experimentally shot it into the gap. It sailed through, only making a small *chink* against the ancient, moldy glass.

Plan in mind, Jade rounded the building and ducked into the little shop. The area was bright and airy, the hardwood floor solid under her feet. A guy in a tank top with a long ponytail was in the process of hammering some boards onto what was going to be a long counter that stretched the entire length of the room. An older couple in cheerful T-shirts looked up from a bunch of open cardboard boxes, pottery bowls clutched in their hands.

"Sorry, we're not open yet," the male of the couple said.

Jade stuck her hands in her pockets and put on her best non-offensive smile. "Yeah, sorry to bother you nice folks." She rubbed a hand through her hair and hoped they bought the next lie she was going to come out with. "I dropped my ring out back and I think it went into your cellar. The window's cracked open." Jade decided to go the whole nine yards and blustered on. "It's not all that valuable but my girlfriend would be heartbroken if I lost it."

"Oh that's terrible." The woman bustled over. "Is there anything we can do to help?"

Kindness Café indeed. Jade mentally raised an eyebrow. "If I could just take a look downstairs that would be great. I know you're busy and I'll be out in a jiffy." Jiffy? Who the hell said that anymore? Jade tried to relax her stance as if a river of sweat wasn't going down her back.

"That's fine." She turned to the ponytailed guy and said, "Paul, how about getting that flashlight and giving our new friend a hand?"

"Sure thing, Miz Yanovsky." The aforementioned Paul straightened up and went into a cubby off the main room. He made cheerful rummaging sounds for a bit before he came back with an industrial-looking flashlight in his hands.

"Do be careful, there's prolly bugs and stuff down there," said the man, who Jade arbitrarily decided was Mr. Yanovsky. He showed them over to the ancient door, and it creaked open in a suitably spooky way. "Don't kill any spiders if you can help it, now y'hear? Friendly little critters."

"Thanks a lot," Jade said. She tried to give off an air of grateful-yet-sheepish as they went down the ancient wooden stairway, Paul and his flashlight in the lead. His beam illuminated the unfinished dirt floor and messy, cluttered space. The air was thick with dust and the smell of damp earth. As they descended, Jade winced as a hollow, keening wail started up.

"Never been down here before," he said. "This place gives me the creeps." The yellow beam swept over the huddled, dusty forms of abandoned boxes and something that looked like it could have been a typewriter in a previous life. The air was colder than could be accounted for by the weather.

Okay I'm here, give me a hint buddy.

Flashes of pain welled up in her mind. The wailing presence brought disjointed images behind her eyes.

"Whereabouts you lose this ring?" Paul's voice filtered through Jade's intense mental listening, causing her to jump.

She dragged her hair back into a clip as it swept up a fine array of cobwebs. With half-closed eyes, Jade allowed her body to drift through the musty cellar as howls of anger and pain moved through her. There was a definite pull toward one end of the cellar.

"This corner here. I think there's something under this big crate-thing here."

The cold was sharp, the temperature dropped with every heartbeat. Jade could almost see her breath in the wan shaft of light courtesy of Paul. Jade grabbed a corner of the wooden crate and gave a heave. It didn't budge. She tried again, this time with her entire weight behind the shove. The crate rocked forward a bit then tottered back to its original position. Jade curled her tongue in her mouth to keep the stream of profanity she wanted to spew in check.

"Here, lemme give you a hand. That looks heavy," he said and set the flashlight on a dirt-caked stool.

"No, I've got it."

"You sure it's down here?" He hugged his bare arms to his chest and looked around with a nervous expression as if he was somehow aware of the breathy wails that filled Jade's ears like cotton.

Her boots dug into the ground and found purchase. Jade gathered herself and shoved the splintery boards with her shoulder. Something gave and the crate lurched backward an inch, then one more. With a quick jerk, the crate turned over. Dirt and pebbles scattered over the packed earthen floor.

"Holy shi—" Paul was the first to react. His arms wheeled as he fell backward and landed sprawled at the bottom of the stairs.

Half-buried in the dirt was a human leg bone, attached to a foot, still clad in a rotting leather shoe. Jade sat back on her heels and studied it with a satisfied smirk. A thundering sound behind her told the story of Paul's escape to the ground floor. Above her, footsteps rattled and voices babbled. Even though she didn't have a lot of time, Jade reached out a hand and pawed through the dirt until she found the round skull.

She gave it a pat and said, "We found you and you're gonna get out of here. Sorry to have kept you waiting so long, sir."

"That was quite a long ouch." Jade looked up to see a dark-skinned, neatly bearded man standing placidly in the middle of the room, arms crossed over his natty suit. He relaxed his stance and lifted his hat. "The name's Ephram Coyle and I'm much obliged to you, ma'am."

"Feeling better now?" Jade stood up and dusted off the knees of her jeans.

"Oh yes, very."

"Think you want to take the next step? Go to a better place?"

He rubbed a large hand over his face and said, "I know I should, but I've kind of gotten used to being here. I'd also like to make up for being in such a foul mood all this time."

Jade leveled a finger at him. "That's fine, but you have to be good to this place. Treat these people well, look out for them and stuff or I'll come back and put you in a jam jar."

With a nod and a wispy "Okey dokey!" Ephram vanished into the shadows. Jade became aware of someone calling her from the top of the stairs.

"Are you all right down there?"

"Sure," Jade said in a cheerful voice before she could dredge up more acting ability. She shrugged at her lapse and bounded up the stairs to meet the concerned trio. "My girlfriend can buy me a new ring," Jade declared and she certainly didn't picture Vickie. The only one that came to mind was Connie and it was the most natural thing ever.

"I'm calling the cops," the mister of the house said. He crossed the room in a few energetic bounds. "Paul, shame on you for leaving a lady in distress."

"It's okay," Jade said. She gave up the pretence. "I'm used to that kind of thing."

"Are you with the police?" Mrs. Yanovsky asked. She had a pitcher of something brown and murky in her hands.

"No," Jade said. "More like spiritual forensics."

"Oh my," Mrs. Yanovsky said with a puzzled look on her face. She held up the pitcher. "Why don't you sit down with us and have some nice Oolong tea? It's organic and fair trade. After that shock, I think we'd all like a nice cool beverage."

"Thanks, but I gotta go," Jade said.

"Are you sure?" Mrs. Yanovsky asked in a trembling voice. "I mean, you should probably be here at least until the police arrive. You were the one to find...that poor thing moldering away downstairs. I don't know what to do, if we should even be here."

Jade looked around at the three people, they all looked worried and scared. Normally, Jade would have turned on her heel and gotten the fuck out of there without a backward glance, but something stopped her. That new giving-a-shit about others kept her from leaving them all in the dust. She grimaced. "Okay, I'll stay until the cops come. Most of them know me anyway."

"Thank you so much," Mrs. Yanovsky said. While Mr. Yanovsky spoke on the phone in a low voice, she poured glasses of tea with a shaking hand.

Preoccupied with her own thoughts, Jade sat down on the somewhat sawdust-covered stool Paul offered. She yanked out her phone and dialed. "Hey," she said as soon as Vickie answered. "Look, um, a situation's come up here, maybe we should just cancel—"

"I can wait," Vickie interrupted. "Jade, I've been looking forward to our coffee date so much. You can't just cancel on me."

Jade pictured Vickie's pout as she spoke. "Okay, I'll try to be as quick as I can. Later."

"Pardon me for eavesdropping," Mrs. Yanovsky said. "But was that your girlfriend? I apologize for keeping you."

"Oh no, that was just..." Jade trailed off. "Nobody."

AS SOON AS the polite, uniformed officer left, Jade was out the door and on the sidewalk. She ran like she was being chased by bulls and quickly made it to the diner across from the office building. After she caught her breath, she made the short phone call and waited for Vickie in one of the booths. While Jade didn't like the inferred intimacy of the enclosed space, she also didn't want to sit at the counter. She felt too exposed with her back to the door. Dixie brought over a glass of water and a menu, which Jade ignored. She already knew what she was going to order.

"Sorry to keep you waiting," Vickie slid into the booth across from Jade. Her made-up face sparkled in the glow from the line of neon lights that arched over the counter. Her blonde curls sported a barrette shaped like a heart.

"No problem, it was me who was late to begin with."

"What can I get you gals today?" Dixie was back with her order pad.

Vickie wrinkled her nose at the menu before she ordered fruit salad and a mineral water.

"I'll have a piece of that good apple pie, please Miz Dixie," Jade announced. She turned back to Vickie and said, "I am really looking forward to having some pie. It's been ages. Pie is the best and most efficient food ever. It's like salad and the main dish and dessert all at the same time. Like you have your fruit, which has fiber and vitamins, and the acid in the apples is neutralized by the sugar." Jade held her hands apart to demonstrate. She didn't even care that Vickie fiddled with her phone as she spoke. She couldn't hold back the words any more. "The crust is the perfect delivery vehicle for all that nice filling especially when it's heated up so the juices come out and react with the crust making a kind of third layer. It's like a shock absorber for when you cut it. And as an extra bonus, that layer also kind of acts like a glue to keep the bits together while you get it to your mouth. Like I said, the perfect food. No ice cream though. I'm a purist. That would be mixing genres."

"Uh, yeah. That's an, um, interesting way to think," Vickie said as she put down her phone. She fluttered her lashes and gifted Jade with a smile that Jade halfheartedly returned.

The food came and Jade was very busy for a while. She shoveled pie into herself as fast as she possibly could, pausing only once to chug down half a glass of milk in one gulp. Once the pie was gone, Jade came up for air to catch Vickie looking at her. Staring, more like, with a spoonful of fruit salad halfway to her mouth.

"You really like pie."

"Guilty as charged," Jade said with a smooth confidence she didn't feel. She turned and called over her shoulder, "My complements to the chef!"

"You're welcome!" The cheerful answer came from the kitchen.

"Can I get you another piece?" Dixie asked from behind the counter. One hand invitingly lifted the glass cover of the pie case.

"Very tempting," Jade said. The look of distain on Vickie's face stole her appetite. Jade slowly pushed her empty plate away. "But I'll pass. I will take a cup of coffee, though."

"Make that two," Vickie said.

Dixie came over with a pot of coffee in one hand and two cups threaded through the fingers of the other. She took two saucers from a pocket in her apron and set them down on the table. She finished by filling the cups with a steady hand. Jade added a couple packets of sugar to hers and stirred. She took a gulp and let her breath go with a satisfied sigh.

Vickie wrapped her fingers around her cup and cradled it just under her pink sparkly lips. She'd drawn them to emphasize her Cupid's bow and Jade was fascinated. All the fashion magazines she'd read mostly out of boredom while on the inside hadn't prepared her to be so up close and personal with a perfectly turned-out girl.

"Has there been any news about Connie?" Vickie looked young and lost, and Jade almost felt bad for not going along with the charade that there could be anything between them. "I mean, have they—did they find her yet? There's been nothing in the news and we haven't heard anything."

"I can't give out any details," Jade said and swirled the coffee around in her cup. "Let's just say the police are in on it and there's been a good development recently."

"Did Gord have anything to do with it? He came in really late today and was kind of, well, crying in Mr. Butters's office. He was saying things about the police. Murel said he was asking about getting a lawyer. Oh my God, he didn't have to, well, you know, identify Connie?"

"No, nothing like that. He's just made himself interesting to the police, that's all."

Vickie continued speaking but Jade's attention drifted to the pie on the counter. The apple filling glistened richly in the orange light from the setting sun. From where she was sitting, she could see into the sacred spot where the pie was cut into and left open to the air in an invitation to anyone to bask in its revealing glory. The view was hypnotizing, the sweet perfection beckoned to her. At that moment, Jade wanted nothing more than to have that pie, to feel the soft gush of apple filling explode so softly, so gently into her mouth. To taste the sweetness of the apple dancing along with the layered perfection of the crust, leaving tiny but precious flakes on her lips. Her body ached for it. Her mouth wished to receive the pie and her stomach rumbled, ready to hold the pie and cherish it. Her hands flexed, ready to be put to work segmenting that pie and bringing it into herself.

"You are an angel," Jade groaned when Dixie brought over a plate and wordlessly set it down in front of her. It was a large slice, slightly warm and beautiful in its fragrant, syrupy perfection. After inhaling the sweet, spicy aroma, she closed her eyes in enjoyment. Then she found her fork and slowly, reverently, became one with the pie.

"I've never seen anyone put away a piece of our good apple pie like you," Dixie said from her post at the counter.

"I'm coming back here every day," Jade declared after she swallowed the last crisp bit of crust. "Do you have any coupons?"

"We got coffee tickets, if that's what you mean."

"I'll take them. In for a penny, in for a pound."

While Jade waited for Dixie to come back with her book of coffee tickets, she turned back to Vickie, who sat still with her half-finished salad in front of her.

"Sorry, what were we talking about?" Jade asked.

"What's going on with Gord? He's not a suspect, is he?"

Jade lowered her voice and leaned closer as she said, "I found out he was stalking Connie. He'd somehow gotten into the apartment down the hall from her and was squatting there."

"I knew Gord was up to something shady. He's always been really quiet. He just stared at Connie all the time. And there were things he said. Nothing specific, but he just seemed to know things about her that nobody else did. Not even me and I'm Connie's friend." Vickie's eyes swam with tears. "Oh my God, Jade, I'm so scared. Why can't the police lock him up right now? Before he hurts anyone else."

"Apparently they need a bit more evidence to do that," Jade

said. "Look, it's only a matter of time. Both me and the police are working on this."

"Let me know if there's anything I can do to help. Maybe I can get into his computer and check his emails or something like that."

"No Vickie, I can't let you do that." The round and pleasant feeling left over from the pie ebbed. "I don't want to get you involved any more than you already are. This could get dangerous. Why don't you take a couple days off work and lay low?"

Vickie sank back, hugging herself. Jade couldn't help but notice how Vickie used the action to push her breasts up in a move that had to be on purpose. Jade kept her eyes resolutely up.

"No, I won't run away." Vickie held her head up. "Connie was my friend and I want to see this through."

"Please don't take any risks," Jade said. She took a deep breath and twisted the napkin in her hand. She'd avoided the topic, but she had to bring it up. "Actually, I was thinking about us." Us. Jade winced at the word. She shifted in her seat. "Look, I don't think we should —"

"I was thinking about us too," Vickie said, her deep blue eyes fixed on Jade's face as the words died in Jade's throat. "And I just want to say I feel so much better with you here, going through this by my side. I mean, it's been really hard." Vickie raised a hand to her face and Jade sucked in a breath as she thought she detected the shine of tears. "Connie was like my first friend here and now she's gone. What if what happened to her happens to me?" Vickie sniffled as she looked across the table. One hand reached out and Vickie's fingers wrapped around Jade's own. "You don't know how much this means to me. I'm grateful to have you in my life."

"Uh, yeah, don't worry about anything," Jade choked.

Coward. The word echoed in her head. She eased her hand from Vickie's grasp and got to her feet. She snagged the check on her way up. Vickie gazed at Jade with guileless trust in her eyes. Jade felt like the biggest heel on the planet as she went over to the register to pay.

Chapter Seventeen

JADE WAS IN the middle of a good dream about climbing a mountain of apples when a dark, smothering presence fell over her. She thrashed about in panic and opened her eyes to her case wall on top of her.

Once Jade recovered from her initial heart-seizure, she heaved the Post-it covered paper to the floor. After the coffee date-that-wasn't-a-date with Vickie, she'd been up half the night adding stuff about Gord and the things she'd found out about the bridge before she crashed on her cot. Now it was Sunday, and Jade was still waiting for Detective Young to get back to her with the phone info. She could only hope it led to something positive. Nobody had called while she'd been asleep, Jade noted with a sigh. She got a certain cool prickling feeling and looked up from her phone. Connie hovered in the doorway. The young specter looked equal parts ashamed and guilty.

"Hey Connie, come on in."

"That was my fault," Connie said in a rush. She pointed to the case wall, which was currently the case floor. "Sorry for scaring you, Jade. I was just trying to straighten it and the whole thing came down."

"No problem, sweetie." Jade motioned toward the wall of the closet. "Look how I've rigged up a system of clips and hooks so it's easy to put the wall back up. Sometimes I like to take it down and lay it out on my desk in the other room. Hey, wait a minute." Jade looked up and a smile broke over her face. "You actually moved something physical. That's great!"

"I guess I did," Connie said. "I wonder if I can move anything else?"

She vanished. A bang followed by three shrieks brought Jade to her feet in an instant.

Alarmed, Jade pounded down the stairs and exploded into the bookstore. She stopped short as she saw Benny and Jordan clutching each other in a horizontal naked tangle in front the coffee counter.

"Oh my God." Jade covered her eyes. "Sorry guys. I thought I heard screaming."

"This place really is freaking haunted!" Jordan jumped up. He turned around and started yanking on his clothes, which consisted of shiny gold hot-pants and a white leather vest. It didn't take too long for him to finish as he didn't seem to be encumbered by underwear.

Jade was suddenly glad of the modest T-shirt and drawstring pants combo she'd changed into before passing out on her cot the previous night. Benny didn't reach for his own clothes. Instead, he lounged on the carpet underneath a rainbow flag.

"I told you we had a bad case of the spookies, Jojo," Benny said, unperturbed. "Don't worry about our ghost. Remember she's into women. One specific woman to be precise." He aimed a knowing look at Jade as he said the last bit. She just sighed and fixed him with a glare.

"Oh Lord, that's Connie?" Jordan perched a pair of pink heart-shaped sunglasses on his mop of curly hair. "She seemed more like a curse from hell than Jade's girlfriend."

Jade didn't bother to correct Jordan. She just raised her eyes to the ceiling and asked, "Connie, what did you do?" When there was no answer, Jade asked, "Ben, can you tell me what went down here?"

"We were getting cozy," Benny said and rose up in a regal motion, somehow he kept the rainbow flag sexily open at one side but still in a genital-covering position. "And suddenly there's this big cold wind that hits all the windows at once and the office door slams shut. No biggie. Jordan got freaked I guess, because he always gets a bit edgy just after he comes."

"I didn't need to know that," Jade said.

A blonde head popped up as Connie peeked from behind the cash register, looking sheepish. She ducked back down and only her voice remained as she said, "I didn't know anyone was here, and I didn't think it would work so well. I also forgot it was Pride weekend. Jade, could you apologize to them for me? I messed up big-time."

"It's okay, sweetie," Jade said. She turned to the young men. "Sorry about that, guys. Connie's harmless, really. She feels bad about scaring you two."

"Don't worry, honey, it's all good." Benny joined her behind the café counter and got out a trio of mugs. Jordan collapsed onto one of the stools in front of Benny. The appearance of a mug of coffee and a cranberry muffin on the counter in front of him seemed to settle Jordan down.

"Just another day in the life of Spooky the Private Eye," Benny said.

"Not you too," Jade gritted her teeth as she received her own coffee, pre-sweetened just the way she liked it. Jade took a mouthful of the hot beverage and felt the tension leave her. Connie was still hiding under the register, looking miserable. Jade set her mug down as she got an idea. "Ben? Do you have any audiobooks you think Connie might like?"

Benny hummed into his mug before he answered, "I've got *Naughty Nurse Tales* on my tablet." He shrugged. "I haven't listened to it, not my cup of tea, but it's pretty popular with the ladies."

"Great," Jade said. She got up and let herself into Benny's office. The tablet was lying on the desk where Benny usually kept it. She queued up the file as Connie peered into the room. "Hey Connie. How about hanging in here with a nice book?"

Connie's face lit up. She curled up in the desk chair as Jade hit play. As the first strands of the narrative began, Connie asked, "Are you going to listen to it with me?"

The shy, hopeful tone undid Jade. There was no way she could refuse. She grinned and said, "Sure thing. Just let me get my coffee."

Jade backed out of the office and faced Benny and Jordan again. They were both staring at her with looks of disbelief. "What?" Jade asked. "Connie likes it here. I don't want to kick her out. She's not bothering anyone in there, got it? Just relax and enjoy your day, okay?"

While Jordan looked the opposite of relaxed, Benny said, "We'll try. Oh Jade, why don't you come out with us tonight? There's going to be a bunch of us getting together for a post-parade bash at Bob the Cowboy's beer hall. You're welcome to come and par-tay with the best."

"I'm not really a big par-tay person," Jade said. She picked up her coffee cup plus a couple napkins to take with her.

"If you do decide to come out tonight, I'll buy you a drink," Benny said. "Give me a call and I'll let you know where we are."

"Thanks, but I'll probably hang out here where it's quiet."

"Okay, but if you want quiet, you'll have to stay upstairs."

"Why?"

"The parade route is right in front of this place and we always get a ton of customers wandering in," Benny said. He rubbed his hands together and cackled, "We're gonna make a fortune selling rainbow stuff."

"Thanks for the heads-up," Jade said. Benny wandered behind the counter in his flag where he piled a few muffins into a basket. Jade looked at them with suspicion. "Isn't it breaking some kind of health law to be serving food without wearing pants?"

"We're not open yet," Benny said with a twirl that made her reflexively avert her eyes. "And it doesn't count as without pants because I'm fabulous!"

"I can't argue with that," Jade said. She grabbed a muffin and ducked back into the office. She waved off Connie's offer of the chair. Instead she perched on the desk and fed herself muffin pieces while the narrator's sexy voice described a naughty scene involving speculums. Connie listened with her eyes closed and her chin resting on her clasped hands.

Only a few minutes into the story, Jade's pocket buzzed. She scowled and pulled out her cell phone. If it was Vickie, she was prepared to ignore the call, but after she saw the name, she lunged and paused the recording. Connie looked up, her eyes questioning. Jade hesitated for a split second before she put the call on speaker.

"Morning, Detective Young. What's up?"

"Sorry to bother you so early, but it looks like we've got a situation."

"What? What's happened?" Jade was on her feet in an instant.

"You remember that young fellow you brought in?"

"Tell me Gord's not pulled a runner," Jade said. She fell back against the wall. The hand holding the phone shook with her sudden anger.

"Not exactly," Young said. "Are you sitting down?"

"Just give it to me straight, Young. What's going on?"

"We got a call from his place early this morning. Landlord was checking a noise complaint and found him dead in his room."

Connie gasped. Jade's knees buckled and she dropped into a startled crouch. "Shit. How?"

"Looks like he drank himself stupid and hung himself from his bedroom doorknob."

Jade pressed a hand to her face before she hauled herself upright once more. She heaved a few deep breaths before she slammed a fist down on the desk. "Great. Just fucking great."

"I don't suppose you'd be able to go down there and you know..." Young began.

"Maybe," Jade said. "Depends on the guy in question. I'm not a OUIJA board. Where's his place at?" She scribbled the address Young gave her down on a coffee-ringed napkin before she ended the call. Jade met Connie's gaze.

"I can't believe it," Connie whispered in a broken voice that had Jade's entire body aching to reach out to her. "I wasn't a huge fan of Gord, but I never wanted anything bad to happen to him. Jade, what if he *is* still around? I don't think I can—"

"It's not your fault. Let me take care of things over there," Jade said. "Will you be okay here?"

"Sure," Connie said. Her face and posture expressed relief. "Don't worry, I'll be good and not bother Benny and Jordan."

"Okay then, enjoy the book," Jade said. She restarted the audiobook and slipped her phone into her pocket as she backed out. The sadness in Connie's expression ripped at her heart. Before she could stop herself, Jade said, "Everything will be okay, sweetheart. I love you." She froze in the doorway. Connie stared at her, lips parted in surprise.

"Did you mean to say that?"

"It kind of slipped out, but yeah, I did." Jade chewed her lip. "Shit, I gotta go, Connie. But we'll discuss this later. That's a promise."

Face flaming, Jade ran out of the office and pounded up the stairs. She got dressed in a hurry and yanked the strap of her bag over her head. A quick trip up to the third floor resulted in receiving the keys to her aunt's car plus a guilt-trip about Addie being "stuck at home" all day.

Even without the GPS, Jade found Gord's place quickly. It was an old-looking three-story building that was once a stately Victorian home before being converted into apartments. A path made out of cracked concrete patio stones weaved through the root-choked dirt of the front yard. Jade paused on her way up the wooden steps to the front porch and peered into the mailbox marked with Gord's name. It held a few pizza flyers and something that could have been one of those fridge magnets the odd-jobs companies like to give out. Nothing significant enough to justify Jade shoving her fingers into the slot to try and fish them out.

The front door was unlocked and led into a small entrance hallway. The carpeted floor was soft, the floorboards yielded in places. Gord's apartment was on the second floor and Jade creaked her way up the stairs and made her way to Gord's room. Identifying it was easy due to the crime scene tape across the door. Jade was about to reach for the door knob when a voice stopped her.

"Are you here with the police?"

Jade whirled. A slightly built guy in brightly patterned leggings and grey cutoff sweatpants was standing in front of the door next to Gord's. An unzipped jacket of the same grey material hung from his shoulders. Underneath it, his T-shirt had a picture of a mountain on it with the words "Because it is there" printed in faded letters. He carried a cloth bag in one hand. The logo indicated a local grocery store. Jade narrowed her eyes as she studied him. He looked uncomfortable as he shifted his weight from foot to foot and fiddled with the snap closure of the bag.

"Kind of," Jade said. "You a friend of Gordon Holloway?"

"Not really, but I know — uh, knew him." He had his shopping balanced on one raised knee as he fumbled with a ring of keys on a carabineer attached to his belt.

"You got a name, kid?"

He eyed Jade with a scared look on his face before he said, "I'm Eric Chow. Uh, look, did he really die? I mean, I saw the ambulance and everything. What happened?"

"Maybe you could tell me." Jade crossed her arms and leaned back against the wall. The aging wallpaper was rough against her back. "Were you here last night?"

"Yeah," Eric said. "Gord was out for a couple hours then he came back with some girl."

"Who?"

"Dunno. I didn't see anything, I just heard them. The walls in this place are paper thin. They were talking for a while and then the girl left."

"Do you know what they were talking about?"

"Not sure." Eric shifted the bag from one hand to the other. Jade saw a packet of crackers and some kind of dried fish in there. "He had his music on pretty loud."

"How about the woman with him? Did you get a look at her?"

"Nope, just heard her. Laughing."

"Like they were having a good time?"

"No, it wasn't in a nice way. It was kind of, I don't know. Mean laughing. After she left all I heard was his music. All night. I guess someone complained because the landlord was here, banging on his door this morning. That's when he..." His face drained of color. "Found Gord. Do you think someone killed him?"

"That's for the police to decide," Jade said. "Do you know if the door was locked or open?"

"It was locked all right. Hasheem, the guy who lives right over Gord, came down at like three in the morning and was rattling the knob and yelling at him to turn the volume down. No answer though. I guess he was maybe already..." Eric trailed off and swallowed hard.

"Is the landlord around now?"

"No." Eric shook his head. "I haven't seen him since the police left. I bet he's out getting drunk. I know I would be, after seeing what he did."

"Not pretty, was it?"

"He sure as hell shrieked loud enough. And that's his puke over there."

Jade grimaced.

"Okay, thanks Eric." Jade pulled herself away from the wall and took a few steps toward Eric. She reached out and patted him on the shoulder and gave him what she hoped was a reassuring smile. "People are looking into things, all right? Just go back to your place and relax. Take care of yourself and just keep going on as usual, okay?"

"Yeah, sure."

Jade waited until Eric's lock clicked shut before she tried Gord's front door. She was pleased to find it unlocked, which saved her and her lockpicking tools a few minutes' work. Jade ducked under the tape and eased herself inside. She hadn't enjoyed meeting Gord in the flesh and certainly wasn't looking forward to getting up close and personal with his eternal soul, if it was even lingering there.

The room was pretty standard for a single person just out of school. It boasted worn brown carpets and a sofa that looked old enough to have had Henry Hudson's ass on it. Her footsteps didn't make any sound as she picked her way through the small apartment. The reek of spilled booze was thick in the stale air. She felt a cold whisper brush across the back of her neck and let a grim smile pull at her mouth.

Without turning around, she said, "So you *are* still hanging around, Gord. You worthless piece of — "

She didn't get to finish the sentence as something that felt like a thin cord snapped tight around her neck. She grabbed at her throat as she tried to claw some air back into her lungs, but Jade only dug her nails into her own skin. The invisible garrote tightened. Jade flung out a hand as she was jerked by the neck to her knees. Her lungs ballooned in her chest. Jade fought the panic that drove all reason from her head.

Let me the fuck go!

Jade speared the thought toward her attacker, but only got a hard jolt at her throat for her troubles. The carpet burned against her legs as she was dragged across the floor in short, rough jerks. Jade's hands clawed at the carpet, grabbed at the sofa legs, anything she could reach but nothing stopped her journey over to the bedroom door. Her butt left the carpet. The doorknob hit her on the back of the head and Jade twisted her body but couldn't get her legs underneath her.

Her body arched in helpless anger as her shirt and sports bra whipped up to her neck. Cold air struck her bare breasts but Jade was beyond caring about modesty. Darkness crowded her vision and she reached out desperately as she saw, for the first time, the shadowy figure standing over her. It was Gord's body, but his face was swollen and purple, bloated almost beyond recognition. His tongue hung out of his mouth and his distended eyes stared at her with a sick hunger.

Suddenly the air was filled with light. It chased the shadows into the farthest corners and threw the room into sharp relief.

The grotesque face turned away from Jade.

Connie radiated a pure, golden light as her hair waved about her face. Her teeth were bared in a feral grin, her hands curled into claws. Even as Jade's consciousness hovered on the edge of darkness, she reached out with one last burst of strength. Connie shone with a force Jade had never seen before. She was magnificent.

"You have no power here! Go away!" Connie thundered and swiped the air with one hand. The resulting bolt of raw energy jolted Gord's apparition back a few steps.

Just as soon as it started, it was over. Released, Jade landed on the carpet and promptly keeled over. She coughed and breathed in the smell of socks, arms crumpled underneath her body. Jade became aware of Connie's wavering form, back to her usual washed-out state as she knelt down in front of her.

"Jade, are you okay? Please be okay."

Even though she couldn't speak yet, Jade nodded. She concentrated on getting air back into her lungs. Connie looked so lost and alone Jade wished she could gather her up and just hold onto her for a good long while. As soon as she could move again, Jade sat up and yanked her clothes back into decency.

"Connie, you saved my ass. Where did you get all that power?"

"I don't know, but I'm glad I could help." Connie gave Jade a shy smile that filled her with light.

"Maybe you really are my guardian angel," Jade said. She got to her feet and looked around with a defeated sigh. "That was a fiasco. I didn't get anything from Gord other than he really is a piece of shit, both alive and dead."

Chapter Eighteen

JADE STUMBLED OUT of Gord's apartment. Her mind whirled with conflicting thoughts. Her body ached and she desperately wanted to sit down. A small coffee shop appeared in front of her and Jade lurched into it.

"What'll you have today?" a young man asked her from behind the counter. The walls were decorated with old movie posters and Jade felt that Benny would approve of the place.

"Uh, a coffee please."

"What size?"

"Oh jeez, medium, I guess."

"We have petite, quaff, draft, and snifter."

Jade just stared at him in complete non-comprehension. The barista sighed and pointed to a series of cups on the counter.

She bit back an avalanche of curses and said, "Make it a quaff."

"And which blend would you like? Today's features are French Mission and Ethiopian Yirgacheffe."

"Ghezunteit!" Jade cracked, however the barista didn't seem all that amused. "Tough crowd. I'll have the, uh, the second one."

"Good choice."

The price flashed up on the register and she handed over a mittful of change. The barista passed Jade her receipt and directed her to the pickup window.

"Goddamn, can't a person just get a normal cup of coffee nowadays without it being a whole wagonload of fancy-shmancy bells and honking whistles?" Jade addressed the room in general while the barista made up her drink. Only a few university student-types were in the café at that hour of the morning and none of them answered Jade's question. However two girls looked up from their cell phones and made "OMG" faces at each other. On the inside, that kind of look would earn you a beating. Jade surreptitiously cracked her knuckles.

"Here's your coffee. Be careful, it's hot."

"Yeah, thanks."

Jade stood at the condiments counter and doctored her coffee before she found a table. The coffee really did smell nice and Jade was hoping it would live up to its not cheap price tag.

She took a moment to mentally review the case. She thought about the people she'd talked to in turn and what kind of motive they'd have for harming Connie. It was hard for her to think about it. The Connie she'd gotten to know was funny and cute and not a threat to anybody at all. Maybe it was something else, Jade mulled. She swirled the coffee in her cup so that the cream she'd poured in drifted about on the current. Maybe they wanted something she had. Maybe Connie was just an obstacle.

"It's not worth it."

"What's not worth it, sweetie?" Jade looked up from her coffee to see Connie sitting in the empty seat across from her. She was barely there. She flickered badly. Her face was creased in concentration as if she had to focus all her energy just to exist.

"Solving my case isn't worth getting you hurt or—worse," Connie said. "If it puts you in danger, I don't want you to continue. Nothing will change what happened to me. So what if whoever did this gets away with it? You'll be safe and that's all I want."

"You worry too much," Jade said. She leaned back with her quaff-sized cup in her hands. "I have yet to find anybody, dead or alive, who can take me down. And with you on my side, that goes double."

Connie nodded. She leaned her chin on her hands and looked straight into Jade's eyes. Time slowed. Jade's breath caught in her throat as reality shifted.

Janebeth shoved her way into the café with her reusable tumbler in one hand and her briefcase in the other. She barked her usual order and checked the text message from her assistant while the barista prepared her coffee. Their bid for the takeover was successful. The owner contacted the firm at 4:00 a.m., not unusual when they were dealing with a family-run business teetering on the edge of bankruptcy but still doggedly hanging on as if waiting for a last-minute miracle.

They usually mulled and squirmed and finally came to their senses in the wee hours of the morning. She allowed a small smile to warm her usually stoic face. She'd chop Johnson's Textiles into pieces and sell the scraps off to the highest bidders. Not a bad Sunday morning. She stuck her platinum card into the reader and keyed in a twenty dollar tip for the barista, just because she could.

She snagged her tumbler and claimed a table by the window so she could see when April came in. Whenever that would be. Sometimes Janebeth swore that woman forgot a meeting time wasn't just a vague suggestion. At least she was never late to pick up their son from daycare or ferry him to and from his various lessons and practices. She sighed and rolled up the starched cuff of her dress shirt to check the time but stopped in confusion. She bared both wrists and gaped at them as if she expected to see something other than the unmarked, unblemished skin and expensive watch. She studied the thin platinum wedding band on her finger as if she'd never seen it before.

Unnerved, she shook her head and raked back her short-cropped hair with one hand. The motion brought another jolt of odd surprise as she had almost expected to feel a heavy twist held in a plastic clip. Janebeth took a glance into her tumbler just to check that she hadn't accidentally ordered some kind of mind-altering substance instead of Ethiopian Yirgacheffe.

The door jangled open and Janebeth looked up, expecting to see her wife of eleven years bustling in with her usual flustered apologies. Instead she saw a slim young woman standing alone in the doorway as if unsure whether to go up to the counter or bolt right back out to the street. She held a laptop to her chest. Her short blonde waves framed a face that was both sweet and shy. Her lips were soft pink and looked delicately kissable.

Janebeth's heart gave a jolt as the young woman turned her head and their eyes met. With that one look, Janebeth's entire body came alive. Her muscles twitched with the urge to leap up and pull the young woman into a crushing embrace, kiss her breathless, and never let her go. Nobody had ever made her feel like that, not even April who came into her life as a comforting presence rather than an earthshaking romance.

Shocked at herself, Janebeth dropped her eyes back to where her hands were clenched around her tumbler on the table. She had no idea who that young woman was and she would never allow herself to find out. April would show up and they'd go to Tremaine Department Store where Janebeth would wait as April dithered over the new tablecloths and towels she'd decided they needed. They'd pick Hunter up from junior kendo and go back to the townhouse on Village Street where their cook and house-keeper Helga would have dinner waiting for them. Life as usual. No surprises, no danger. Just money, business, and family. The way things should be.

A storm of giggling from the OMG girls yanked Jade back to reality. Connie was gone, but the lingering warmth of her presence stayed. Jade stood up and swallowed the rest of her coffee with resolution.

Fuck woolgathering and all that bullshit with alternative timelines. She had stuff to do. Things to look for. People to bother. With that thought, Jade returned her mug and threw out the pile of napkins she appeared to have gathered in her brief stay before she strode out of the coffee shop.

SHE BLEW INTO the police station and surprised Detective Young who was at his desk with his hand on his phone.

"Jeez Mayflower," he said as he retrieved his hand. "Can't you make appointments like normal people?"

"No," Jade told him.

"Look, I was just about to call you."

"And I appeared." She struck a diva pose. "Today's your lucky day."

He looked like it was quite the opposite as he sank down into his chair.

"Get anything with the Holloway fellow?"

Jade pressed her lips together and shook her head.

"Ah well, it was a long shot anyway." Young sighed and knit his fingers together behind his head. "I heard back from the phone trace people, looks like the earliest they can get the records is tomorrow."

Jade swallowed the stream of profanities that wanted to erupt from herself. "What am I supposed to do until then?"

"I dunno," Young said. "How about go out and enjoy your Sunday? It is Pride, after all. Aren't you right on the parade route? Should be a good show."

Jade gaped at him for a moment before she could speak.

"Yeah, I might do that." She stood and stuffed her hands in her pockets.

Jade got home just before the roadblocks went up. Already the sidewalks on both sides of the street were filled with rainbow-bedecked people and the air was buzzing with excitement. The bookstore had never been so busy. Even though Benny had warned her, Jade found it nerve-wracking. She looked around, but Benny and Jordan were nowhere in sight. Jim was selling rainbow bracelets and bottled water at a breakneck pace inside the bookstore and barely gave Jade a nod as she hurried through the milling crowd.

She poked her head into Addie's domain to return her aunt's car keys and received a Tupperware container of cooling tuna casserole with a spoon stuck into it.

"Don't eat that standing up," Addie said.

"Why would I?" Jade asked, even though she already had the spoon in her hand.

"Watching the parade. They'll be coming by any minute now," Addie said. "I'm gonna be watching from my place. First time I'm not seeing it on the TV. Can't wait to see all those pretty guys and drag queens in real life."

Jade paused with her eyebrows raised and the spoon in her mouth. She went back down to her place and dutifully plopped onto a kitchen chair before she shoveled in her food. The washed Tupperware had just landed in her dish rack when the first strains of Samba music filtered through the air.

"Jade! The parade's starting!" Connie's voice brought Jade over to the window in a single bound.

Jade shared a grin with Connie as she opened the window and leaned both elbows on the sill. Connie hovered next to her, occasionally flitting around Jade. Courtesy of Benny, the building was decked out in Pride colors and rainbow flags flapped merrily in the breeze on either side of the window. On the second floor, Jade was treated to a great view of everything. She didn't know what to expect and sucked in a hard breath at the sight of the colorful floats and organized groups. Every type of person Jade had ever imagined was there. Most of them displayed some kind of colorful flag, some held signs, some danced. All of them were smiling and waving, proud and bold and free in the sunlight.

Emotion choked her. Jade pressed a hand to her mouth.

"Are you okay?" Connie asked.

"Yeah," Jade said. She blinked a few times. "It's just a bit of a shock, you know. I'm not used to all this...celebration and openness, you know? This is my first time seeing the parade, I just missed it last year. It's cool, really cool how much things have changed."

"I think so too," Connie said in a small voice. "I can't believe I nearly threw this all away."

Jade wished she could put an arm around Connie.

A float came into view. It was decorated with plywood clouds and held a herd of children, each dressed in a different color. Seated in the middle on a raised throne-like cloud was Ross wearing a halo made from gold tinsel. His long hair and beard spread out over his robes. He smiled benignly down over the crowds. As he passed Jade's building, he looked up and gave them a big grin and wave.

"Looking good, dude!" Jade hollered out. "Praise Rainbow Jesus!"

"There's Sky," Connie said. She leaned out farther and waved enthusiastically as if she'd forgotten she was invisible to most people. Jade stifled a laugh at her bubbly eagerness. It was a marked change from the miserable, lost specter that appeared in Jade's office only a week ago.

Below them, Sky popped around and threw wrapped candies into the crowd, looking like she was having the time of her life.

"What a cutie," Jade said.

"Have you ever thought about it?" Connie asked in a small, introspective voice. "Starting a family."

"Not seriously, but if I had a guarantee it'd turn out like Sky," Jade said, "I'd consider having a kid."

"You would?" Connie turned to look at her. Her lips quirked up. "You'd definitely be the fun parent, not the strict one."

"Maybe," Jade said. She leaned her chin on one hand. "How about you, Connie? Ever thought about becoming a mother?"

Connie shook her head. "Not really. I don't know if I'd be any good at it."

"You know what, I think you'd be a wonderful, understanding, and cool mom. Not to mention sweet and damn cute."

Connie's hands came up and covered her cheeks the way she did whenever Jade gave her a compliment. "It's kind of moot, now. I never had anyone I wanted to have a family with." She glanced at Jade and asked, "Would you adopt or go the old-fashioned route?"

Jade focused on the parade in front of them as she said, "Definitely adopt. I don't want to deal with crying and diapers and all that shit. If I ever do the family thing, I'd get an older kid, maybe eight or ten years old. After all, I'm coming to this motherhood thing kind of late, so it makes sense."

"That's wonderful and generous of you," Connie said. "I don't know if I could do that. Be responsible for an entire human being. Making them into a decent person and releasing them into society."

"When you put it that way, it sounds kind of serious," Jade said. "But going the whole kid route is only one option. I'd be just as happy with a shelter dog or a hamster or even a friendly cactus, as long as I've got someone I love in my life. That's all I need."

Connie went quiet and started flickering and fading away. Jade had done it again. She ached to see Connie leave.

Thinking quickly, Jade said, "Wanna hear a secret? Ross and me go way back, like to kindergarten. We were each other's first kiss in junior high school."

That did the trick. Connie's form solidified and the flickering stopped. She stared at Jade in wonder.

"See, we both liked girls and decided to try it out," Jade said as a float full of drag queens passed by. She had to speak louder to be heard over the thumping dance beat. "Ross was still presenting as female back then. When we kissed, it was okay but something was off, you know? Kind of answered a bunch of questions for both of us, though. For the record, you have nothing to worry about, Connie."

"I'm not worried," Connie said with an adorable flush. "But thanks for telling me anyway."

Jade knit her fingers together and turned her attention to the scene in front of her. She wanted to bring up the words she'd let slip earlier but didn't want to shout them over the cacophony of music, shouts, and the occasional tooting horn. As precious and limited as their time was, Jade couldn't bring herself to speak.

"Hey cutie! Over here!"

Startled, Jade turned her attention onto a passing float, which

held a number of bikini-clad dancers. One of them, a stunning tat-
tooed violet-haired beauty, looked Jade square in the eye before
she yanked up her top and flashed Jade.

"Janie, get that nice young lady's number! I think she likes
you," Addie's voice filtered down to them.

"Thanks for the show, but sorry," Jade called out as soon as
her voice came back. She leaned closer to where Connie was hovering and said in a low voice, "I've already got my eye on someone. That is, if she's willing."

Jade didn't turn her head, but she heard Connie's little
shocked gasp and laugh. This time, Connie didn't vanish.

Chapter Nineteen

AFTER THE LOUD music faded and the crowds drifted off, Jade sleepily got ready for bed. She finished tying her drawstring pajama pants and shook out her hair. Even though Benny called her a number of times, each in an increasing state of drunkenness, with invitations to par-tay at several different establishments of no doubt ill-repute, Jade refused. She wanted to bask in the comfort and silence of her room. Silence, but not solitude. Even after everything Jade said, Connie was still hanging around. Jade poked her head out of the bedroom and caught Connie sheepishly hovering in the kitchen.

"Sorry, it's late. I'll go," she said.

"No, it's okay, I don't want you to leave." Jade held out a hand and said in a gentle voice, "How about coming in here?"

"Are you asking me to..." Connie looked both nervous and excited.

Jade wrinkled her nose in the expression she'd inadvertently picked up from Connie. "I'm not propositioning you. I, um, don't think I could tonight. I just want to feel you next to me." Jade took a step back and held the bedroom door open. Her heart banged in her chest but she kept her expression soft. "Come and lie down with me."

Jade didn't wait for an answer before she flipped the light switch and flopped down on her bed. In the darkness, Jade burrowed under the comforter with a sleepy sigh that turned into a yawn. She wasn't sure if Connie would, or even could, accept her offer but not even a minute passed before Jade was aware of a cool softness beside her. The presence was thinner than Jade remembered, more elusive. She fought the nagging fear that Connie was losing the battle, that she was slowly fading away. She couldn't think about that. Not tonight. Jade closed her eyes and simply enjoyed the closeness. It wasn't nearly enough, but Jade knew it would have to do.

She was just drifting off when Connie's voice roused her.

"What do you think it's like?"

"What is, sweetie?" Jade mumbled.

"Dying."

Jade took a deep breath and rolled over onto her back. She crossed her arms behind her head and glanced over to the translucent young woman next to her. Connie lay on her side, curled up on top of the comforter with that same lonely, lost kitten look she had the first night Jade met her.

"I can't say for sure," Jade said with a wry twist of her lips. "But I don't think it's unpleasant. Being stuck in between has to be worse."

"I'm scared. I don't want to just vanish. What if I'm trapped in darkness forever? What if I just—become nothing?"

"Sweetheart." Jade's heart ached. "Think about what it was like before you were born. Yeah, it was probably dark, but it's not like you minded. I don't think we vanish. I think we go somewhere we don't have an individual consciousness. Like some kind of primordial ocean out there and this thing we call life is just a tiny blip on the entire, endless scope of everything, from infinity to infinity. Think about returning to an eternal hug where you'll never be alone because you aren't a single being." She paused and shot a grin at Connie. "Bet you didn't think I was this full of woo-woo bullshit, did you?"

"If I could pick up a pillow, I'd be hitting you with it," Connie propped her head up on one hand. Her delicate lips quirked up and Jade had the almost overwhelming urge to kiss the dimple that appeared with the smile. "Thanks."

"No problem," Jade said and yawned again before she could stop herself.

"I'm keeping you up, go to sleep. Good night, Jade."

Jade mumbled and buried her face into her pillow.

WHEN SHE WOKE, Connie was gone. The room felt empty and Jade got a slight frisson of unease as she wondered if Connie was all right. She decided to head over to the hospital right away. Jade threw on some clothes and blew into the bookstore, which looked like a hurricane had hit after the festivities of the previous day. Jade exchanged a rushed greeting with a somewhat hungover Benny who was cleaning up the masses of glitter someone saw fit to sprinkle liberally over the entire bookstore.

"Care to give me a hand?" Benny asked in a pathetic voice.

"I, uh, aw shit, Ben." Jade paused with her hand on the front door when her phone buzzed in her pocket. It was Detective Young.

"Mayflower," Jade answered in a clipped voice.

"I got the phone records if you want to swing by and take a look-see."

"I'll be there ASAP," Jade said. She ended the call and called over her shoulder, "Sorry to bail on cleanup, but I gotta go."

He waved limply and continued sweeping.

Since Addie and her car had already left for the day, Jade dashed into the street and flung herself onto a bus that had just pulled into the stop in front of the building. On the way, Jade fidgeted and tried not to pace too much within the confines of the bus as the early-morning commuters glanced at her. A few minutes later, Jade pounded into the station. She didn't slow down until she was in front of Young's desk.

Without looking up, Young pulled a printed sheet of paper from the piles on his desk and handed it over.

Breathlessly, Jade scanned the paper. Someone made a call two hours before the 9-1-1 call. She stared at the number and spat a phrase that, loosely translated into polite speech would be, "Great Scott!"

Suddenly it all made sense. Who was the most helpful, practically shoving suspects and motives her way? Who was almost too interested in the case, going to great lengths to keep abreast of the latest developments? It was all too convenient. And Jade had a feeling she knew why.

"I've got to get out of here. Mind if I keep this?" Jade shoved the paper into her bag.

She was already in motion and barely heard Young's voice behind her. "Help yourself. It's on the house."

Jade tried frantically to hail a cab with nothing to show for it except a few strange looks from a group of joggers pushing baby strollers. A nondescript navy blue car pulled up beside her. Young was behind the wheel.

He leaned over and unlocked the passenger's side door. Shocked and more than a little grateful, Jade got into the car.

"Buckle up," he said.

"Yes sir!"

"So where are you off to in such a hurry?"

"You know where Connie works, that office building on Bruin and Gable?"

"Out by the Public Gardens? Yep."

"You need to get us there as fast as you can. Step on it," Jade said and pounded on the dashboard. "You got a siren in here? And turn on your green-light changer thingy too."

"We can't just turn lights green, you know." Young sighed as he took a corner at a suitably dangerous pace. "What's the emergency then? Something I need to know about?"

"I can't believe I was so stupid," Jade muttered under her breath. She cradled her head in her hands. "I can't believe I didn't know. Fuck me, I'm a useless fucking idiot!"

"Hey, don't beat yourself up, kid."

A large hand landed on Jade's shoulder. She looked across at Young. He retrieved his hand and focused his gaze on the road. The old nickname brought Jade back from the dark place she was headed.

Young said, "You know a lot. More than any of us should maybe. That's your gift and your burden. But nobody can know everything. You're doing the best you can."

"Thanks, big guy." Jade pulled herself up straight. Strength flowed through her limbs. She still had time to make things right. It wasn't too late.

The building appeared in front of them. Jade bolted out of the car before it was fully stopped, which earned a warning from Young.

Jade hauled ass into the building and left a trail of shocked people milling about in her wake. She stabbed the elevator button with her finger a few times before she gave up and raced up the stairs. She took them two at a time and sometimes three when she got a good leap in.

Jade barreled into the office like a runaway locomotive. She locked eyes with Vicki for an instant and couldn't stop the raw, feral growl that echoed from the depths of her soul. The next moment, Vickie whirled and bolted. She scampered out to the fire escape and clanged down it.

In a blind rage, Jade shoved people out of the way in her haste to get to the fire escape. She ripped open the safety doors and stumbled onto the landing. Her boots clanked against the iron mesh grating. Jade looked down and saw a slim form pattering downward a few floors underneath her.

Jade whipped out her cell phone and dialed faster than she ever had in her life.

"Young!" Jade hollered into it the second he picked up. "Get your ass in motion! We got a runner heading down the fire escape. East side of the building."

She shoved her phone into her bag. Vickie had a head start but Jade was in good shape and her longer legs closed the distance between them until Jade was only half a floor behind her. As Vickie reached street level, Jade jumped the remaining steps.

She staggered but still managed to propel herself forward. Her bangs fell into her face and Jade impatiently shook them out as she pounded after the fleeing young woman.

Vickie looked over her shoulder at Jade before she grabbed a bunch of garbage cans and threw them down onto the sidewalk. Without slowing, Jade kicked the cans out of the way, spilling wadded-up papers and fast food containers everywhere.

Once she was clear, Jade hollered, "Just wanna talk, Vickie! Nothing bad!"

Vickie kept running as if she hadn't heard. Jade blew out curse words left, right, and center as she followed.

A bus roared past, dangerously close and Vickie stumbled, giving Jade the chance to catch up with her. She lunged and snagged Vickie by the collar of her uniform vest.

"Let go of me!" Vickie shrieked. "I didn't do anything." She kicked and squirmed as Jade dragged her off the road. People around stopped and looked at them.

"I just want to talk to you," Jade said. "If you've done nothing, then you've got nothing to be afraid of."

"Why don't you give up?" Vickie hissed. She tried to pull away but Jade held her tightly. Vickie turned to the people who were gawking and shouted, "Help! Get her away from me! I didn't do anything!"

Jade let out a resigned sigh. She got Vickie into a wristlock and shoved her face down onto the sidewalk.

"If you didn't hurt Connie, then why did you run?"

"You were the one chasing me like a deranged lunatic." The cute and sparkly Vickie was back. Even with her face inches from the pavement, she didn't give up her act. "Come on, you know I never would do anything to Connie. And you're hurting me. You don't have to be so rough. That's not my kink."

"Uh huh. Tell that to the judge."

The navy blue car pulled up beside them. Young rolled his window down and hooked his arm over the side.

"What's going on here?" Young asked.

"I need you to apprehend this suspect for the attempted murder of Connie Mason."

"All right, we can take her in for questioning. But I'm warning you, this had better be solid. We don't want a repeat of what happened to Holloway."

"Yeah, that really was too bad," Vickie said. She raised her head from the sidewalk with a mean smirk. "He was too chicken to go to jail."

"How did you know about that?" Jade breathed.

For the first time, Vickie looked worried. Her eyes darted around. "People talk."

"I'm sure they do." Young got out of the car and crouched down beside Vickie. "Are you going to give me an excuse to cuff you, young lady?"

"You wouldn't," she pouted.

"Wanna try me and see?"

"No." Vickie sulked as she let herself be guided into the car.

"Buckle up," Young said over his shoulder. Vickie rolled her eyes at him and didn't comply as the car pulled into traffic.

"What did you do to Connie?" Jade gritted. She twisted against her own seatbelt to glare into the backseat.

"Look, this is all a big misunderstanding." Vickie leaned forward and put one hand on Jade's shoulder. "Come on, Jade, talk to me. You've been so nice to me until now." The sweet tone of her voice sickened Jade and she jerked away.

"Then tell me where I'm getting the idea that you had something to do with Connie's, how shall we put it, accident?"

"I don't know what you're talking about," Vickie said. She rose up against the back of Jade's seat and stroked her finger down the side of Jade's neck. "Don't be mad, okay?"

"Sit your ass down," Jade snapped and shoved her away. "Before I make you."

Vickie plopped down onto the seat and crossed her arms. "Now you're just being a bitch because you couldn't get into my panties."

"Oh yeah, that's it," Jade said.

Jade's leg jiggled irritably as Young stopped at a red light. The light changed to green and Jade noticed two things at the same time as the car rolled into the intersection. The first was a red ball wedged into the space between her seat and Young's, the second was the slamming of the car door behind her.

"Shit, Young stop the—"

She never got to finish.

The smoke grenade exploded into a wall of white foam. Young slammed on the brakes and the car behind smashed into them. The front wheels jumped over the curb and the car impacted with something. Jade let out a shout as the airbag deployed in her face and everything went dark.

When Jade woke up, it was through a white haze. The sound of rushing water filled her ears. The windshield in front of her was cracked and torrents of water gushed down over the glass. A few icy rivulets spurted through the cracks. Jade tried to get her breathing back under control as she took in the situation. She felt like she'd run into a wall. Twin bands of pain radiated across her chest and hips from the seatbelt.

Beside her, Young was sprawled over the driver's seat with the deflated airbag hanging from the steering wheel. The powdery stink of the inflating agents crawled up Jade's nose and down her throat. He groaned and stirred against his seatbelt.

"Jade!"

She looked up to see Connie. Her face distorted into a raw scream.

"Something's wrong. I can't see. Something's taking my air! It's coming for me—"

"Connie, baby hang on," Jade said. She reached over and grabbed Young by the shoulder. She gave him a quick shake. "Wake up, big guy."

"What happened?" Young gasped. He rubbed at his chest.

"She had one of those smoke grenade things on her," Jade said. Young's glasses had flown off somewhere, but he was awake and seemed relatively unhurt. Her heart pounded. Jade had to get out of there. She had a choice, try and find where Vickie had run off or go to Connie. It was no choice at all. Jade paused with her hand on the door handle. "Are you gonna be okay?"

"Don't worry about me," Young said. "Go."

Jade didn't need to hear any more than that. She wrenched the door open and her boots hit the pavement. Freezing water dashed the breath from her lungs the instant she left the car.

"My friend's in there," she shouted over her shoulder as she shoved her way through the gathered crowd. "Take care of him."

The hospital was only a block away.

Jade took off at a dead run as Connie's cries rang in her ears.

JADE RODE INTO the hospital on a wave of pure adrenaline. The nurses and a few patients in the lobby gave her alarmed looks.

"Get off! I'm not here as a patient," Jade hollered and shoved at a uniformed woman who came at her with a clipboard. She shouldered past the woman and pounded down the hall. She heard lots of "Hey!" and "Watch where you're going!" plus a few instances of "No running in the hall!".

Jade burst through Connie's door. The air was alive with warning bells from the various machines around her still form. The slowly jumping line on her heart monitor was weak and jerky. Vickie stood over Connie with her back to the door. Galvanized by rage, Jade launched herself across the room. She grabbed Vickie in a stranglehold and twisted back, away from the bed. They landed in a tumble on the hallway floor.

Jade got up onto her knees. She seized Vickie by the collar of her vest and slammed her up against the wall.

"How did you know Connie was here?"

"Let go of me, you insane bitch! I have every right to be here. Connie's mom called and asked me to make sure Connie was okay."

A cold, sick feeling grabbed Jade. Of course, Connie believed Vickie was her friend. Maybe even her best friend.

Vickie slapped at Jade. "This is assault, you know. Somebody help!"

"Nobody's gonna help you," Jade hissed. She was so angry her arms shook.

"Whatever. I don't need help," Vickie said. Her eyes flicked over to the room where Connie lay. Vickie pulled the corners of her lips down in a mockery of sadness. "Not as much as she does.

Poor thing."

The coldness in her eyes chilled Jade. Even on the inside, she'd only seen that kind of cold calculation in a very rare brand of person, the kind who did things that made people want to reinstate the death penalty. Suddenly a piercing alarm split the air.

Shouting preceded a group of doctors and nurses who raced into the room with a crash cart between them. They didn't spare a glance to the two women in the hall.

"What did you do to her?" Jade whispered.

"I didn't do anything," Vickie said. She twisted in Jade's grip. "I was just here at a lucky time. Check the security cameras. I didn't have time to do anything before your crazy Amazon butt barreled in and started freaking out. Besides, it looks like you're going to be out a client soon. Shouldn't you be, like, saying good-bye or something?"

"She dies and you're a murderer."

"I don't think so." Vickie looked much too confident.

The realization hit Jade. If Connie never woke up, the case would die with her. True or not, ghostly visions were not considered valid evidence of foul play.

Jade's fist tightened on the front of Vickie's vest. She lowered her head until they were nose-to-nose in what would be an intimate gesture if Jade's teeth hadn't been bared in a snarl. She spoke in a low, barely controlled growl, "You were there, at the bridge. Connie knew you were there and she called you for help. Your fucking phone was the last thing Connie heard, right before you bashed her across the face." Jade's voice was raw. "She came to you for help and you pushed her off that ladder. You smashed her hands and let her fall. And the whole time you were sexting some random jerkoff like the soulless cuntrag you are."

"Oh, aren't we Sherlock Fucking Holmes," Vickie spat the words. In disgust, Jade turned her head slightly to avoid the spray. "I don't know how the fuck you know what she heard, but nobody's gonna be able to prove it. Looks like the only witness isn't with us anymore."

Vickie smirked in triumph. The air was broken by a single sound. The still, deadly tone of a flat line.

Jade heard someone cry out in her own voice. The room tilted and sounds came at her as if though a bottle were held to her ear. Her throat closed. Her hands went numb. Jade was peripherally aware of Vickie yanking herself away but her only thought was for Connie. She pressed a hand to her face to shut out the frantic activity, unable to fight the gaping maw of loss that followed the silence after every shouted "Clear!".

It was unthinkable that Connie had been taken so soon, her voice silenced before she could even begin to speak. Jade closed her eyes and clenched her hands into desperate fists as she wished she could join Connie. Something broke inside of her. She *slipped*.

Jade didn't feel her body hit the floor.

Icy, howling wind tore at her like claws. Jade fought her way across the shuddering hospital room. She didn't even flinch when a team of orderlies ran right through her. Her goal was a small, ashen column of light by the window.

"Connie!" Jade screamed into the maelstrom.

The young woman turned dead eyes to her.

"Jade, you shouldn't be here."

"I couldn't let you go," Jade said. She dragged her sleeve across her face. "Not without telling you how much I meant what I said in Benny's office."

"You love me?" the words were barely audible over the roaring wind.

"Yes I do," Jade said. "Connie, I loved you from the first time you said Fuckity McFuckfurters and everything you've done and everything you've said just makes me love you more."

Connie turned away. She buried her face in her hands. "I waited so long to hear those words but now I wish you'd never said them. *I'm* the reason why I was alone. I always found reasons not to text people back. I was busy whenever anyone asked me out. That's the person I was out there and not who I am here. I changed. You changed me, Jade." She whirled to face Jade. "If I go back, what if I lose everything that happened here? What if I don't know you? What if I push you away like I did to every single other person who gave me a chance?"

"If you don't remember me, I'll introduce myself," Jade said.

Each word was a battle.

Her chest felt heavy.

Every breath was harder than the last. "If you don't answer my texts, I'll call. If you're busy, I'll wait and ask again. I won't pressure you, sweetheart. I'll give you as many chances to say no as you want. If you say yes, I'll bring you flowers and cook for you and invite you on drives to the ocean." Jade struggled to speak. "But if you're determined to stay here, I will too because I'm not going back without you. I love you and I'm not going to leave you here." She held out a hand. The room around them was fading out. Jade didn't have much time left.

"No," Connie said in a tiny voice. Her head came up and she continued, strong and sure. "Even if I never do anything else, I can't let you die." She lunged and shoved Jade hard in the chest with both hands.

With a wrenching jolt, Jade sucked in a sharp breath. She was flat on her back on the cold floor of the hallway. She batted away the oxygen mask someone was holding over her face and heaved her body upright. She staggered to her feet and tried to push her way into Connie's room but a burly nurse got an arm in front of her and blocked her in the doorway.

"You can't go in there," he said.

Jade struggled to get past him. She couldn't leave, she had to know. He was strong and determined, but so was Jade. The activity around Connie's prone form hadn't ceased. If anything, it was more frantic than ever.

"Connie!" Jade shouted and made a lunge against the nurse's arm.

The room fell silent for a blinding split second.

Then she heard it.

Blip.

Blip.

Blip.

The heartbeat was back. A shock of joy filled Jade.

The figure in the bed struggled against hands that pulled the breathing tube from her throat. The young woman coughed. She rubbed at her throat as she drew in a breath.

Connie.

Heart pounding, Jade fell back and watched through the Plexiglas window as if in a dream. She bit her lip as a load of feelings landed in her gut. Surrounded by bustling nurses, Connie blinked and twisted around in confusion. Her face was pale. She looked shockingly young.

Jade froze as if breathing would break the spell.

"That was quite a show you put on," one of the nurses said, not unkindly. "How are you feeling?"

Connie moved her mouth. Nothing more than a croaking sound came out.

A scuffle beside her caught Jade's attention. Vickie stood in the doorway. She fixed Connie with the kind of expression one would have upon finding a nice, toasty rat carcass baked into your meatloaf.

Connie raised a battered hand. She pointed a finger at Vickie. "You," she mouthed.

Quick as a fleeing snake, Vickie took off at a dash down the hallway. Jade whirled and barreled after her.

She didn't get far.

With a squeak, Vickie collided with a scruffy and unmoving man. Young.

"Not so fast, miss," Young said as he held Vickie still with a long-practiced grip. "I think it's time you told us what this is all about."

"That stupid bitch should have died!" Vickie shouted and struggled in Young's grasp. "Okay, yeah so I bricked that pathetic, plain-Jane loser," she screamed the words at Jade, who fell back a step. Vickie laughed and continued, "You should have seen her dragging her sorry self up that ladder, all crying and looking like an old dishrag. Just gasping for air. No wonder that ugly pug-nosed cow was single as fuck. She sucked at being a dyke. Who would want to get near someone who was such a fuckup they couldn't even kill themselves?"

Jade's face twisted with rage. She twitched with the urge to smash that grin off Vickie's face.

Vickie spat, "Living was too good for her. Just like that pathetic loser Gord. They're both better off dead."

"So you admit you killed Gord?" Jade rasped.

"No way. I just listened to his troubles," she gloated. "Got him drunk and let him know what to expect from prison. The rest he did himself. I didn't even have to drive him to a bridge or slip roofies into his drink or anything. He was much easier than Connie. That took *months* of planning."

Jade staggered back a step. She felt as if she'd been stabbed in the chest. Jade said, "You were her friend. She trusted you and you fucked her over."

"Not literally," Vickie said with a snort. "I've never been that desperate."

"Connie is twice the woman you'll ever be," Jade snapped. "You don't have the slightest clue what a special, wonderful, funny, and unique person she is."

"What makes her so special?" Vickie shouted with her arms flung wide. "What makes Connie Mason so special she gets the best desk in the whole office? Why does she get to be the score-keeper for billiards, huh? And leading Gord on like that? Being so nice to him and swinging her hair in his face and all? That little slut was just making him think he had a chance with her when she was only leading him on! I should have told Gord when I had Connie's stupid trusting ass drugged and in his car so she could have actually gotten a little rape—" She didn't get to finish as Jade let loose with a backhand across her face.

"Don't use that word lightly around me," Jade said through clenched teeth. "Ever."

It wasn't even the hardest Jade could have hit, more like a prac-tice tap, but Vickie crashed down to the floor in a boneless heap. Vickie held her hands over her face and her shoulders shivered.

"You hit me," Vickie said in a shocked, quivering voice. "Nobody hits me! Everybody likes me!"

"Guess what," Jade said. "I don't."

Vickie's head came up. Jade saw the soulless killer flash through her eyes again. The real Vickie. That time might not land her on the inside for long—or at all—but eventually she would cross that line. Jade was sure of it.

Suddenly Vickie turned to Young and whined, "She hit me. You have to arrest her!"

"Sorry," Young said, "I didn't see anything just now. Come on, let's get going. I'm afraid I'm going to have to ask you to wear these." He dug out a pair of handcuffs and snapped them into place before he led her away.

As Vickie passed Jade, she sneered, "I had to brush my teeth a hundred times after kissing you once. You're a disgusting pig. Watching you eat is like seeing someone puking backward."

"Uh huh. You might want to try the speed-eating thing," Jade said with a knowing arch of one brow. "It'll come in handy on the inside."

Young left with Vickie and a feeling of disbelief settled over Jade. While she ached to go inside the room and see Connie, a part of her was terrified at what might be waiting for her.

"You have to leave now," one of the nurses said. "Just for a bit, okay? This is ICU after all. Don't worry, you can see her in a little while."

"Okay, okay. I'm going."

As Jade backed away, she caught a glimpse of Connie through the Plexiglas window. She looked so small and lost and scared in the middle of all that bustle, it took all of Jade's will-power not to run back into the room.

Someone ushered Jade to a utilitarian waiting room a ways down the hall. Jade collapsed onto the molded plastic bench and dropped her head into her hands. Her cheeks were wet with tears. She let out a shaky breath as she tried to get herself together.

After a moment, Jade ducked into a washroom where she splashed her face with cold water and stood under the hot-air dryer until she felt somewhat human again. On her way back, Jade dialed Trevor's number.

"Greene here."

"Hey, it's Jade Mayflower," she said.

"Oh, hi! What's up? Any news?"

"Yeah. Good news." Jade let out a shaky breath. A smile broke over her face. "That girl you called the ambulance for? She just woke up. She's going to make it. You saved her life, my friend."

"That's great. Thanks for letting me know."

"No problem." Saying the words made it real. Connie was awake. She was going to be okay. Now all Jade had to do was fig-ure out what the hell to do with herself.

After what seemed like an eternity, a nurse came into the waiting room.

"We've finished with Ms. Mason if you'd like to see her."

"Yeah, I do. Thank you," Jade said as she got to her feet. A rush of nerves made her knees want to give out but Jade managed to get herself back to Connie's room.

Connie looked up as Jade entered. She was free from the breathing machine, but the gauze and bandages and the rest of the wires and tubes were still there. Her hair was lank and dirty and her face mottled with bruises. Connie was more beautiful than Jade had ever seen her. Alan hovered at Connie's bedside, but when he saw Jade, he stepped back with a knowing look and busied himself with something in the corner. In silence, Jade shuffled into the room and stood awkwardly beside Connie's bed. Their eyes met. Jade swallowed the rush of nerves.

Connie looked at her with wide eyes. Jade couldn't tell if she was scared or confused.

Jade's heart pounded. Her breath came hard and fast. Her hands shook. She was scared — not as scared as she'd been standing in front of the judge waiting for that gavel to fall, not even as much as she'd been on the bus that took her down the long road to Dorvelle, but still plenty scared. She had to know, but the words didn't come.

Connie was the first to break the silence.

"Jade. Mayflower," Connie whispered. Each syllable of her name hit Jade like a bolt of pure joy.

A rush of relief ripped Jade's fear in two. Jade blinked back sudden tears and said, "You remember me."

Connie's lips quirked into a quicksilver grin that sent another shock of joy through Jade. She could only catch her breath. Connie wrinkled her nose in the slightly shy way that never failed to steal Jade's reason.

"How could I forget you?

Slowly, reverently, Jade held out her hand. Connie looked at it for a long moment before she reached out and placed her fingers in Jade's palm. The young woman didn't move as Jade took her hand in the gentlest grip she could. An electric thrill rippled through her with the first brush of Connie's skin on hers. The healing scabs were rough against Jade's fingers but she didn't give them a second thought.

"I was afraid you were a dream," Connie said in a soft, bruised-sounding voice.

"I'm no dream, sweetheart. I'm right here and I'm not going anywhere, not unless you want me to." Jade fidgeted, still holding onto Connie's hand. "I mean, you've been through a lot all at once. You might want some time to yourself."

"No, I want you to stay with me. Please, Jade."

Jade wanted to sing and shout. A huge, goofy grin broke all over her face.

"Are you still going to call me?" Connie asked.

"Hell yeah," Jade said. "I'm going to call you and text you too. I'm going to bring you flowers and home-cooked dinners and take you on drives to the ocean."

"Are you going to kiss me?" The light of mischief Jade knew so well danced in Connie's eyes.

"If you want me to." Jade thought her heart would burst through her chest.

"Yes, I do."

Slowly, aching with the effort to restrain the wave of need that urged her forward, Jade reached out and cupped Connie's face. With the softest touch she was capable of, she drew her thumb over Connie's lip, which elicited a short gasp. Jade leaned down and, just as softly, pressed her lips to Connie's. The first kiss was chaste and light. Connie moved to meet her, opening her mouth the smallest bit and Jade leaned into the next kiss.

Jade was in heaven. She wanted that moment to last forever. She fought to hold back the rush of desire that burned through her. Connie made a soft sound in her throat and Jade drew back. Connie pressed a bandaged hand to her chest with a look of discomfort on her face.

"I'm sorry, babe, did I hurt you?" Jade's words caught in her throat. She wanted to kick herself. "Aw shit, I didn't mean to come on too strong. After what you've been through, you must feel like hell."

"I'm okay," Connie said. "It hurts but I'm alive, Jade. The pain will go away soon, but I won't." She took a shaky breath and met Jade's eyes. She was glowing with strength. "I'm back and I'm not going to run away from life again."

Jade couldn't help but reach out and cradle Connie's face in her hand. She couldn't speak, but words weren't necessary.

Epilogue

"WHY THE HELL did I let you talk me into this black tie beach shit again?" Jade asked.

Benny tossed his head and put his hands on his hips, a pose which was at odds with the sleek black tux he had on. "Because it's fun and you spend every single day at the hospital. You need to get some fresh air and sun. Just be glad I'm not making you ride the subway with no pants on."

"I look like a penguin."

"You know you make a damn sexy penguin."

Jade had to crack a grin at that.

She tugged at her white tuxedo jacket and flapped the tails around her legs, also clad in the finest white. The only splash of color was the sea foam green scarf she wore at her opened collar instead of a bow tie. The scarf matched the delicate silk rose in her buttonhole. Both items were from Benny who produced them with an air of mystery Jade was still puzzling over. She'd pulled her hair back into a long ponytail with a white bow and even though Jade was complaining, she felt pretty good in the formal-wear.

A figure came into view. Benny waved an arm and called out, "Over here, Jordie!"

In a black tuxedo that matched Benny's, Jordan trotted over. He almost fell into the sand as Benny greeted him with a running hug. Jordan accented his own tux with a metallic purple cummer-bund and matching bow tie. With a patient and gentle air, he lifted his chin as Benny tutted over him and fiddled with the tie.

Satisfied, Benny struck a pose with his boyfriend, arm in arm. "How do we look?"

"Like the top of a San Francisco wedding cake," Jade said. She broke down and gave them an indulgent smile.

"Pose for the 'before' pic!" Benny sang as he held his phone at arms' length. Jade complied with a sigh.

Once the photo-documentation was over, Jade gave Benny a gentle shove. "All right, go off and play now. Be good."

"Of course." Benny grabbed Jordan's hand and they both scrambled off. Their laughing voices melded with the shouts of the crowd and the hiss of the waves. All around Jade, people in tuxedos and flowing dresses enjoyed the beach. Some of them threw beach balls and Frisbees. A few brave souls waded into the frigid Atlantic waters where saltwater soaked the luxurious fabrics.

Jade looked out over the flat grey expanse of the ocean and let out a long breath. The tableau was missing one important piece. Connie's physical therapy was progressing very well, but it had only been a month since she'd woken up from her coma and they were taking things slow. With her hands stuffed in her pockets, Jade kicked at the sand with the toe of her white, slightly scuffed tennis shoe.

Things were moving slowly between her and Connie as well, out of necessity. Connie was moved into a lower-intensity ward and was sharing a room with three other patients. Privacy become a rare commodity.

With a long-honed talent for finding secluded spots, Jade discovered a number of good places for some time alone with Connie — seldom-trafficked so as not to piss off the nurses. Her lip quirked up as she remembered the passionate kisses they shared just the day before in their favorite linen closet. Jade never thought her twenty years in prison would come in handy when finding ways to sneak kisses with her girlfriend.

God, did she, ex-con and professional ghost detective Jade Mayflower, actually have a girlfriend? And what a girlfriend. Connie was beautiful, strong, and sweet. She loved the home-made food Jade brought over in Tupperware containers and even laughed at her jokes. The way she gazed up at Jade made her feel like there was nothing she couldn't do. Once they actually met in person, Addie became a huge fan of Connie as well and Jade had to fend off unsubtle jabs about "Ms. Right" and "don't let this one get away" whenever she was around. While Jade did want to discuss the future with Connie in more detail, she didn't think the time was quite right yet.

Jade shaded her eyes and scanned the beach for Benny and Jordan. She found them involved in a lively game of catch with another young couple and a golden retriever. Jade returned their wave then dropped her hand. The wind whipped her tails around her legs. Watching the happy couples, Jade felt quite alone.

"Jade. Mayflower." The voice behind her caused Jade to freeze. Her heart gave a great kick. "You are absolutely stunning in that tux."

Jade spun in her tracks. Her breath caught in her throat. Connie stood a couple meters away with a pair of strappy sandals hanging from one hand. Her soft golden hair fanned about her face in the ocean breeze. She was a vision of classic beauty in a simple dress of sheer cream lace over the finest sea foam green silk that hugged her slim body and fell to her ankles. Suddenly everything made sense. Jade understood why Benny insisted she wear that scarf and Jordan drove there in his own car. The three of them must have been plotting the surprise all along. Jade was impressed and humbled.

"They let you out?" was the only thing Jade could think of to say.

"Yes." Connie gave Jade a knee-melting smile and spun around. The hem of her dress billowed out around her legs. She hopped over to where Jade was standing dumbstruck. She pressed up against the sleek white jacket and threaded her arm through Jade's. "Not that I don't love spending my days sneaking around like we're still in high school, but it would be nice to have some actual privacy and no time limit."

"Yeah, it would," Jade said.

Connie dropped her sandals. She drew close to Jade and whispered in her ear, "Because I want to try out what we've been practicing in the linen closet in my bed. Or yours. It doesn't matter where, just someplace without interruption."

"Connie," Jade breathed. "Yeah, I'd like that too. Very much."

Jade couldn't be still anymore. She reached out and took Connie's face in her hands. Desire and love flared into life as she lowered her head for a slow, lingering kiss. A passing guy catcalled them but Jade didn't care. She gave a low moan as Connie's hands slipped under her jacket and slender arms wrapped around her waist. One hand drifted lower and cupped her backside. Connie gave her a squeeze, which led to Jade whispering, "Naughty girl," while nipping Connie on the neck. Jade finished off by kissing the sweet little dip between her collarbones.

"So, do you want to go find the guys?" Jade asked. She sank

back a step and tried to get her breathing under control. "We can play in the sand and wreck these fancy-shmancy second-hand outfits."

Connie nodded and they headed back toward the beach where Jordan was being buried in the sand by a gleeful Benny.

"I see Connie found you. Did you like our surprise?" Benny crowed as they came over.

"Yes," Jade said. She reached out to mess up Benny's hair. "You're a sneaky little shit, you know."

"Tee hee!" Benny twirled. "Hey, I didn't say you could get up yet."

"I'm getting sand up my gears," Jordan said. Sand rained down as he shook himself out. "For that, you're going to go swimming with me!"

"Okay," Benny said. He hooted and followed Jordan into the surf.

Not to be outdone, Jade bent down and swept Connie up into her arms, lifting her clear off the beach like she was a princess. Jade's gallantry was rewarded with a cute squeak of surprise.

"How about we join them?" Jade asked, secretly grateful of all those hours she'd spent pumping iron.

"That depends." Connie wrapped her arms around Jade's shoulders. "How cold is the water?"

"One way to find out!" With her arms full of a laughing Connie, Jade waded in up to her knees. "Not cold at all," she gritted. "It's actually quite tropical."

"Yeah, I see your teeth chattering," Connie said. She surprised Jade with a swift kiss on the lips. "No sign of hypothermia yet, so you can't stop here. Up to your waist then."

Jade watched carefully for any sign the impromptu dip was upsetting the woman in her arms as she slogged in deeper. Benny and Jordan frolicked some distance away, splashing each other and calling out encouragement to Jade.

"Last chance to stay dry," Jade whispered into Connie's hair. She kissed one temple and nuzzled against her.

"Too late. I'm already wet," Connie purred. She trailed one hand from Jade's shoulder and stole under the silky length of the scarf. Her deft fingers stroked over the curve of Jade's breast.

"Jesus, Connie!" Jade said with her eyes bugging out. "I almost dropped you! Okay, for that we go deep."

Connie gasped and kept her arms tight around Jade's shoulders as Jade lunged into the icy Atlantic waters. She stopped when the water was at chest-level. Jade cradled Connie's body against her and stood strong against the small, grey waves that jostled around them. While her back was freezing, her front was quite warm and happy.

"Don't let go," Connie said.

"I won't," Jade breathed. She looked deep into Connie's eyes. Her entire universe narrowed to those green depths.

A volley of splashes interrupted before Jade could say anything more. Connie lowered her head to Jade's shoulder and laughed as Benny and Jordan came over.

"Benny! You little—" Jade gasped as Benny poured a bucketful of seawater down her back. "Come on guys, thanks for interrupting a nice moment."

"Yeah whatever," Benny said as he shook wet hair out of his face like a freshly-bathed poodle. "Anyway, Jordan's driving me home so you can have as many nice moments with your honey as you want."

"Okay, Ben. In that case, I forgive you."

They splashed each other and played in the water. Eventually Connie left the safety of Jade's arms. Jade watched as she swam around with Benny and Jordan, her strokes powerful and sure even in the long dress. In the midst of the joyful group, Jade wondered at the events that had led to that moment, that place in time and space. Her introspection was interrupted by a surprise splash attack from three sides. Jade retaliated and chased them out of the ocean to the beach where they made sand angels and gathered up giant piles of seaweed.

Benny and Jordan draped trailing handfuls of the purplish stuff over their heads and put on an impromptu show, which included a selection of musical hits and pop tunes. A bunch of bedraggled black-tie-clad people joined Jade and Connie as they clapped and whistled. Benny assembled them for an "after" picture and Jade, feeling magnanimous, treated them all to hotdogs and buckets of grape soda from a nearby kiosk.

"Okay, I think I'm done," Benny declared as he finished off his double-cheese dog.

"Yeah, I'm ready to head back too. Good day, today," Jade said. She got up and slapped at the once-spotless white tux before she held out an arm to Connie, "My lady?"

"My white knight," Connie replied. The words sent a rush of joy through Jade's chest. Connie took Jade's arm with a calm elegance that belied the fact she was covered with sand and seaweed and bid farewell to the boys with a regal bow of her head.

"Where to?" Jade asked as they sat on the garbage-bag protected seats in Jade's car, for the first time both on the same plane of existence. "What time do you need to get back to the hospital?"

Connie turned to face Jade, her eyes alight. "Never. I checked myself out. I have nowhere to go except where you're going to take me."

Jade lost her breath and her fingers closed reflexively on the steering wheel. She couldn't fight the wave of heat that rose steadily from her belly. With a sideways glance, she cracked a grin. "Okay then. I'll take you back to your place. But first, there's something I want to show you at mine."

"That's fine with me," Connie said. She leaned forward and fiddled with the radio. "Just don't ramp the car like you did that one time."

"Hey, I thought that was pretty cool," Jade said. "But all right, if you insist. All four tires are staying connected to the road." She started the car and pulled into traffic. Jade kept her word and drove with prudence. Soon they pulled into the lot behind Jade's building. Jade jumped out and opened Connie's door for her.

Jade bounded over to the silent and dark bookstore and unlocked the front door before leading Connie inside. She held back as Connie stepped carefully around, taking in the book-lined aisles and the café counter.

"This place is so familiar," she said. She started to sit down on one of the stools but stopped and hauled herself up at the last minute with an apologetic glance at her still-damp dress. "It's like a dream. I felt safe here."

"You're welcome any time, Connie. Consider this place your second home," Jade said. She came up behind Connie and wrapped her arms around the young woman. Jade bent her head and inhaled the salty sea aroma mixed with Connie's own scent. Her heart thundered in her chest and she wondered if Connie could feel it. "The thing I wanted to show you? It's over here."

Jade dropped her arms and took Connie's hand. A few steps

took them over to the glass-paned door leading to the stairway to Jade's office. They stopped in front of it and Connie let out a breath. Emblazoned on the glass were the words: "Mason and Mayflower Investigations".

"What do you think?" Jade asked. She kept her voice calm and slow as she said, "I know you can't see them the way I do, but if you were serious about being partners, I thought it might be nice to make it official. If you don't that's totally okay and this all can come off in a minute. I mean it's just kinda stuck on—"

"Jade." Connie turned to her, eyes shining. That look stopped the excited babble of words spilling out of Jade. "Thank you. I love it. And I'd love to be your partner. In this, and everything else too."

Their eyes met. Connie looked at her with an intensity that knocked the wind out of Jade's lungs. She knew what was coming next. The bottom dropped out of Jade's belly as Connie shifted. She moved even closer as her hands came together behind Jade's head.

"I love you," Connie whispered, her breath hot against Jade's face.

Jade squeezed her eyes closed as she gave into the urge and pulled Connie hard against her. She cradled Connie's head against her shoulder. Overwhelmed, Jade couldn't think of anything to say, but it didn't seem to matter. As many times as Connie hinted at it, she'd never actually said the words. Jade felt something come loose inside herself at hearing them. Jade, being the cool, restrained person she was, regularly blurted out the L-word, but had managed to give the impression she wasn't fishing for Connie to say it back.

"Give me ten minutes to change and we can be on our way," Jade said. She was reluctant to break the moment, but she didn't want to spend too much time there. "You can wait here, or come upstairs." Jade ducked behind the café counter and popped up to address Connie. "Benny's got some muffins left over and there's a carton of cranberry juice in the fridge if you'd like."

"That's all right. I'm still full from that yummy hotdog," Connie said. "I'll just wait here. I don't want to track any more sand and crap around than I have to."

Jade emerged from behind the counter and draped a plastic grocery bag over one of the stools. She bowed as she presented it with a pompous air.

"Your seat madam." She stepped back with a grand gesture.

Connie gave a little hop and perched on it. With a nod, she indicated the doorway. Understanding she'd been dismissed, Jade bounded up the stairs and past her office. She paused only to shed her tux into a heap on the floor on her way to the bathroom. It didn't seem in such bad shape, actually. With a good dry-cleaning, it was probably still serviceable.

Jade blew through a prison-fast shower. Once she was presentable again, Jade turned to leave but paused at the doorway to her room. Without a second thought, she rolled her toothbrush and a clean pair of underwear into a T-shirt and stuffed them into her bag. Luckily it was Addie's bingo night so Jade was saved from having to explain where she was going, not that she didn't want to shout it from the rooftops, but Jade was in a hurry. She barely took a moment to drag her hair back into a clip and was soon back in the bookstore.

Connie was thumbing through one of the poetry collections Benny had on display on the café counter and looked up with a smile that whacked Jade right in the gut.

"Are you ready to go home?"

"Home," Connie said in a small voice. She put the book down with a sigh. "You know, right here is the place where I feel the most at home. Could I just stay here? Maybe I don't want to go back there just yet." She let out a troubled breath. "And I chucked everything out before I — left. The place is bare."

Jade drew Connie to her and stroked a hand over her cheek. After she kissed her softly on the temple, Jade looked into Connie's face and said, "You don't have to do anything you don't want to. But I have another surprise for you. Benny and Aunt Addie and me got some new things for your place. Not anything gorgeous, just some towels and dishes, food and juice too. We didn't know how long you'd be out so it's mostly instant and frozen stuff. We also made some changes to the décor. It's like a different room now. Think of it as a fresh start."

"You decorated?" Connie asked with shining eyes. "All right, I'm curious." She jumped off the stool and soon she and Jade were back on the road. "Jade, you are too good for me. I can't believe you did all that."

"No way," Jade told her. "You deserve everything good and

more. Benny has way better taste than me so he picked out any-thing with a pattern. Oh, and I smudged and warded the entire place courtesy of Amber's House of Woo-Woo." She glanced over to meet Connie's eyes for an instant. "You don't want to be bring-ing work home with you, after all."

When they got to Connie's apartment complex, Jade went over and pounded on Mr. Baldesare's door. She shouted out, "Hey Wally!"

The door creaked open and Wally peered out. "What are you doing here when it's not even the middle of the night? What do you want now?"

"Just coming around to say hi." Jade gave him the biggest grin she could muster. She draped her arm around Connie's shoulder and pulled her close. "And say thanks for all your help. As you can see, Connie's back safe and sound."

"That's good." Wally did look glad to see Connie. "What the hell happened? Did you drag her out from the bottom of the ocean?"

"No way, my good man," Jade said in an expansive way, "Just made sure she had a place to come back to. Mind if we get the key from you? The one Connie left here."

Wally shuffled around in the lock box before he pressed the key and its battered dolphin charm into Connie's outstretched hand.

"Thanks," she said and gave Wally a cute little smile.

"No problem at all," Wally replied with a fatherly expression Jade approved of. He fixed Jade with a sharp look and said, "So I guess it's goodbye then."

"Nope," Jade said. She thrust out her chest. "You're going to be seeing a lot more of me around here."

"Oh no, that's just what I need," he moaned and threw up his hands. The door eased closed in the middle of his long-winded griping.

"Do I want to know what you did to that poor man?" Connie asked.

"Nah, we're cool," Jade said. "Me and Wally are old buds."

Connie didn't reply, just lifted a cool brow. They arrived at the sixth floor and Connie unlocked the door to her apartment. She hesitated for a fraction of a second before she went inside. Once over the threshold, she let out a breath and turned slowly as she took in the changes. The once-white walls were a lovely shade of blue. The old, dull curtains had been replaced by rough, hand-woven ones in a delicate green shot with yellow and red. Cheerful placemats decorated the table. The sofa was covered with a crocheted throw and piled with cushions.

Jade said in an excited rush, "Ben called in a bunch of favors and got a whole crew here to help paint and stuff. It was like a Pride parade with brushes."

"It's wonderful!" Connie reflected Jade's excitement as she bustled around the room. She ended up in the kitchen where she opened the cupboard and found the collection of rough, interestingly-shaped pottery bowls and plates inside. "Wow, these are great! Where did they come from?"

"The folks at this place called the Kindness Café sell hand-made stuff on the side," Jade said. "I got those when I went to their grand opening. Kind of tree-huggers, but the food's really good. Vegan, I think they said it was. If you want, we can go there for lunch someday. Let me know in advance, though. For some reason the place is super popular. I got an in with the owners but we still should make a reservation."

"That sounds great," Connie said.

"Aunt Addie made this throw here," Jade said as she fell into the comfortable lap of the sofa. "And the cushion covers were my mother's."

Connie stopped her tour and settled down next to Jade. She picked up one of the cushions and looked down at it. Her fingers traced the cross-stitched design. "I don't know what to say."

"It's not a big deal," Jade said as her face got warm. She felt just as nervous as she had back in the seventh grade with her first crush.

"It is a big deal. I never thought I'd ever come back here." Suddenly she jumped to her feet and looked down at her dress. "And I'm getting sand all over Aunt Addie's nice throw." She hurried off toward the bathroom. "Sorry. I'll be right back."

"Take your time," Jade said.

With the sound of the shower in the background, Jade wandered into to the kitchen where she dug out a can of frozen juice concentrate and quickly made it up in a plastic pitcher. She set two chunky mugs on the counter and filled them with ice and juice. They'd forgotten to get coasters so Jade improvised with folded paper towels. She was back on the sofa sipping her juice when Connie returned with damp hair curling around her face, in a T-shirt Benny donated with a sparkly unicorn on it and a well-worn cotton skirt that survived the apartment-purge and had been sleeping in the dresser all that time. Connie looked relaxed and happy and absolutely beautiful.

A jolt of desire race through Jade.

"Have some juice," Jade choked and tried not to look as stunned as she felt. Shit, she wasn't good at this whole seduction stuff. Jade tried to remember those sappy romance movies she'd mostly slept through and fought the urge to fidget.

"I love the towels Benny picked out. You're right, he has excellent taste," Connie said. She took a sip of juice. "Oh, mango. That's really good." She put her cup down and picked up a small blue bottle that was decorating the table. "Did you and Benny do all this?"

"The knickknacks and stuff? Everybody who came over to paint brought something with them." Jade jumped up and pointed to a neat bundle of rolled-up papers next to the front door. She said, "Ben's theater friends donated a bunch of posters and Jordan put together those dried flower things. Anything you don't like, feel free to chuck."

Jade dropped back onto the sofa. She'd actually tried to slip her own donation in with everyone else's, but Benny had thrust it back into her hands and said, "You give that to Connie in person the first time she brings you here, got it?" Before she could change her mind, Jade rummaged around in her bag and pulled out the bulky rectangular package that, incidentally, Benny insisted she'd bring with her that morning. That alone should have tipped Jade off he was up to something, but she'd been too preoccupied in getting herself ready for the event to really think about other things. Without any kind of grace, she passed the package to Connie.

"This is from me." Jade felt like a complete dork. She cleared her throat as Connie untied the ribbon that held the brown paper closed. "I made it a couple years ago when I was working in the wood shop. They let me take it with me when I left. It's not great, but I thought maybe you could use it." Suddenly shy, Jade stopped and worriedly rolled her cup between her palms.

The paper fell away and Connie gazed down at the gift in her lap. It was a three-part photo frame, hinged so it could stand alone. The wood was good Canadian maple that shone like polished honey in the room's soft light. Jade remembered the time she'd taken sanding and staining each piece. It wasn't the most gorgeous thing in the world, but it wasn't your average grade-school piece of crap either.

"It doesn't have any pictures in it," Jade found herself explaining unnecessarily. "Not yet anyway. I figured maybe we could—" She had to stop talking at that moment as Connie quickly and very thoroughly kissed her. Jade closed her eyes and gave herself to the embrace. She drew her hands up Connie's back and held her close.

"Thank you." Connie's breath was hot against her lips.

Jade held Connie's face in her hands and looked into her eyes as a rush of love and the hot wash of desire rose within her. She didn't even get to say, "You're welcome," before Connie was on her, claiming her mouth with a passion Jade had only glimpsed in the weeks they'd been together. Jade let herself be pressed back into the cushions. She gave a soft moan as Connie's hands stole up to her collar and popped the buttons open.

Cool air hit her skin. Jade threw her head back. She arched against Connie's insistent hands and mouth that kissed a line from her collarbone down. Shockwaves echoed out from each point of contact. Her shirt fell off her shoulders. The kisses let up just long enough for Connie to drag Jade's undershirt and sports bra over her head.

Okay, so she was a bottom, Jade managed to think to herself. So fucking what? There were definite advantages to being in that position. Jade bit back a cry of pleasure as Connie drew a throbbing nipple into her mouth. At the same time, nimble fingers opened the button of her jeans and slid the zipper down. The motions stilled as Connie hesitated.

"Don't stop, Connie," Jade gasped. Her body was on fire. She arched back as a hand slipped past the opened waistband. Jade wished for nothing more than to feel those slender fingers on her. She was spread out on the sofa with Connie nestled between her legs. Jade had never felt so vulnerable, or so safe. So desired and loved.

With one hand stroking Jade through the damp cotton of her underwear, Connie whispered against her neck, "Would you like to stay the night?"

"Sure. I brought my toothbrush," Jade panted. It wasn't the smoothest answer, but she wasn't exactly in the most eloquent of moods at that moment.

The pressure on her body left. Jade looked up as Connie stood and held out her hands. Understanding, Jade clasped the proffered hands and got up as well, glad Connie hadn't gotten her jeans down too far.

Her body thrilled and her heart pounded as Jade let Connie lay her down on the big, comfy bed. Jade scooted backward to prop herself up on the cheerful pile of pillows at the headboard. Connie reached up and released Jade's clip. Jade gave her head a shake. Her long hair spilled over her shoulders and spread out on the pillows. She opened her arms and Connie fell into them.

Hungry lips met each other. Jade closed her eyes. She lost herself in the deep kiss. Connie ran her hands up and down Jade's belly, drifting lower until Jade was gasping, begging Connie to touch her and claim her body. Connie didn't comply for a good long time. She stripped off Jade's clothing piece by piece. Finally Connie stood. Slowly, she pulled her own T-shirt over her head and dropped her long skirt to the floor.

Jade lost awareness of anything except for the beauty of the woman standing bare before her. She rose to her knees on the soft bed. Connie let out a little squeak as Jade grabbed her and rolled her down onto the quilt. Using her weight, Jade pressed Connie down underneath her, feeling every single place where their bodies met. Connie molded herself to Jade, her arms wrapped tightly around her as if she would never let go.

Okay, maybe she was a switch, Jade thought to herself. Oh hell, who cared about labels? The only thing that mattered was she loved Connie and Jade wanted to share every bit of herself without hesitation or guile. Connie's harsh breathing in her ears only jacked up Jade's desire. Connie's body was soft and willing against her. Jade guided Connie's fingers to her, crying out at the first contact. Jade shifted so Connie was lying on her. She loved the weight of Connie's body on hers, the feeling of Connie within her. She couldn't help it as she threw her head back and bucked her hips.

"Put another one in me," Jade whispered.

"It won't hurt you?"

"Oh hell no," Jade said. She let her breath out in a hiss of pleasure as a second finger slipped into her. She put her hands on Connie's hips, pushed her thigh between Connie's and rocked them together in an instinctive rhythm as old as life. Between Jade's legs, Connie's touch was sure and she found just the right spots. She teased Jade with her fingers, stroking her into a fiery passion.

"Oh shit, Connie that's so fucking good," Jade panted out. She glanced up into Connie's pink-cheeked face. "Uh, sorry for the potty mouth. I can tone it down if you want."

"That's okay, I like it," Connie said. Her own breath came out in short, fast pants. She gave Jade a slight, naughty grin and said, "This is the kind of situation where 'Oh Gosh' isn't going to cut it."

The time for talk was over.

Jade arched her back as she let Connie explore her. Even as Connie unlocked the secret areas that brought moans to Jade's throat, Connie's eyes grew unfocused with need and her slender body tight with building tension. Jade lay back and draped her hands over the pillows at her head, letting Connie set the pace. Jade never had the luxury of taking her time with a woman before, and she'd certainly never felt anything like that. Not only was her body involved, her soul was too. It was intoxicating. She wanted nothing more than to give all of herself to Connie.

Her breath hitched when Connie picked up the pace. She drove her hips into Jade's. Shocks of pleasure lanced through Jade with every movement. Every thrust drew Connie's slick fingers in and out of her. Jade was barely aware of Connie's lips on her face, her neck, her breasts. She was too far gone to care and bit down on the "Sweet Jesus!" that flew out of her mouth.

The peak hit Jade right in the gut and rippled through her entire body down to her toes. Her head arched back into the pillows as her body let go. She felt more than heard Connie's exclamation of pleasure as she came as well. After the initial shockwaves died down, Jade coaxed Connie onto her back and knelt down between her legs where she gave Connie a few more reasons to grab at the pillows and let loose with the cute, saucy cries Jade was beginning to love.

They ended up wrapped around each other under the quilt. Sweat-damp and limp as a banana peel, Jade had her arms around

Connie's waist with her head resting on Connie's shoulder. Under the covers, their legs tangled together. Every one of her slow, calm breaths had Connie's softness rising and falling against her.

"Holy Mary mother of God that was great," Jade said. She rose up to brush a strand of hair from Connie's brow, then bent to kiss her temple. Jade reveled in the contented sigh Connie gave at the soft caress. Jade flopped back down and asked, "Did you know you were a top? Because you certainly did me better than anyone ever has."

"No, before you I never even tried," Connie said. She slowly drew a hand up and down Jade's back as she snuggled closer. Her flush spread from her cheeks to the delicate skin of her throat and chest. "You know my history, Jade. I barely have any experience. I honestly don't know what I'm doing so don't feel like you have to sugar-coat it if I'm terrible."

"*Pfft*, you don't have anything to worry about, sweetie. You do everything just right for me. And for the record, I haven't exactly been doing my own Masters and Johnson research these past twenty-odd years either," Jade said. She reached out and twined her fingers with Connie's. "But I must have done something pretty awesome somewhere along the line to end up with someone as great as you."

"I must have too, because you're pretty great yourself." Connie's voice was low and amused. She shifted and gave a little laugh as her body molded to Jade's in a smooth, intimate caress. She took a deep breath, then said, "I am going to love falling asleep in your arms, and waking up next to you tomorrow morning, but you know what I want right now?"

Jade raised her head. She dragged her long hair back with one hand. She met Connie's eyes and they both said in unison, "Pie."

"How about a little trip to Miss Dixie's?" Connie's face was alight.

"That's one amazingly perfect idea." Jade jumped to her feet and gathered up their discarded clothing. She piled it onto the bed before she allowed herself to be distracted by Connie and a big fluffy towel. Jade ended up standing with Connie in her arms in the shower as hot water coursed down over them.

They got dressed in a flurry of activity. Jade cracked jokes and basked in their easy camaraderie.

Jade drove them to the diner, and they sat across from each other in a booth with generous slices of pie in front of them along with two icy-cold glasses of milk that Jade had negotiated in exchange for two coffee tickets.

"This pie is almost as good as sex," Jade declared. Her mouth bulged around a large number of apples. She swallowed and said, "But with way more calories."

Connie put a hand over her face as she let out an unladylike snort. From behind the counter, Dixie shook her head.

"You two do beat all," she said. "It's good to know my pie's got a couple of devoted fans at least."

"That's for sure," Jade said. She looked across the table and didn't care about the two truckers sitting at the counter or the busboy rattling around with his tray full of cups in the booth next to them as she reached out and took Connie's fingers in hers. Softly, Jade rubbed her thumb over the back of Connie's hand. Their eyes locked.

"Goddamn," Jade breathed. "Connie, I think I love you more than this pie."

Connie let loose with her beautiful laugh. She said, "I know you do."

It was the absolute truth. Jade knew that nothing less than that would do. She was complete, and that was in no small part due to the woman across from her. Whatever the future brought, Jade knew they would meet it halfway and kick its ass if necessary. Connie was here to stay.

THE END...?

About the Author

Mildred Gail Digby has a BSc in geology, however Takarazuka, pachinko, and no laws against drinking beer outside lured her to teach in Japan. Her favorite thing to do is add lesbians to any situation and make a novel about it. She dreams one day of working as a professional beer taster and devotes a good deal of her time honing her skills in that area which, to an uninformed outsider, appears to be simply drinking a lot of beer.

She shares her non-angst-filled life with her wife of nearly ten years where the most excitement they have is deciding where to eat and forgetting where they parked their bicycles. Mildred is a sucker for oddball characters, opposites attract, and women getting what (and who) they want. She will squeeze a happy ending out of anything and still blushes when she writes love scenes.

Other Mildred Gail Digby titles to look for:

Perfect Match: Book One

After a tragedy derailed her life, Dr. Megan Maier crawls back to the land of her birth to take a job in a private Jewish hospital. There, she meets Syler Terada, a pediatric surgeon with a brash attitude and a lack of respect for authority who incidentally rocks a tuxedo. She captivates Megan with one glance. Conservative culture and rules against fraternization can't stop Megan. However the secrets she's running from can. The weight of her guilt prevents Megan from making the promise of forever, even though that's the only thing Syler wants from her.

ISBN 978-1-61929-414-1
eISBN 978-1-61929-415-8

Perfect Match: Book Two

Dr. Megan Maier is on her way to happiness and professional success when a hurdle to both appears in the form of Charles Brockman, the son of the hospital's president who has decided that Megan is the perfect partner for him and proposes to her. Megan turns him down cold, certain nothing could make her even consider his offer. Nothing except for Megan's secrets. Incriminating documents go missing and Megan has to face the truth that the cost of protecting herself, and the victims of her shattered past, is betrayal of the woman she loves.

ISBN 978-1-61929-416-5
eISBN 978-1-61929-417-2

Phoenix

What would it take to make you ditch your career, your pride, and run from everything you believe in? In private investigator Ashe Devon's case, it's the fact that her client ended up dead while under her protection. Out of the P.I. business, Ashe is just trying to survive the daily grind of her boring, vanilla life when her former boss calls her out of retirement for one last job: protect a local DJ from a violent stalker. Ashe is fully prepared to turn down the case until she meets the client.

Mystral Galbraith, aka Phoenix, is unashamedly gay, just a tad awkward and musically brilliant. Ashe is instantly captivated by her and can't ignore the fierce young woman's plea for help. Neither can Ashe ignore the stirrings of long-forgotten emotions that set both her heart and her boxer briefs on fire. While Ashe struggles to keep her relationship with Mystral professional, the tension between them simmers just beneath the surface.

More than Ashe's pride is involved — failure could cost Mystral her life. But is Ashe the right person for the job? If she doesn't get her hormones under control, the undeniable pull between them could compromise her judgment and open the door for history to repeat its tragic lesson.

ISBN 978-1-61929-394-6
eISBN 978-1-61929-395-3

MORE REGAL CREST PUBLICATIONS

Brenda Adcock	Soiled Dove	978-1-935053-35-4
Brenda Adcock	The Sea Hawk	978-1-935053-10-1
Brenda Adcock	The Other Mrs. Champion	978-1-935053-46-0
Brenda Adcock	Picking Up the Pieces	978-1-61929-120-1
Brenda Adcock	The Game of Denial	978-1-61929-130-0
Brenda Adcock	In the Midnight Hour	978-1-61929-188-1
Brenda Adcock	Untouchable	978-1-61929-210-9
Brenda Adcock	The Heart of the Mountain	978-1-61929-330-4
Brenda Adcock	Gift of the Redeemer	978-1-61929-360-1
Brenda Adcock	Unresolved Conflicts	978-1-61929-374-8
Brenda Adcock	One Step At A Time	978-1-61929-408-0
K. Aten	The Fletcher	978-1-61929-356-4
K. Aten	Rules of the Road	978-1-61919-366-3
K. Aten	The Archer	978-1-61929-370-0
K. Aten	Waking the Dreamer	978-1-61929-382-3
K. Aten	The Sagittarius	978-1-61929-386-1
K. Aten	Running From Forever: Book One in the Blood Resonance Series	978-1-61929-398-4
K. Aten	The Sovereign of Psiere: Book One In the Mystery of the Makers series	978-1-61929-412-7
K. Aten	Burn It Down	978-1-61929-418-9
Georgia Beers	Thy Neighbor's Wife	1-932300-15-5
Georgia Beers	Turning the Page	978-1-932300-71-0
Lynnette Beers	Just Beyond the Shining River	978-1-61929-352-6
Tonie Chacon	Struck! A Titanic Love Story	978-1-61929-226-0
Sky Croft	Amazonia	978-1-61929-067-9
Sky Croft	Amazonia: An Impossible Choice	978-1-61929-179-9
Sky Croft	Mountain Rescue: The Ascent	978-1-61929-099-0
Sky Croft	Mountain Rescue: On the Edge	978-1-61929-205-5
Mildred Gail Digby	Phoenix	978-1-61929-394-6
Mildred Gail Digby	Perfect Match: Book One	978-1-61929-414-4
Mildred Gail Digby	Perfect Match: Book Two	978-1-61929-416-5
Mildred Gail Digby	Stay	978-1-61929-416-5
Cronin and Foster	Blue Collar Lesbian Erotica	978-1-935053-01-9
Cronin and Foster	Women in Uniform	978-1-935053-31-6
Cronin and Foster	Women in Sports	978-1-61929-278-9
Anna Furtado	The Heart's Desire	978-1-935053-81-1
Anna Furtado	The Heart's Strength	978-1-935053-82-8
Anna Furtado	The Heart's Longing	978-1-935053-83-5
Anna Furtado	Tremble and Burn	978-1-61929-354-0
Melissa Good	Eye of the Storm	1-932300-13-9
Melissa Good	Hurricane Watch	978-1-935053-00-2
Melissa Good	Moving Target	978-1-61929-150-8
Melissa Good	Red Sky At Morning	978-1-932300-80-2
Melissa Good	Storm Surge: Book One	978-1-935053-28-6
Melissa Good	Storm Surge: Book Two	978-1-935053-39-2

Melissa Good	Stormy Waters	978-1-61929-082-2
Melissa Good	Thicker Than Water	1-932300-24-4
Melissa Good	Terrors of the High Seas	1-932300-45-7
Melissa Good	Tropical Storm	978-1-932300-60-4
Melissa Good	Tropical Convergence	978-1-935053-18-7
Melissa Good	Winds of Change Book One	978-1-61929-194-2
Melissa Good	Winds of Change Book Two	978-1-61929-232-1
Melissa Good	Southern Stars	978-1-61929-348-9
Jeanine Hoffman	Lights & Sirens	978-1-61929-115-7
Jeanine Hoffman	Strength in Numbers	978-1-61929-109-6
Jeanine Hoffman	Back Swing	978-1-61929-137-9
K. E. Lane	And, Playing the Role of Herself	978-1-932300-72-7
Jennifer McCormick	Tears of the Sun	978-1-61929-396-0
Kate McLachlan	Christmas Crush	978-1-61929-195-9
Kate McLachlan	Hearts, Dead and Alive	978-1-61929-017-4
Kate McLachlan	Murder and the Hurdy Gurdy Girl	978-1-61929-125-6
Kate McLachlan	Rescue At Inspiration Point	978-1-61929-005-1
Kate McLachlan	Return Of An Impetuous Pilot	978-1-61929-152-2
Kate McLachlan	Rip Van Dyke	978-1-935053-29-3
Kate McLachlan	Ten Little Lesbians	978-1-61929-236-9
Kate McLachlan	Alias Mrs. Jones	978-1-61929-282-6
Lynne Norris	One Promise	978-1-932300-92-5
Lynne Norris	Sanctuary	978-1-61929-248-2
Lynne Norris	The Light of Day	978-1-61929-338-0
Kelly Sinclair	Getting Back	978-1-61929-242-0
Kelly Sinclair	Accidental Rebels	978-1-61929-260-4
Schramm and Dunne	Love Is In the Air	978-1-61929-362-8
Rae Theodore	Leaving Normal: Adventures in Gender	978-1-61929-320-5
Rae Theodore	My Mother Says Drums Are for Boys: True Stories for Gender Rebels	978-1-61929-378-6
Barbara Valletto	Pulse Points	978-1-61929-254-3
Barbara Valletto	Everlong	978-1-61929-266-6
Barbara Valletto	Limbo	978-1-61929-358-8
Barbara Valletto	Diver Blues	978-1-61929-384-7
Lisa Young	Out and Proud	978-1-61929-392-2

Be sure to check out our other imprints,
Blue Beacon Books, Carnelian Books, Mystic Books, Quest Books,
Silver Dragon Books, Troubadour Books, and Young Adult Books.

www.ingramcontent.com/pod-product-compliance
Lightning Source LLC
Chambersburg PA
CBHW071835020726
47502CB00004B/1360